After the Fire

Eric Horridge

After the Fire

Copyright © 2019 by Eric Horridge

All rights reserved.

Front Cover Design: Michael Horridge

Back Cover photo (paperback): Rebecca Hudson

Book design by Eric Horridge

No part of this book may be reproduced in any form or by any electronic or mechanical means including information storage and retrieval systems, without permission in writing from the author. The only exception is by a reviewer, who may quote short excerpts in a review.

This book is a work of fiction. Names, characters, places, and incidents either are products of the author's imagination or are used fictitiously. Any resemblance to actual persons, living or dead, events, or locales is entirely coincidental.

Eric Horridge

After the Fire

DEDICATION

This book is dedicated to my sons, Michael and Matthew, who have brought me nothing but joy and love.

After the Fire

After the Fire

CHAPTER 1

She normally ran with her head bowed down, looking a few feet ahead of her. Occasionally if she sensed someone or movement around her, she would look up to avoid bumping into them or she would glance to where there was any activity that may be of interest.
The music in her headphones kept a beat that she tried to keep a rhythm to while she jogged along Queens-walk on the south bank of the Thames. She was a few minutes late this morning but had increased her pace a little in order to catch up and be back at her flat at her normal time in order to shower and change. She would grab some breakfast near the office.
The sky was a muddy grey, the dawn breaking, the dome of St. Paul's cathedral only a distant silhouette, the rest of the city still sitting in a darkened bowl where dawn's fingers had not yet been able to penetrate. The rain overnight had eased but had left numerous puddles of standing water that she splashed through in order not to break her stride. It was still a cold morning, exactly as predicted by the weather bureau, a range expected of 2 degrees overnight to about 11 by mid-afternoon, nothing unusual for mid-November. At least it was an improvement on recent weeks when the rain had been almost unending resulting in flood warnings in various parts of the country.
As she passed the OXO building heading towards Waterloo bridge, which was halfway, her turning point, where she would cross the river and head back towards Blackfriars and then onto her flat, she looked towards her right noticing that the river was already quite low. At 6:45 in the morning she wondered if the man who made sandcastles and sand sculptures every day on the 'beach' just outside the ITV studio would be there this morning? She saw him most days. Sometimes he had been there for a while, already busy by the time she passed him, other times it seems he had just arrived. She always wondered how he made a living as he was there every weekday, even out of season when the tourists had all gone, so he must be able to survive somehow she thought.
As she moved closer to the railing to look down to the 'beach' she noticed what appeared to be a large plank of wood being pushed towards the sand by the waves of the river. The tidal movement and the eddies created by the various boats moving along and across the water seemed to be pushing the plank from the waters grasp, ejecting it onto dry land as if regurgitating something it didn't want to swallow.

After the Fire

She had no intention of stopping her run, but something about the object made her slow down for a second. She squinted in the light to get a better view, removing her headphones as she did so, noticing that the object now seemed to have developed from an oblong shape to an amorphous mass with various parts moving in different directions as the waves continued to push it up onto the sand.

She looked around at the few people walking along the promenade, some towards her and others passing her, jogging, walking, all keeping to themselves. Being so early in the morning it was still very quiet. Most of the people she saw, she guessed were from the local hotels heading to breakfast or like her, having an early run before their day started. She doubted if any of them would really want to get involved with something she wasn't even sure was an issue just yet.

She decided to take a closer look. Hopefully, the 'sand sculpture' man would be around soon.

She found the steps she needed, a further 50 yards along the promenade and quickly ran down them, taking them two at a time.

As she landed on the sand, she saw the object more clearly, it was only 20 yards away. She realized it was not a wooden plank at all. It was a human body, lying face down. The head was rolling from side to side as the waves continued their incessant movement, the arms of the body rising and falling.

Approaching with trepidation, she again looked around towards the promenade. She tried to see if any of the passersby had noticed her. She was about 15 feet below where they would be walking, surely someone would be able to see her?

She edged closer to the body. Previously the cold weather had not bothered her, but fear now gripped her, chilling her to the bone. She knelt down a foot from the body. She could see it was a man from his size and clothing. Again, she looked towards the promenade but no one was watching her. 'What do I do?' she thought to herself.

She began to panic and as she reached into her tracksuit for her mobile phone to call the police, she dropped it onto the back of the head of the body. "Shit!" she exclaimed, shock beginning to filter through her. She was beginning to shake uncontrollably, tears beginning to drift down her cheeks. 'Where the hell is the Sandman?' she thought.

She stretched for her phone, but as she did so the body was hit was another wave which twisted the head that had previously been facing down and away from her. The head now turning towards her.

The face, if there was such a thing was only half there. The right-hand side was missing. A black hole where the eye should have been and most of the cheek was gone. All she could see was a mass of skin, tissue, and bone, all congealed into an ugly mass of flesh.

As she stared at the sight, she fell backward, and in her haste, her state of fear, she pushed herself back up the sand, crab walking on her hands. Moving as quickly as possible to get as far away as she could. The head was still facing in her direction. A Cyclops. The left eye was open, almost pleading with her for help, yet it was obviously way too late for any possible assistance.

Suddenly and without warning she retched, her empty stomach mercifully having nothing to expel. The only thing coming from her throat, thankfully, was a piercing scream!

CHAPTER 2

"All this bloody rain has been a nightmare," exclaimed Mike Cannon to his head lad 'Rich' Telside. "It looks like both Taunton and Chepstow are off," he continued, pointing at the computer screen they were facing.

It was just after midday and they were sitting in Mike's office. A room Mike had been able to commandeer from Michelle while part of the house was being rebuilt. This, following the attempt by an arsonist to burn it down nearly two years prior. The room faced towards the short driveway that was used as a temporary car park for visitors to the stables. Mike and Rich were trying to find the best races in which to place the horses in their care that were fit and well, but needed a run. Outside, the sky resembled used dishwater as the grey and dark clouds swirled, scattering themselves on an easterly wind. The threat of rain remained, but at least the seven-day forecast showed promise of a change coming. A change bringing some improvement. During late winter one could never be sure about the weather. Dry and hard frost. Maybe some flurries of snow or sometimes worse, large dumps of it. Or rain, lots of it.

It was the latter that was of concern. Over the past few weeks, opportunities to race had *dried up*. Ironic in a way, given the cause of being unable to race was the wet weather and the continuous battering of the UK by storms from the Atlantic. Disruption to travel, the washing away of roads and infrastructure and more importantly to Mike and his team, the flooding of racetracks in the west of the country had been particularly devastating.

The past two seasons had been pretty lean. Winners had been relatively scarce and some of his owners had moved their animals away to other trainers. This was not unusual, but as a small stable, the loss of any horse was not good. Of course, it wasn't only about training winners. It was about growing your brand, increasing your profile, developing a name that owners could trust. The big stables would always get the cream of the crop, the best horses because they had wealthy patrons who plowed millions of pounds into the racing game. What was a worry more broadly across the industry was the larger stables were getting much larger and the smaller ones were left struggling. Many trainers having to leave the sport, the sport they loved, as there was not enough money in it for them to make a reasonable living.

Cannon sat back and sighed, "What do you think Rich?"

"Well, it looks like Newbury is expected to be on at the end of the month, and Uttoxeter should also be okay next week, so we do have a few options. Hopefully, other courses will be suitable as they dry out over the next few days. Let's hope the rain stops soon. At least for a while," he said, looking unconvincingly through the window at the deeply thickening skies outside. "We need better ground for *RockGod* to have a couple of runs if we want to finally qualify him for the National."

"Agreed, probably Newbury on that Saturday will be a better bet. There's a three-mile chase that will be a good test for him, plus he will be up against a reasonable class of opposition which I think he needs. The last two races were too easy for him, but it was good to see him win. Christ! We really needed those."

Telside nodded in agreement. This year's tally of wins to date was just short of twenty. A far cry from two seasons ago when the stable achieved just shy of sixty winners. Since then, and after the fire at the house and the impact on the running of the stables, the trend had been downwards. Cannon had hoped that while the house was being redesigned and rebuilt that it would not affect how the horses would run, but unfortunately it did. Last season only brought twenty-eight winners, less than half he had hoped for following on from the previous year, his most successful. The goal had been to at least match what they had achieved in that season. The reason for the decline wasn't clear. Was it the disruption caused by the building works being so close to the stables? Were the horses being impacted in some way? Neither Cannon nor Rich could see any direct correlation but it was clear the owners had their own views. At least fifteen of them decided to move their investments to other trainers. Fortunately, at least a dozen owners moved their animals from other stables to Cannon, so the merry go round at least brought some form of equilibrium on the training income front. At least enough to keep the wolf from the door. Thank God Michelle was still teaching. Although it didn't bring in much, at least being at a private school she was able to earn more than those teaching at a government institution.

Another Godsend was that Cassie was now away at university. Studying law at York. She had been away since September. This being her first year she was sharing a house with new classmates and fortunately had been able to secure a grant and a loan to finance herself, at least for most of what she needed. Cannon and Michelle were able to support her to some extent, but money was tight and the lack of success of the yard had resulted in Cannon having to lay off some of his staff, including some of the stable lads and girls. Those on whom he relied to look after the horses, to take them out each morning and ride work every day, schooling them over fences then cleaning them off afterward, mucking out their stables, giving them feed and generally ensuring the stable worked as it should. When he had to let some of his staff go, Cannon was really disappointed in himself and deeply regretted having to make the decision he did. He had tried to put it off as long as he could until he had no other choice. The winners weren't coming,

After the Fire

and the abandonments and cancellation of meetings just added to the financial nightmare.

Thank God the house had been insured. Now all the builders needed to do was finish the bloody thing!

Unfortunately, and as expected as far as Cannon was concerned, the *tradies* were 'almost' finished, as they regularly advised, but 'almost' never seemed to become 'finally' completed.

"Another couple of weeks Mr. Cannon," Pavel had said when Cannon enquired, and that was seven weeks ago! At least the rains were hopefully beginning to ease, and this would mean no more excuses from them. He wasn't convinced however, Cannon still hoped that what was left to be done would be completed soon and the scaffolding at the end of the house abutting the road would quickly be gone. This would mean that the entrance into his stable driveway from the road, would once again be clear of debris. At least that's what he hoped. However today there was not one builder to be seen, despite promises that they would be available. The lack of progress was the source of increasing friction between himself and Michelle. A yard full of builders, painters and decorators one day, and then no-one the next. It was extremely disruptive and frustrating.

Cannon himself looked out at the darkening sky. Despite it being eleven-thirty in the morning both Cannon and Telside were not confident that they would see a clear sky before dark, no matter what the forecasters were predicting. Already the lights from the study shone onto the gravel outside as the gloom deepened.

"Shit!" said Cannon, "Is there no end to this?"

Before Telside could comment a beam of light reflected across the side of the stables, then turned inwardly towards the house. A dark green car turned from the road, drove across the driveway and the detritus still around from the renovations and pulled up directly in front of the study, the headlights of the car blinding Cannon as he tried to see who was driving.

"Anyone you know Mike?" asked Telside, standing up to peer through the window, his right hand above his head like a salute angled downwards to protect his eyes while he squinted into the light.

"No," answered Cannon, "I'd better go and see who it is. Maybe a new owner?" he smiled.

"Okay," came the reply, "I'll leave you to it. I'm off to see how the lads are doing. Nearly time for most of them to be off for their break".

Despite the stable staff being sixty percent female, Telside still referred to everyone as a lad. He had been head-lad himself for Cannon for a number of years, and his assistant trainer for the past two. Liked by everyone in the stable, he was fair but firm and Cannon relied upon him completely. Looking after the running of the stables, setting staff work rosters, feed

times, and then making sure that the training regimes he and Cannon had agreed upon per individual horse were implemented. It was a large part of what Telside did each day. It was his life and he loved every minute of it.
More importantly, he was very good at it!
Cannon gave a cursory wave to Rich as he walked off towards the stables. Cannon himself walked towards the car. The driver was pulling on a dark grey overcoat as he stood next to the open driver's side car door. The engine had been silenced but the car headlights remained bright.
Cannon reached out a hand just as the man closed the door, clicking a fob in his hand locking the car and dimming the lights. The darkened sky overhead suddenly seemed more threatening.
The man took Cannons' hand in his. His grip was firm.
"Leslie Timms," he announced, "BHA".
BHA, the British Horseracing Authority. Formed in 2007 after a merger of the British Horseracing Board (BRB) and the Horseracing Regulatory Authority (HRA). Basically, a body set up to regulate the sport, from fixture setting to licensing to the integrity of its participants.
"Oh," replied Cannon, somewhat taken aback. He had never had any real dealings with anyone even remotely linked to the BHA. Of course, he had been through its licensing process when he first became a trainer, and received and read the literature they regularly issued to all trainers, but other than that he had no experience or dealings with them.
Suddenly, his previous life as a former policeman, a former Detective Inspector, a life he had tried to forget, began to raise some alarm bells. He anticipated that visits from the BHA weren't something that occurred as a nicety, especially one unannounced.
"Pleased to meet you," continued Cannon, "should we go inside?" he said, pointing at the threatening sky.
Timms was a tall man, around six foot three inches, about one meter ninety, skinny with very long legs. He had a ruddy face and a slightly greying well-kept beard. He had a good head of hair, cut close, with just a touch of 'salt' flecks throughout. His eyes were grey/green and he had a slight scar just below his left eye. A nick from a stone or a ball perhaps thought Cannon
Cannon led the way to his study, offering Timms the chair that Rich had previously occupied.
Timms removed his coat before sitting. Cannon took the opportunity to turn the computer screen away from Timms' gaze and quickly look over his guest, as he used to do when he was assessing victims or an *accused* in his prior life. He had no reason for personal concern but he wanted to assess the body language of his visitor.
"So, what can I do for you Mr. Timms?" enquired Cannon.
"Leslie, please," came the reply, "call me Leslie. Much more informal don't you think?"

Cannon knew from experience that Timms' reply was a way of charming and disarming him. He had done it himself many times. He didn't fall for it, keeping himself on his guard and not revealing to his visitor in any way his gut instinct, his suspicion, as to why Timms was here. He quickly realized though that Timms had probably been trained in such techniques himself somewhere. Army perhaps?

"Okay Leslie," he went on trying to sound relaxed, "to what do I owe the pleasure?"

Timms looked around the little room and cleared his throat before asking, "Mr. Charles Flint. Do you know him?"

"Of course, he's one of my owners. Has a couple of horses with me," answered Cannon, "why do you ask?" he continued.

Timms shifted slightly in his seat, seemingly uncomfortable. Cannon waited for him to speak. He knew that Timms was playing a game with him, remaining quiet and allowing the silence to eat into Cannon's conscience until he had to speak, or his body gave away any subtle clues or signs that Timms was looking out for in relation to the original question.

Cannon gave away neither. He had nothing to give away anyway. He knew very little of Charles Flint outside of the two horses that he had in work with him and the fact that Flint paid his bills on time. They had met very briefly a year or so before. He knew Flint was a stockbroker in London, rarely attended race meetings to see his horses run, but did drop a thank you note by email to Cannon whenever one of his horses ran into place money. In fact, it was Flint who owned *RockGod* the one horse who had done so well for the stable in recent times, keeping Cannon's profile up in the owner's ranks.

Eventually, Timms crossed his long legs, took a deep breath and got to the point. "Well we've been doing some investigation into recent betting anomalies," he said, "and Mr. Flint's name and his association with certain horses has cropped up so I've been sent here as HRA inspector to make some inquiries."

"Inquire away, and by the way, call me Mike. Less formal don't you think?" said Cannon sarcastically, his arms wide with a cheeky smile on his face. He had nothing to hide and he was enjoying the game. It was something he used to enjoy when asking the questions as a DI. Now he was enjoying being on the receiving end. While he understood that he and Timms were on the same side, he took umbrage to anyone thinking that he would be involved in any act of deception when it came to his profession. Any such thought went against his very being and he felt slightly pissed off that Timms or anyone from the BHA would even consider such a thought. He let Timms continue.

"Mr. Flint has several horses with various trainers, and obviously the two with you. *RockGod* and……?" he let Cannon answer the question.

"'*Youcantcatchme*'"
"Yes, that's right."
"What of it?" asked Cannon.
"Well, to be direct…Mike…during our inquiries we have some evidence that suggests certain trainers or their stables may have been aware of certain *activities* shall we say, that indicates that they may have been involved in or been aware of a scam."
"You mean a plunge?" asked Cannon. "Nothing wrong with that as far as I know, as long as people aren't betting against their own horses."
Timms was silent for a second, before continuing, "Aah, here's where the rubber hits the road," he said, his tone changing, sounding much more formal. "We believe that's exactly what's happening."
Cannon looked straight into Timms' eyes. Neither man flinched. The anger inside Cannon rising, however, he tried not to show it.
"You're stable has been having a lean time of it recently," went on Timms, his eyes still on Cannon's face.
"Yes."
"We think that some of your horses have been sent out with the intent of not trying to win."
"What?!" exclaimed Cannon, "are you accusing me of deliberately losing races?" he shouted, the anger within him too expansive to contain. He pointed a finger at Timms, who remained passive as he was trained to do, letting Cannon's emotions get the better of him.
"No, I'm not suggesting that at all," answered Timms noting the ferocity of Cannon's response, "what I am saying though is that there appears to have been some manipulation of the race results that a few of your horses have contested, resulting in someone benefitting financially from the outcome of the race."
"And you think this was my doing?"
"Again Mr. Cannon, er Mike, I'm not implying anything, I'm just making initial inquiries at this stage of the investigation."
"Very diplomatically put," said Cannon, "but you must have some evidence to back up your suspicions otherwise you wouldn't be asking these questions," Cannon replied, drawing on his own experiences. "You don't start an *investigation* unless you have a theory, a premise and something to go on. Am I right?"
Timms sat silently for a few seconds, his face and entire body almost statuesque, immovable, his expression impenetrable.
Cannon smiled inwardly. He knew that he had rattled Timms somewhat.
"Let me put it this way, and I can't say any more than this," answered Timms, "based on the information to hand, we believe that one of your owners, Mr. Flint to be specific, has profited substantially from some of his horses not running up to form and that includes the two in your stable."

"He can't have made too much from my horses. *RockGod* has won both his outings this season, but at very short odds, and *Youcantcatchme* has also had just a couple of runs but ran miserably both times."

"Well, we think he did. Remember he has a number of horses with other trainers and despite what you say, we believe he has profited handsomely on a number of the races that your horses have competed in."

Cannon considered this for a second, remembering his earlier frustration at not being able to find races for his horses to run in.

"Then all I can say Mr.Timms," he replied, ignoring the earlier informality, "is that I run *my* horses to do their best, to race fairly and if possible, to win! I don't ever send them out with the intention of cheating. Maybe some owners, some bookmakers and some other trainers and jockeys try to beat the system, but not me, nor my staff!"

Silence sat like a heavy blanket between the two men. Enveloping them. For a tense few seconds, and with the darkening sky outside making the room and the atmosphere even more oppressive, neither man's eyes left those of the other. Finally, Timms spoke.

"I appreciate your candour, Mike. It's noted. As my investigation continues and should I need to contact you, I will do so. However, for now, I'll say my goodbyes and be off. Please be aware though, this is a serious issue."

Both men stood, then exchanged mobile phone numbers, the earlier animosity between them simmering still, bubbling under the surface.

Cannon understood that Timms was just doing his job, one which in practical terms was best for all trainers and the wider industry at large, however, he didn't like being accused or implicated in anything untoward.

He knew though that despite all the innovations introduced over the years to stop corruption, where money was to be made and people with huge bank balances and egos wanted to play, it could never really be stamped out.

The two men said their goodbyes, a brief smile crossing Timms' lips as he shook Cannon's hand and quickly ducked back into his car to escape the cold and damp. Soft rain, the initial splattering of what was to come, had just begun to fall. The low cloud that had been threatening for a while decided now was the time.

Cannon nodded briefly towards Timms as the car reversed and headed out of the stable yard onto Combe Road, turning east towards the small town of Woodstock and then ultimately, he guessed would head south towards London.

He ran back inside to escape the rain that once again began to pound the area, adding more moisture to the already sodden ground. The rain's intensity growing with every passing moment.

He entered his office, the large screen of his computer shining like a beacon in the gloom of the room. Cannon replayed the conversation he had just had with Timms in his mind. It was both disturbing and intriguing. His experience as a DI began to set off alarm bells. He knew that Timms would not have visited him unless there was something going on. He knew that somehow his own horses were part of some larger scheme. But what? And by whom? And for what purpose? Greed? Or just because it could be done? A challenge, a gauntlet thrown down to the racing authorities perhaps?

Cannon knew that where there was an undercurrent of doubt in relation to racings' integrity and especially towards a stable or a specific person, then very quickly things could go downhill and livelihoods and careers could be lost. He didn't have a lot but what he had was his. More specifically he had his reputation and he valued his integrity.

Since he had left the force, he had experienced the highs and lows of life, including losing a wife to cancer, to being a single parent and to falling in love again. After all his years of policing, through sheer hard work, sweat and guts he had built up his stable from nothing but an empty paddock, to what he had now. Yes, it was still small, and it would never likely be large like those who had grown up in the industry all their lives, but it was what he had worked for, and nobody was going to do anything to make him lose it.

In addition, Michelle had moved in permanently after the fire. She had supervised the rebuilding of the house and continued to do so despite the unfinished parts, still seeming to be taking forever. With Cassie heading off in her own direction, Michelle and Cannon's relationship was now much stronger. They had been through a lot together over the past couple of years and Cannon was determined not to allow anything to threaten his personal happiness.

He stood up from his chair and began pacing the small room, he had a feeling, a sense of dread. He felt like he was experiencing cabin fever. With all the recent cancellations his days had been more indoors than out. He was feeling claustrophobic, restless, his mind now racing. He needed to get out. The sooner he was legging up a jockey onto one of his charges the better. He turned back towards the window as the rain began to lash against it.

"Fuck!" he thought to himself, "more of this across the country and there will be no racing at Newbury in a fortnights time, and certainly nothing suitable for *RockGod* before then."

As the rain began to hammer down even harder, Cannon decided to make a few phone calls. He needed to find out a bit more about Charles Flint and why the best horse in the stable was potentially being used in a possible conspiracy that had been brought to the attention of the BHA. To do that he needed to do some background research on his rather reclusive and elusive client.

After the Fire

CHAPTER 3

"Who is he?" enquired Detective Inspector Jeremy Walsh.
"We are not sure yet," came the reply, "there was no ID on him at all, no wallet, no keys, nothing. Even the clothes he was wearing were pretty basic. No distinguishable brands, not even any shoes."
"Anything else?"
"Apparently a poor attempt was made to file off his fingerprints, probably as an afterthought."
"Christ!" said Walsh.
The two men were sitting in Walsh's office in the Tooting police station, an imposing, brown brick five storey art deco building on Mitcham Road. Not a popular place to visit and the locals less than happy with the service being received from its occupants.
Walsh was an old fashioned 'copper' who was happy doing leg work if needed. He had come up through the ranks over nearly thirty years. A thin man, tall at six foot two, dark hair with bushy eyebrows that always seemed to be moving. Like hairy caterpillars on a leaf. A widower for 15 years now. He always wore a black suit, white shirt and tie every day, no matter the temperature or season. His colleague, Sergeant Matthew Sedgefield, a diminutive man in comparison to Walsh, was a mere five foot nine. He was more a square than round. A family man, popular in the station and more so with his two young children who saw him as a hero. They were about to start a meeting, the wider team slowly assembling in the ad-hoc briefing room set up just outside the office. Ongoing renovations to the 'station' had reduced the number of available rooms and everyone was constantly trying to find suitable accommodation to facilitate their investigations.
What didn't help either was that the phone system was being updated, and due to technical problems, which BT and the IT department were still struggling to resolve between themselves, had resulted in communication with the outside world was a nightmare.
"At this rate, we'll never find out," complained Walsh, "can't even contact the lab, the morgue or even the Chief Inspector," he said, the latter thought bringing a smile to his face. "Bloody softphones, whose idea is that?" he went on, unable to hide his displeasure. "Can't even phone the local curry house for a takeaway either! Thank God for mobiles," he concluded holding up his own in his left hand before placing it back on his desk.
"All part of the usual cost-saving exercise we keep going through each year," replied Sedgefield. "Derick in IT says that using digital technology, like a softphone on your desk to make calls through the network, will save a

fortune."

"Network?" responded Walsh, "Network? The only bloody network I want to work with is a human one. One where I can talk to a warm body and see the whites of their eyes. Talking of which, let's get this show on the road, can't keep the team waiting," he nodded towards the group of men and women assembled just outside.

Making a deep coughing sound from his throat, Walsh slowly managed to hush the assembled group of men and women and gain their attention. Some of the group leaned against or sat on tables, a couple stood arms folded, waiting, and a few others had been able to find a chair. It was just after 10 am the normal time for daily briefings. Including Sedgefield and Walsh himself, there was a total of nine people. Two of these were non-operational staff, those employed by the police to do admin work, such as capture and collate data that police officers had been able to establish or uncover during their investigation. The others in the group included a Detective Constable, Paul Fitch. A police support officer who would act in a community liaison role, Wendy Carmichael, plus two junior constables dragged in from other investigations and finally Adrian Windsor, the *nerd* from IT.

Walsh gave Adrian a brief look, making a tutting sound before he issued a final grunt from his throat and began addressing the team.

"So, you all know what this is about I'm assuming?"

A quiet muttering stirred from his audience.

"It's about this!" he continued, holding up an A5 size photo showing a close-up of a head with only half a face. "Not pretty is it?" he asked rhetorically. "Now we don't know who he is yet, but from what we do know by the time the body was found just outside the TV Studio's on Southbank, he had been in the water at least twelve hours. Forensic and Pathology have established an approximate time of death of around 8 pm on Sunday night. That was three days ago, so if you pardon the pun, a lot of water has gone under the bridge since then."

A brief chuckle escaped from the group. Walsh knew that to keep people sane in this job, a bit of levity was often needed. It was vital to keep his team motivated and on his side. With investigations often running on far longer than expected, and this one hadn't even really started yet, he needed everyone to focus and for them to pay attention to detail. The powers that be wanted results. The general public demanded to be safe in their homes and on the streets. With constant battles about budgets, and with limited resources, many of which could be taken away at any time if a higher profile case was deemed more important, Walsh knew that time was against him and the team. Solving the case quickly was what was expected. If not, everyone moved on, new cases were started and those remaining cases still unresolved were labelled as such, details filed and stored, and maybe one day someone may relook at them. He nodded towards Sedgefield to continue.

"Just for you who prefer something in your hand, I'm going to pass around a couple of photos that Dr. Davidson the head pathologist down at the lab has taken of the body. What they show are a couple of distinctive marks which may mean something or at least could be recognizable to someone." He passed a pile of copies to one of the junior constables to hand out to the team. As the photos were being circulated, Sedgefield brought up a replica image of the photograph on an electronic status board. Further detail would slowly be added onto it as the investigation unfolded.

Another place where technology was taking over. No more pinning pictures to boards and linking them with pieces of string. That was long gone. Much to the chagrin of many of the longer serving officers. Most of the information needed on an investigation was now being shared electronically.

If only they could get the phones to work, Walsh thought wryly.

Pointing at the image on the board Sedgefield went on, "This first mark is a very distinctive tattoo." All eyes trained onto the picture. He gave a summary of what they were looking at.

"As you can see, it looks like an anchor with the shaft of the trident longer than is normal and curling quite clearly into a letter P at the top. What this is, is a Polish military tattoo. It's a lot smaller than it looks on the photo and it's taken from the upper left thigh of the body. Obviously being on the leg, and in the position that it is in, very few people would actually notice it. Even if the person was wearing shorts it would be very difficult to see."

"So, are we thinking the victim was in the Polish army at some point?" interrupted DC Fitch.

"Not necessarily Constable," he answered, "many people have tattoo's that imply one thing, an association or a membership of some group or other, but are essentially just a tattoo that they like, nothing else. Plus, we suspect that if he was in the Polish armed forces, a soldier would normally want to show it off or at least have a bigger version than this one is. Normally this type of tattoo one would expect would be more prominently placed on a forearm rather, not on the top of a thigh."

"Should we not...?" said Fitch.

"I know," interrupted Sedgefield anticipating Fitch's question, "contact the Polish authorities via Interpol? See if they have any information that could be relevant?"

"Yes."

"It's a bit early for that just yet, we don't even know if he is Polish. But we will certainly be following up once we have made more inquiries locally," replied the Sergeant. Turning back towards the digital board, he pressed a remote in his hand. A second photograph popped up into the screen.

"Now this picture is the one that interests me," said Walsh, taking over the conversation. They were looking at a second tattoo taken from the dead man. "It's much less distinct and obviously a lot older, but we can just make out the letters S or Z, then something that's unclear," he said pausing, "then there is an L, then two letters we can't work out yet, an N an I, and then some form of a squiggle at the end. You can tell from the way the tattoo has been drawn onto the body, in this case, the right forearm, that it must have meant something to the victim to be so prominent. Especially when compared to the location on the body of the first tattoo," he concluded. He waited for a second allowing the team to think about what he had said. "The issue we have is that we can't make out what it really says or is supposed to mean. However, someone will know it, someone will recognize it. What we now need to do is to find that person or persons," he stated, pointing at the team.

"Excuse me Sir," interrupted Windsor, "let me do some 'googling', some further investigation on those letters, maybe I can find something on-line that might help?"

Walsh, who wasn't totally a technophobe, nodded affirmatively towards the IT representative in the team.

"Whatever you can find that is useful, we would all appreciate it," he stated, casting a glance across the assembled team. "Right, we need to get going on this, but before we do, a few other things," he went on. "Initial forensic reports and autopsy findings have apparently been sent to you all this morning by email. They should be accessible to you through your inboxes," he said.

He was on a roll now. He wanted action. "Okay, next thing...Fitch...!"

"Yes, Sir?" answered the Constable.

"I want you to be the coordinator of all the data being collected. Work with Windsor here to implement the usual processes. I want an update on this case every morning or even earlier if anything breaks."

"Yes, Sir."

"Sergeant Sedgefield here should be the first port of call if I'm unavailable. I'm just wrapping up the 'Sandra Moore' case but should be shot of that by close of business tomorrow," he continued.

"Yes, Sir."

"And another thing, if you need me, call my mobile, even if I'm in my office. These bloody softphones do my head in!"

A murmur, mimicking soft laughter spread across the team. Even Sedgefield smirked.

"Ok Sergeant," said Walsh, "I want you to have a detailed look at what we have so far. Give me an overview at the end of the day. I'll be in my office," and with that, he turned on his heels, walked back into his office and closed the door.

As Walsh sat down, looking at the pile of paperwork about the Sandra Moore murder on his desk, he sighed and opened the top folder. A pop-up icon appeared on his desktop computer screen. It was an incoming phone call, and the handset wasn't ringing. He ignored it.

CHAPTER 4

The man had his back to the office door. He stood with his hands behind him, the left held by the right. He was looking out of the full floor to ceiling window on level 25 of the *'Cheesegrater'* building on Leadenhall Street. Through the rain streaks on the glass, he tried to follow the progress of a Thames Clipper as it wound its way through the dirty brown water towards Westminster. The volume of traffic churned up the river, white/grey plumes spat out from the back of the various vessels sending ripples towards the banks, each disappearing before they got there as they smashed into those created by other boats. Grey clouds twisted themselves around the building obscuring his view and with a sigh, he turned around 180 degrees just as his secretary gently tapped on his door and entered without waiting for an answer.
"It's that man again," she said.
Henry Perkel, Queens Counsel, nodded and picked up his phone. Before pressing the button on the console to take the call, he put his hand over the receiver's mouthpiece and said, "Okay Sandra, I'll take it this time."
Looking at the door he motioned with his eyes that she should leave the room, "and close the door, will you?" he said as she reluctantly departed.
"Henry Perkel," he said nonchalantly into the phone.
"Aah Mr. Perkel, how are you today?" came the voice down the line, "I've been trying to reach you for the past couple of days. You are not avoiding me, are you?"
"Of course not," answered Perkel, "I've been very busy on a case I'm handling and have been unavailable due to my being required in court."
A short silence followed. It was something that always unsettled him. Eventually, the man spoke again. Firmly. Threatening. "Tomorrow you will receive a letter at your home address. In it will be my requirements and for you the final piece of the jigsaw."
The line went silent. The voice taunting him now gone. Perkel slowly put the phone back onto the consol's cradle.
Will this nightmare never end? he thought.

CHAPTER 5

"What do you think?" asked Cannon.
Rich Telside considered his reply before responding. They were sitting in Cannon's office again barely 18 hours since the visit from Timms.
"I must admit Mike, I'm gobsmacked. How anyone could think you would pull your horses or not try to win with them is beyond me. We haven't had the best of seasons these past two years as it is. We need all the winners we can get."
"So bloody true," Cannon answered. "after Timms left yesterday I made a few phone calls to a couple of people I know to hear whether the investigation Timms is leading has any other trainers in his sights and whether it includes other horses as well," he said. "I didn't find out very much, unfortunately, however, when I spoke with Michelle last night and told her the names of the horses that Timms referred to, she highlighted a couple of things about the way those horses had raced at the time, that I had forgotten about, and that got me thinking."
Mixed with Michelle's observations Cannon had mulled over Timms' comments and subtle accusations. He had spent a restless night tossing and turning. Timms had got to him and the inference was bothering him. He could sense that there was something going on. Something that could impact him. It was in his bones. What it was though, he couldn't yet put his finger on.
"And?" asked Telside.
"I'm not sure yet Rich," he replied, "I need to do a bit more thinking first," he went on, "and I need to call Charles Flint at some point. Something about Timms' inquiry doesn't add up."
"Be careful Mike. If Timms and his team are conducting an investigation, especially in relation to Flints' horses, the last thing you want to happen is to be stuck in-between the two of them. If there is any doubt on Timms' behalf about what we do here and the way the stable is run, he'll have your license suspended straight away!"
"You absolutely right Rich, but I am already being tarred with some type of brush. Timms' visit was more of a warning. Letting me know that the BHA is watching."
"Would they have got the police involved yet?"
"No, I don't think so. They will need to collect a lot more evidence of any wrongdoing before they engage the police. As you said, the BHA can easily

have us shut down if they believe we have broken any of the rules of racing. It's not a Police matter currently as far as I know, but if I lost my license, even temporarily, we wouldn't be able to continue. It would mean that we would have to let the horses go. With no horses, logically that would mean we would need no staff and given the state we're already in financially I'd likely have to sell the place."

"So, what do you want to do?" asked Telside gloomily.

Cannon considered this for a second, then with a smile despite his resigned sigh said, "First things first. Given the weather has improved, let's see if we can get a few miles into the legs of *RockGod* and the others. I'll consider our next move after that."

The pounding of hooves over the shared gallops that Cannon and his team used took away some of the concern churning inside his stomach.

The squelching and the slipperiness of the ground beneath their feet made the standing and watching of his charges unpleasant, but at least he was out of his office and doing what he loved.

"Send them around again," he shouted to Rich who was standing a couple of hundred yards further up the gallops. Cannon was eager to get as much exercise into his top five runners as he could. While there was still the possibility of meetings being cancelled, he wanted to make sure that where he could, he would ensure all the owners would get the best out of their horses when the time came for them to race.

An icy blast blew from the west. Cannon shivered despite wearing a heavy padded jacket, jeans, and heavy boots. Underneath his clothes, the thermals he had put on earlier to protect him from the cold only seemed to make him sweat, the material sticking to his skin. The dark muddy clouds that had brought rain overnight had begun to break up, scattered and thrown around the sky by the swirling wind. A pale sun shone in the sky, weak, but at least showing signs of making a bolder appearance over the next few days. Hopefully, as the wind crossed the country it would help dry up some of the tracks, allowing racing to start again soon.

Cannon watched as *RockGod* and *Harvester*, two of his best *chasers* continued their work. Aligned to each other, they bravely attacked the schooling fences, soaring across each in a fluid motion. The way each horse approached the fences, urged on by their riders, then leapt off the ground and within a second landed on the other side continuing onwards onto the next barrier, was pure grace. Poetry in motion. It was a sight that Cannon never tired of. In his last race, which *RockGod* had won, the horse had pulled up lame. Despite the injury, his in-bred will to win had prevailed. Cannon remembered the race like it was run yesterday. The horses' bravery

After the Fire

had provided Cannon with confirmation in his own mind that *RockGod* was definitely a *National* horse.

"Let *TheMan* and *Visitation* go next," he called to Rich who was now standing next to the first fence of three that Cannon used in the horses training and schooling. Rich was to record each pair on camera as they jumped the fence, "Once they've gone, send *Youcantcatchme* and *Whitehall Kid*." Cannon continued. "After that, give them all a brief three-quarter gallop up the hill turn them around and let them canter back. We can take them home once they are all back".

Rich nodded and passed on the necessary instructions to the young riders who eagerly put the animals to work.

Cannon looked to his left where *RockGod* and *Harvester* had pulled up to a walk and were waiting for the others to complete their schooling before all of them would go again in their same pairs to complete the last part of the days' exercise.

Despite the gloom of the day, Cannon could see the steam rising from the bodies of the horses even though he was a quarter of a mile away from them. He noticed how the steam mingled with the breath of the jockeys.

Jump jockeys were a hardy lot, but the young men and women who rode work each day for very little money were even tougher. Paid a pittance compared to many other jobs available, they were the backbone of horse racing, whether they were linked or involved with jumps or flat racing. They started each day early, they exercised and looked after the horses, yet the glamour of the race day itself basically eluded them. Perhaps in time some of them would be lucky and become jockeys, but in most cases, they would miss out and remain stable-hands, stable-riders.

"Most of the horses are looking good," he shouted to Rich, "no sign of lameness or problems with any of their actions, must be the rest they have had over the past few weeks?" he questioned.

Rich smiled as Mike walked towards him, slowly covering the short distance between them, his boots sinking into the soft ground. "I think your right Mike, too much feed and not enough exercise. These buggers would really have enjoyed being in their stalls."

"Well let's get them home and get the second lot out here. Hopefully in the next week or so we'll be able to go racing?"

"I hope so," answered Rich, "I bloody well hope so."

CHAPTER 6

The men stood in front of a wall of grey steel doors each with a large handle that protruded out from the base and stood parallel to the floor.
There was a chill of death emanating throughout the room. The cold used to slow the dead from decomposing sneaked into the bones of the living. Walsh and Sedgefield along with Dr. Davidson waited for the assistant to open up the bay where the body was kept after the post mortem had been completed.
"Ah, here we are," said Davidson, with too much gusto for Walsh's liking, "our Thames mystery man."
The body had been sewn back together again after the autopsy and with the exception of the face looked almost normal.
"So, what was so important Inspector that you wanted to see the body, *in the flesh* so to speak?"
Davidson's attempt at humour was not lost on Walsh, but he just ignored it.
"It's the tattoo on the arm that intrigues me, I wanted to see it *in situ* rather than just on a photograph as its quite indistinct otherwise. Any idea how old it is?"
"It's hard to say," answered the Pathologist, using gloved hands to turn the bodies arm gently towards Walsh, thus allowing both he and Sedgefield to peer closely at the writing. "All depends on the quality of the tattoo artist and the type of needles used, the ink quality and of course the ageing of the body."
Walsh stood up straight after checking the tattoo and nodded imperceptibly suggesting Davidson continue.
"There are certain trends in tattooing which may give one a rough timing as to when the work was done. For example, in the Eighties, there was a trend in tattooing towards flowers and animals. In the Nineties, it was more tribal type tattoos. Since the start of the millennium, it was barbwire bands and neck tattoos. Then that trend seemed to morph into full sleeve and pacific island motifs for some reason."
"And our man here has none of that," indicated Walsh
"No that's right. So, given we have estimated his age to be in his early thirties it seems as though generally he wasn't a *dedicated follower of fashion*," chuckled Davidson at his own joke. Walsh did not respond.
The Pathologist carried on, giving his opinion. "As you would be aware from the other tattoo, it is highly possible that he may have had some other

After the Fire

association. Though that's just my view."

"Yes," said Sedgefield, "we think it's a Polish army tattoo."

"Polish eh? I see lots of marks on the various bodies I encounter, but I haven't seen either of these before."

"So, what does this look like to you then?" asked Walsh of Davidson, pointing at the words on the arm.

"Well if it's Polish then I can't help you. Not one of my *specialties* I'm afraid, and the way it's been needled on, it's very difficult to really make out all the letters."

"I realize that," answered the Detective, "however while we get our experts looking at it, can you get me a blown-up copy of your picture?"

"Already done," answered Davidson, "it's included in the 60 to 70 pictures of the body we took and sent through to your team yesterday. They should be accessible via your computer. You should be able to zoom in extremely close onto both tattoos. We use high definition camera's at 4K resolution now."

Walsh took the information on board. He knew he should be more willing to embrace the technology the force gave him, but ever since the softphone debacle started, he refused to touch his PC.

"Okay, thank you, Doc," Walsh said. Turning to Sedgefield he asked, "when we get back to the 'station let's see if *whatshisname* from IT.....?"

"Adrian?"

"Yes, Adrian. Let's check with him to see if he has been able to work out if the tattoo is a word or has a meaning of some sort."

Sedgefield smiled at Walsh's poor recall of names, then said, "What happens now, Doctor?"

"Well as you can imagine we are pretty busy here so with all the budget cuts and limitations of facilities and space, unfortunately, we can't keep the body here forever. The council in this area allows us to keep it for 10 days and then after that we move those unclaimed bodies to our overspill facility."

"For how long?" asked the Sergeant,

"Sixty days. After that, we dispose of the body."

"Cremation?"

"Normally, yes. If no one by that time has come forward to claim the body."

As he spoke Davidson's mobile phone began to ring. He put a finger to his lips to suggest to Sedgefield and Walsh that he needed to answer it. He listened into his earpiece and then mouthed off that he had to go, nodding as he did so to the assistant to close the door of the chamber into which the mystery body would again be stored.

Walsh & Sedgefield shook his hand, thanking him for his help so far. The assistant showed them towards the exit.

After the chill of the morgue, the cold outside felt positively balmy. The fresh breeze and the speckled sunlight peeking through the breaking clouds seemed almost tropical.

"I'm not happy about this one, Sergeant. There is something about the way this poor soul was killed that suggests something big is going on," said Walsh, "just as well we have closed off the Sandra Moore case."

"Agreed Sir," answered Sedgefield

Just then Walsh's mobile buzzed. He had put it on silent the previous evening and had forgotten to turn it back on to ring, basically because he hated the hip-hop ringtone that his eldest daughter had set up on it a couple of days earlier. He didn't know how to change it.

Taking the phone from his inside jacket pocket, he pressed the answer button and placed the phone to his ear.

"Walsh!" he shouted to be heard above the wind and the passing cars.

Sedgefield stood around, waiting as Walsh took the call. While he did so, he wondered why Walsh had not yet begun to use wireless earpieces? He noticed his bosses' facial expression change as he listened to the caller. Something was up.

After finishing the call and without hesitation, Walsh said, "Sergeant, it never rains but it pours doesn't it?" He looked up at the miserable sky, thinking how relevant that saying was given the incessant drenching the country had received over the past few weeks.

"Sir?"

"That call," he said, indicating the phone in his hand, "another body, in the Thames. We're needed. Let's go."

CHAPTER 7

"Somethings not right," muttered Cannon.

He was on the couch in the living room where he and Michelle sat most evenings when there were no race meetings to attend the next day. If there was, he would be in his office planning logistics, tactics or making other arrangements. The room had been redecorated over the past twelve months. The fire that had torn away most of the roof of the house at one end of the building had also damaged the interior through the smoke damage. Michelle had used the opportunity to revamp some of the rooms. New furniture, new wallpaper, and carpets were evident. Though building work on the outside still continued with new guttering, downpipes, slate tiling and painting still being done. The house was now livable again.

They normally had the TV on but most evenings it was just background noise to their conversation. Only the evening news or the odd comedy or sports event were really of interest.

Instead, they loved to share their time together to talk about the days' activities. Whether it was Michelle's day, with all the problems of the 15 and 16-year-old pupils at the private school she taught at just outside Charlbury, in the Cotswold Hills, or Cannon's summary of what had happened at the races he had been to. If there were no race meetings then the conversation was often just how things were going with the running of the stables.

"What do you mean?" she answered.

"I've been going to…," Cannon stopped, interrupted by the home phone on a side table starting to ring. The shrill of the instrument stopping the words before they escaped from his mouth.

He got up from his chair.

"Hello?" he said into the mouthpiece.

"Hi d…!" came the reply. Unclear. Indistinct.

Cannon pressed the phone harder to his ear, hoping to get a better sound from it. What was coming from his speaker was both loud and garbled.

"Hi dad! Can you *hear me!?*"

"Cassie! Yes, I can, but can you find a better spot to call from, the background noise is just unbearable?"

A sound of crackling, voices mixed with laughter and cheering, *'excuse me's'* reverberated in Cannon's ear. Eventually, Cassie's voice came back on the line.

"Hey dad, is that better?"

"Yes, that's much better," he said, eyes rolling heavenwards as Michelle looked at him quizzically, wondering what was happening.

After the Fire

She reached for the remote to turn off the TV.

"Are you okay?" asked Cannon.

"Yes, all good. Sorry to bother you," Cassie replied.

"Where are you?"

"Oh, in a pub, 'The Graduate.' Well, I'm outside now. It's crazy in there, but so much fun," she said.

That explained all the noise, Cannon thought.

"It's Simone's birthday, so we are having a bit of a celebration," she went on.

Cannon remembered the name from Cassie's last visit home a few weeks ago. Her first since she had moved up to York. Simone was one of several girls that Cassie had befriended there.

"What about the studying?" answered Cannon, still not sure what Cassie was calling about, other than to say hello.

"Yeah, yeah dad, I'm doing that..." she trailed off.

"And to what do I owe the honour then of the call?"

For a few seconds, there was silence on the line. Cannon could hear Cassie breathing through the microphone headset she was probably using. He could imagine the cogs in her brain working overtime, trying to work out what to say.

Eventually, she continued, "Dad, I'm sorry to bother you, but could I get some...money?"

Cannon's initial reaction was to say *no*. He couldn't understand the logic of people without any income like Cassie spending what they didn't have. Especially students. Here she was in a pub with her friends, yet she was crying poor and was asking him for money so that she could enjoy herself. It was just like those people he saw on news programs complaining about hard times, yet maximizing out credit cards and complaining about being in debt, yet they were out drinking, partying or had just come off expensive holidays and were driving new cars.

Cassie knew that things were tough right now for the stable, they had discussed it several times on her last visit home.

"Cassie, you know things are hard for us right now. How come you can afford to spend money at the pub, when I'm guessing that what you want the money for is for something else, like food maybe?"

"I know dad, I'm sorry to have to ask, but...but...if you can't well..." she trailed off.

It was the age-old dilemma of parenting. When to say no and when to give in.

"What's it for? And how much?" asked Cannon eventually breaking the silence between them.

"A hundred pounds,"

"For what? Not another night at the pub?" he asked sarcastically.

"No, it's for a dress."
"A dress!" he answered, almost apoplectically.
"Yes, for a ball. A law-school ball."
Cannon felt himself getting angry but decided not to let it cloud his judgment. His relationship with his daughter was precious after all they had been through over the past 10 years or so. Cassie had grown up to be a sensible young woman. She had seen her father change careers from that of a senior policeman to a horse racing trainer which was a risk to the entire family. Had lost her mother to cancer and had been the victim of a kidnapping. This could have sent her off the rails, but it hadn't and Cannon was thankful for that.
"Just a second," he said into the phone.
Cupping his hand over the mouthpiece he turned to Michelle. "She wants some more money."
"How much?"
"100 quid…for a dress, for a ball."
Michelle smiled to herself.
"What's so funny?" asked Cannon.
"Mike, you don't get much for a hundred pounds these days. If Cassie can get a dress that's suitable for her for that amount, then good luck I say."
Cannon slightly exasperated and confused said, "So you are okay with it?"
"Mike, Cassie has done most of the work for you by getting a grant for herself, and she has a loan that she will need to pay back at some point. All that is for her studies. On occasion she *does* need to have some sort of social life outside of her studies, so if you can't help her just a little then who can?"
Cannon pondered this for a second. "You're right," he said, "100 pounds won't break the bank, I guess, but let's hope we can get some bloody horses running in the next week or so. Maybe we can get a few winners. Certainly, would make the owners happy….and me," he went on.
Michelle nodded, "She's waiting," she said, indicating the phone in Cannons' hand.
"Okay Cassie," he said down the line, "we'll transfer it to you shortly."
"Thanks Dad,"
"Don't thank me," he replied, "you should be thanking Michelle, she's the one who convinced me."
"Will do Dad when I speak to her next. But in the meantime, could *you* do that for me?" The relief in Cassie's voice was plain to hear. Cannon smiled inwardly. He didn't want Cassie to think he was a soft touch anymore. He wanted her to take responsibility for her own finances in addition to looking after her personal wellbeing.
"Umm, I'll see," he teased. "OK love, take it easy, no more drinking tonight hey?"

"I'll be straight to bed," she replied demurely, the joke obvious, in her tone.
"Good. Oh, and Cassie…?"
"Yes?"
"Maybe a part-time job would be worth looking at?"
"I'll see what I can find," she replied.
"Goodnight then."
"Goodnight dad. Love you." With that, she terminated the call.
For a second Cannon held the receiver to his ear, then sighed, put the phone down onto its cradle and turned back to Michelle.
"Another problem solved," he thought, sitting back in his seat.
"Everything settled then?" she inquired.
"Once we've sent the money I'd guess, at least until the next time," he said, "let's hope she is as focused on her studying as she is on the partying,"
"She'll be fine, she's a smart girl."
Cannon nodded in response, his thought process returning to what was bothering him.
"What I wanted to say earlier before Cassie called, is that you were right."
"How do you mean?"
"Well remember the other night, the day Timms came?"
"Yes?"
"Well if Timms is right about Flint's horses then there is something that doesn't gel. Something that flies in the face of his theory."
"And that is?" she asked.
"The whole point of the investigation is to understand why horses were being bet on, through the betting exchanges, to *lose*," he emphasized, "yet *RockGod* won both times, and this despite being lame in his last race. If those under investigation bet on *Youcantcatchme* to lose in his races then that also doesn't make sense. He was unlikely to win anyway. He doesn't have the ability."
"But isn't that the issue," asked Michelle, "that despite this, someone was trying to make money from them *not* winning?"
"Yes, but *Youcantcatchme* was always the outsider of the field in the race he ran in and his starting price on the tote and with the bookmakers was *forty to one*. I'm not sure how anyone could have made any money by backing him not to win."
"Sounds odd to me," she said, "and I'm somewhat confused. How does it work then that someone who is not a bookmaker can bet *against* a horse winning a race?"
Cannon took a deep breath. It did seem odd, and he was concerned that somehow, reluctantly, he was starting to find himself in a place that he didn't really want to be. However, if he didn't act, he may find that he was at the mercy of the BHA and their own investigation as they dug deeper into things. He knew that should that happen, he could be on a very long

and uncomfortable road of accusation, innuendo and of constantly and continuously having to prove his innocence. There could be suspensions, appeals, etc. He could be tied up for years, needing to do things that he didn't need now or at any time in the future. What he needed was for the scandal that was brewing, to be stopped in its tracks. For the tentacles of Timms and his team to focus their energies elsewhere, and for Cannon's horses to run. His focus was his horses.

He was aiming *RockGod*, Charles Flint's horse, the best Cannon had, towards the Grand National. While the Cheltenham Festival was for the racing *elite*, arguably including the better horses, the Grand National meeting at Aintree was the biggest showcase in the world for jumps racing. The *National* was also the most well-known race, with the general public. He had a few short weeks before the race itself, the race which effectively bookending the National Hunt racing season. Accordingly, he needed to find out what was going on. Find out how, by whom, and why, he was being implicated in the deception that Timms alluded to.

Michelle was staring at him, waiting for him to answer. Cannon's mind refocused on her question.

"Sorry love," he said, "mind wandered for a minute." His cheeks flushed slightly. Michelle had a feeling as to where this was going but decided to stay quiet for now.

"Let me explain it this way," he went on. "When a bookmaker offers odds on a horse, it's basically a simple transaction. You place your money with the bookmaker, let's use four-to-one to win for example. If your horse wins you are paid out on that basis. If your horse loses, you lose the bet and the bookmaker keeps your money."

"That's clear," she said, "most people know that."

"True. But what most people don't know is how exchanges actually work. What they do is act as an intermediary, they are not bookmakers like many people think, they don't even offer any odds like in the example I just gave."

"So, what do they do?"

"They find people willing to offer odds of horses to win or lose and match them to each other. If a match is found then the bet is taken."

She looked at him quizzically, eyebrows raised. "And?" she asked.

"So, if a person offers odds of four-to-one on a horse to win, then as with my prior example the same thing happens should that horse win. BUT, let's say the person willing to accept the bet offers MUCH more than the bookmakers are offering on the same horse in the same race. Perhaps they know something that the bookmakers don't. Perhaps they *know* that the particular horse is NOT going to win, so they offer more generous odds in order to attract more punters, get more of the betting stake and ultimately make more money with little risk."

"But how do they know the horse isn't going to win?"
"That's the sixty-four million-dollar question," replied Cannon, "how do they know? Nothing is ever certain in racing so why take the risk of paying out more than they should?"
She was still a little confused. "So how do you bet on a horse to lose then? You've told me how it works to bet on a horse to win, which I think most people understand, but betting on one to lose?"
"This is a bit trickier to explain, but essentially if a horse is say marked up by the bookmaker at one hundred to one to win, it's pretty clear that its chances are small, so conversely its chances of losing are large."
"That's clear,"
"So, when someone wants to back a horse to lose, which you can't do with a bookmaker or the tote, but you *can* do on the exchanges, then the odds offered to lose are much lower for obvious reasons. Why? Because the horse is not likely to win, so much more likely to lose."
"So, what is Timms' concern then?"
"I don't know," he went on, "perhaps someone has been offering huge odds on horses not winning, way above what should be being offered and someone has smelt a rat?"
"And?"
"And, that's what I need to find out," he replied.
He knew as soon as he had said it, as soon as the words had left his mouth, that he shouldn't have been so blunt, so direct.
Michelle had been ready for it however, her intuition spot on. She had known that it was coming. Despite the admission now that he wanted to understand what was going on, get involved, as she knew he would, she felt compelled to raise her concerns first hand even before things escalated.
"Mike,"
"I know," he answered soberly, "it's not my job anymore, and I know I should leave it with Timms and the police to investigate, but somehow I've been implicated in what's been going on and I'm pissed off about it," he said. "I, we, the whole team have worked hard over the years to build a good reputation and a clean yard. I can't just stand idly by and wait to be accused of and charged for something that I haven't done. I can't have this millstone around my neck. It could go on for months, years maybe? I need to do something!"
"You should give Timms and the BHA time to conduct further investigations," she replied, her voice calm and measured, "but I know you won't, because you are who you are, and I know it's in your blood," she said. "A career of nearly 20 years in the police force and many years as a DI don't just disappear into the past and not influence you," she continued. "You need to be careful though, you never know where this could lead and who could be behind it. Where money is involved it brings out the worst in

people."

She was stating the obvious to someone that had seen the worst of human nature throughout his life. The wife beaters, the drug addicts, the child neglecters, paedophiles, murderers and those bastards who had no label at all, but were just too evil to be considered as human. He understood where she was coming from and he loved her for it.

"Thanks for your understanding," he said touching her hair. Then he gently kissed her forehead.

"I'll be fine," he said.

Michelle looked into his eyes, stared for a few seconds until he could no longer hold her gaze.

"I hope so," she said.

CHAPTER 8

As expected, the envelope was in the post delivered that morning. It now sat on the table between the two men. They were seated in a quiet part of the Punch Tavern on Fleet Street. It was just after six pm and the two men had agreed to meet there. It was dark outside, the lights of passing cars and buses occasionally illuminating the front window, though the ornate montage on the front entrance and small lobby hid the pubs interior. The chilly wind of the past twenty-four hours had eased slightly, reducing the wind chill factor. Despite this, London was still very cold at just above four degrees. Pedestrians strolled passed the pub hardly noticing it. Heads down, scarves, gloves, and coats an absolute necessity. Inside, the atmosphere was one of quiet sophistication. Prints reflecting beer types and the promise of what beer could do for you adorned the deep red brick walls. Victorian lamps provided adequate but subtle lighting. A fire cracked and fizzed in one corner of the room, embers spitting inside the grate.

The reason to meet here was that pub was relatively close to the Central Criminal Court, or the Old Bailey as it was better known, where Perkel had been the whole day. It was also just far enough away to limit the potential for him to be seen with the other man at the table.

Both men had seen the contents of the envelope. Both had been shocked by the images.

"This has to stop," said Perkel, through thin lips. His anger tempered solely by his allegiance to the other. "And it has to stop now," he went on.

"I know," said the other man, his voice clear despite him speaking quietly. The man's background, his education, his standing, clear to anyone who would have been able to hear it. "Don't you think I understand that?" he said.

Charles Flint sat up straight on his chair. His posture ramrod-straight. He had an air about him, he had confidence. He oozed money. He was exactly six foot tall. A full head of grey hair. Tanned and neither fat nor slim. He had eyes like those of a rat, dark and deep. He was a very successful man but most people who met him were never totally sure if he was friend or foe. He had an arrogance about him that unnerved many, others liked him. Perhaps those who did saw within him a mirror of themselves? Most people, however, found that they could never really get close to him.

Perkel, on the other hand, was gregarious, friendly, but often seemed like a rabbit in a headlight. Small and round. Fidgety. Balding. In some ways, he was a caricature of himself.

"So why don't we just pay him what he wants and be done with it?" went on Perkel.

Flint stared back at his longtime client and friend. He picked up his glass of gin and tonic that each had ordered from the bar, but neither had yet touched. He sipped at the liquid, placing the glass back down on the table once he had had drunk enough.

"Henry, you know as well I do that paying off this man, this criminal!" he said, expressing his vehemence, "won't end it. This man, his *type*, will want more. It won't end just by paying him, we need a solution, a more long-term solution. Something permanent."

Perkel looked into Flints' eyes. He saw the same coldness, the same steely resolve, the same willingness to go beyond what was right, that he had first seen when they had met at Cambridge some thirty years before. It was a trait that had excited Perkel at the time, a time where he was learning to be a man. A time of excitement and discovery, risk-taking and experimentation. Flint had a predilection nowadays of going too far, and it scared Perkel.

He looked down at the envelope, nodding.

"Can you even remember the girls' name?"

"No, I don't," answered Flint dismissively with a wave of a hand, "why should you care anyway?" he went on.

Flint's arrogance irked Perkel, leading him to say through clenched teeth, and looking around the pub as he did so. "Because Charles, *fucking* underage girls is a *crime,* and your inability to see that is putting us both at risk. Christ, I'm not even sure why I am having this conversation with you," he went on. "Those pictures are dynamite and if the police ever got hold of them, we would be strung up! How old was she anyway, twelve, eleven?"

Flint took another sip of his drink. Still holding the glass in his hand, the lights in the room causing the liquid inside to sparkle, he said, "Henry you used to be so much fun, now look at you. Look at what you've become."

"What do you mean?"

"You've become…you've become..*old*," said Flint searching for the right words that he knew would hurt his cohort the most.

Perkel leaned back in his chair, his mind racing. He needed to find a way out of this mess. "Charles, I've been your friend for a long time now. I've got you out of many scrapes over the years."

"Yes, you have Henry," acknowledged Flint, "and for that, I am extremely grateful."

"Good," replied Perkel, "because this is the last straw. I'm never going to represent you in any capacity at all from now on. Do you hear me?"

Flint finished his drink slowly, dragging out the last few drops from the glass. He noticed that Perkel had not even touched his own drink.

"Are you trying to tell me, Henry, that after everything we've been through over the years, that you've now suddenly grown a spine?" he asked sarcastically.

Perkel's anger rose. It was only his self-control that stopped him from screaming at Flint. He wanted to knock the smirk off Flints' face. However, he knew he never could. He was a weak man. His outrage was a sham and Flint knew it. Flint also knew Perkel would never do anything in such a public place. It was not a clever thing to do. Bringing unnecessary attention to themselves would be stupid.

"I shouldn't even have been there in the first place," answered Perkel. "I wasn't really involved." Tears began to form in his eyes. His body language reflecting that of a defeated man.

"Ah, but you *were*," relayed Flint, his own anger growing, tempered though by his observation of how Perkel was reacting to the situation. Flint, however, grew excited seeing how Perkel's body was slowly convulsing with fear and self-loathing. He looked around at their immediate surroundings. They still needed to maintain their anonymity from the patrons. While the customer numbers had grown in the pub since they had arrived, it was just possible to talk at a reasonable volume to one another without being overheard by others.

Flint made his point. "That's the issue, Henry. We need to stay calm, relaxed. Let's not do anything stupid. So far, we have had no demands for money, or anything at all, despite this," he said, pointing at the envelope between them.

"And no comments either about us not going to the Police," added Perkel, which he thought unusual but kept it to himself.

"Precisely," replied Flint. "So, what does this tell us?" he went on, deciding to answer his own question. "I suspect that a request for money will soon be forthcoming, and when it does, that's when we need to have our plans ready and put them into action."

"What plans?" asked Perkel, feeling very uncomfortable.

"Leave that to me," answered Flint, a sense of menace in his eyes.

Perkel considered what Flint was suggesting and reflected on the earlier part of their conversation. Since this issue started, he had always considered himself an innocent bystander, someone in the wrong place at the wrong time. As a barrister, he knew that in the eyes of the law he was just as guilty as all the others. He *was* involved. While he hadn't participated, he had *watched*. He liked to watch.

He had been invited to a party at Flints' home in Chelsea, and while trying to leave unannounced around midnight, he had walked inadvertently into a room where he thought his coat was being kept.

The sight of Flint openly having sex with the young girl while others stood around, had turned him on. Perkel himself preferred boys, but it was the act that he found stimulating that night. It could have been two men or two women for all he cared, but the fact that it was in full view of others was what fascinated him. There were six other people in the room along with Perkel that night, all of whom were just watching. Three couples, some straight, some gay all who just stood and watched until it was all over. It was the start of the nightmare!

Since that night, only a few weeks ago, Perkel had received three photographs, one every three days. They were parts of a larger picture clearly showing Flint, the girl and watching on, Perkel.

"But we don't know what they really want yet," pleaded Perkel, "so how do we know what plans to make?"

"Because unless we stop this man, whoever he is, we will be watching our backs forever. Believe me, it will be money he is after. If he was a public do-gooder the photos would be in hands of the police by now."

"So, what do we do?"

"We wait. We continue with business as usual. We will see what demands are made when we get the last piece of the photo, and then I'll take it from there. Mark my words, though, with that last piece there will be demands. These people like to play a game. So far, we don't know what he wants but that will come. Believe me, that will come!"

Perkel slowly began to turn pale as the realization of what Flint had said earlier in the conversation about 'leaving the solution' to him. It began to hit home. He knew that whatever Flint would likely do, it would be illegal.

He began to feel sick. "I've got to go," he said, slowly getting to his feet and putting on his coat.

Flint eyes never left Perkels' face as Perkel completed putting on his scarf and gloves before silently turning away from the table and walking straight out into the night. Looking at the empty chair in front of him, Flint sighed, then smiled. He picked up Perkel's still full glass, raised it to his lips and drank the contents in one go.

CHAPTER 9

Walsh was on his own. He had left Sedgefield back at the station to work with the rest of the team, compiling more detail about the original murder. *The man in the Thames.* This second victim had been pulled from the river just under Blackfriars bridge. A police patrol boat had been notified through a 999 call, relayed to them after a passenger on a ferry had noticed the body in the water.

After recovery, the body had been brought to Davidson's mortuary.

"It's the same tattoo?"

"Yes, it is Inspector, and it's in the same place as the one on the other body that we inspected the other day," responded Davidson, "but I'm guessing you still don't know what it says or means?"

They were communicating through a microphone and speaker system that was normally used in the mortuary by students who would watch and study autopsies as they were being performed. Other approved visitors such as the police could also stand or sit to watch an autopsy being performed from a safe distance should it be necessary. The system suited those who were particularly squeamish, as they could see what was going on but without being close to the body. They didn't have to smell the stench of death which seemed to pervade the walls of the autopsy room and the clothes of those conducting the procedure. To Walsh, however, death seemed to creep into the very souls of all those who worked there.

"That's true Doctor" Walsh answered, "but I'm sure we'll find out soon enough. Are there any other distinguishing marks you can see or tell me about?"

"Not really. However, I can tell you that this man drowned," he pointed at the cadaver lying on the mortuary bench, chest opened up, skull partially removed.

Looking up he noticed the frown on Walsh's face. "Yes, you heard me right Inspector. This man drowned. The amount of water in his lungs makes it is obvious as to the cause of death. The difficulty we have in establishing the cause of death when the body has been in the water for a while is whether the drowning took place somewhere else and he was dumped, dead into the river, or whether he drowned in the river itself."

"I thought you could tell the difference quite easily Doctor?" answered Walsh. "I thought that when people fall into the water, the water going into their lungs is that of the river say but if they drown in a pool or a bath then it's the water of the pool or bath that you find in their lungs, is that not right?"

"Well, yes, it is," answered Davidson, "but if they already dead then put into a river, the water still gets into their lungs, especially if they have been

After the Fire

under for quite some time or are weighed under."

"Oh, I see," replied Walsh.

"Yes, it's not like you see on TV. It's not so clear cut," Davidson went on, "and from what I've been able to establish I'm not sure whether this man drowned in the bath or in the river. I just know he drowned, period." he concluded, his voice rising to make his point.

"Anything else?" asked Walsh.

"Well, Toxicology will determine if there were any additional factors that could have played a part in his death. Alcohol, drugs, that type of thing, but until we get those details, we have no other reason than to suggest it is a simple drowning."

"No signs of any external trauma?" asked Walsh.

"Nothing at all," replied Davidson, "but there was something of possible interest"

"And that was?"

"Well, he had some swelling in the throat that seemed a little unusual, but it is difficult to see what the cause was or indeed if it wasn't just a natural occurrence."

"Any ideas?" went on Walsh, trying to find out anything of use.

"It could be a number of different possibilities. Inflammation from a virus, the flu, that type of thing. Though at first glance I would suggest the cause wouldn't be normal influenza. Or maybe he just was unlucky enough to choke on a chicken bone or maybe a fishbone? It's possible that something like that could cause the swelling as well," he stated. "It would be ironic though don't you think if we found out that a dead fish was the cause of his throat to swell. Given his death was by drowning." Davidson chuckled to himself. "Anyway, we've taken some swabs and we'll do some tissue testing to find out more," he went on.

"So, returning to the tattoo, it's...?"

"Yours to decipher I'm afraid Inspector. My job is to determine the cause of death. Your job is to find out why and if anyone else was involved in that person's demise."

Walsh considered this for a second. He knew Davidson was right but wanted more.

"The other day you said you had never seen that type of tattoo before, yes?"

"Yes, that right."

"So, it's quite unusual wouldn't you say?"

"Yes, it is."

"So, seeing two bodies within a few days of each other, with the same tattoo, and both having been in the river, can't be too much of a coincidence can it?"

"I know where you are going with this inspector, and like you, I agree it is

After the Fire

way too coincidental."

"Are they related?" interrupted Walsh, referring to the two individual bodies.

"Too early to tell, we haven't concluded our DNA samples for testing."

"How about on features?"

"On first glance, there are some similarities. Physically they do have a similar build."

"So, any conclusions?"

"I'll let you know late tomorrow or the day after," answered Davidson, "it will be in my report, but at first glance, given this one has a face, whereas the other didn't, it is *possible* that they are related in some capacity but that's just a guess right now."

"Thank you, Doctor, that's all I needed to know."

"Okay everybody," said Walsh, "I need your full attention."

He was back at the station and wanted to relay to his team how urgent the investigation regarding their first murder victim and what now appeared to be a related murder, was becoming.

"Things have gotten a lot more serious over the past forty-eight hours," he emphasized. "As Sergeant Sedgefield would have told you by now, we have two victims, both of whom were found in the Thames and both of who seem to have the same tattoo on their arms. The tattoo that on victim one, was one of two and on victim two was the only tattoo that he had. The tatt' that was made up of letters."

Walsh stopped for a few seconds, letting the obvious connection filter into his teams' consciousness and the ripple of a murmur within the room settle down.

"So, first things first. Fitch! Windsor!" he called out, addressing the Constable and the IT representative in the team, "any luck with the wording of the tatt'? Anything at all as to what it means?"

Windsor turned to Fitch, who was seated beside him, both men perched on the edge of the desks that formed part of the situation room.

Fitch nodded his head slightly, suggesting Windsor should answer the question.

"At this stage Sir, we haven't found much. We've spent the past twenty-four hours plus looking at various websites and used various translation tools, but from the results to date we can't find any Polish words that fit the pattern of the tattoo on victim number one."

Walsh's disappointment was clear to see on his face.

"But we'll continue with our search Sir," jumped in Fitch, "though I think it

After the Fire

likely that it will be best if we contact our counterparts in Poland to see if they are able to help."

Given the current lack of progress the team had made on this part of the investigation, Walsh reluctantly conceded the point, "Okay, get in contact with our friends in Warsaw, let's see what they can come up with. Also, while you are at it, send them a photo of the latest victim, at least he has a face. Maybe they can let us know if they have any idea who he could be. They'll have access to passport and other ID information I'm sure. He must have had one to get into the UK, so hopefully, they may be able to find a match?"

"Yes Sir," replied Fitch, "we'll get onto it right away."

"Sergeant," asked Walsh, "anything else in relation to our first victim? Has anyone reported a missing person anywhere that could match our mystery man?"

"No Sir."

"And have the *boffins* in the lab, been able to work out where he went into the river?"

The *boffins* Walsh referred to were not the scene of the crime teams, but the back-office teams that are able to do further analysis on the crime scene details. For example, looking at blood splatter patterns, undertake ballistic tests on bullets or guns found abandoned that could be or were related to crimes being investigated. The sophistication of today's' techniques, which never failed to impress Walsh, often amused him as well. They could use mathematical models that took data such as tides, rainfall, the river flows, etecetera and could interpret this data to approximate how the body of a victim could end up where it was found. Then taking that information combined with the estimate by Dr. Davidson as to how long the body had been in the river, they could work out a general idea of where the victim first hit the water. Despite all this, Walsh mused, the *tech-heads* still couldn't give him a proper phone in his office. He still only had a dumb softphone option that he couldn't work out how to operate.

He sighed as Sedgefield answered the question.

"No, not yet Sir, but we expect an answer from the smart brigade soon."

"Bloody hell! How long does it take?" retorted Walsh, immediately regretting his outburst. He needed his team to be on his side. He needed them to be focused. He enjoyed a positive relationship with most if not all of them, and he wanted to keep it that way.

The room was silent. Each member of the team knew how progress on a case could turn morale around, making up for the long periods on an investigation when nothing seemed to happen. They knew outbursts from the leadership occurred and the team expected them at times. When they did come, however, it often negatively impacted the morale they wanted to keep high especially when there were resource restraints and increased

After the Fire

demands on each of them. To get the best out of the team they needed support and praise, not criticisms.

Walsh looked around at the assembled group before him., They were all facing him, looking into his eyes, awaiting his next remarks.

"Okay people, I know it's hard, but we have *two* victims now," he said, emphasizing the fact that while the cases may well be linked, at this stage there were two bodies that they needed to identify and two apparent crimes to investigate. While one of the bodies was clearly murdered, the injuries to victim one clearly ruling out suicide, the other victim seemed to have just drowned. At this stage the how and the where was unclear. So, was it a case for the team anyway? The sole fact that the tattoos worn by each man were the same was why Walsh's team had occupancy of the two cases. So, did victim B or number 2 die in the river or somewhere else? Over the years, Walsh, like most cops of longstanding, did not believe in coincidences. He was sure that the two bodies were linked somehow. He just needed to work out how.

"Sergeant, I think we should do a door knock around the Balham, Tooting Bec areas for starters," went on Walsh, "let's see if anyone recognizes either the tattoos or the victim that we have a face for. Victim B. There is a reasonable Polish community around that area and hopefully, somebody knows something that may be of use".

Turning his attention to Wendy Carmichael he said, "Wendy I want you to work with Sedgefield and get out amongst the community. Put up some photographs on a few shop windows, get them on lamp-posts or something, meet with some of the local traders in the area, especially Polish business owners and let's see if they can provide any detail at all. If they can't, then obviously we will need to look in a different Manor. But I'm guessing someone knows something. We just need to find out what's being said on the street".

Carmichael nodded, "Yes Sir, no problem".

Walsh looked around the room. It was still early days in the investigation. He knew it would take a while. It always did.

"Okay," he said, standing up and arching his back, "if there is nothing else, no further questions, then let's get on with it."

The room remained quiet for a few seconds to see if anyone would add anything further. No one spoke. Walsh clapped his hands to dismiss them and everyone moved back to their respective desks, computers, and phones. They all knew what they had to do.

Walsh waved towards Sedgefield, "Sergeant," he said, "my office, you need to show me how to use this bloody phone!"

CHAPTER 10

"Look at this," said Cannon.

They were sitting together in Telside's office in the stable block directly across from Cannon's house. The two buildings separated by a small cement yard where the horses walked around most days in order to stretch their legs before their daily exercises.

Outside the watery sun had won a battle over the cloud, winning itself a temporary reprieve. The clouds had parted, allowing the sun to turn the sky a lighter shade of turquoise blue. The late morning rays pierced the high window behind Telsides' chair, landing themselves on the opposite wall, creating a soft silhouette of the security bars in the window. They looked like those of a jail cell. Cannon noted the symbolism in his mind.

It was still quite cold outside despite the sun trying to give warmth to the day as it traversed the sky in its inexorable journey towards the horizon and ultimately setting around 6 pm. It had been even colder overnight than in the last few days. As the sky had cleared, an easy frost had formed and had been on the ground when the different lots had been taken out for their exercise. The soil had not hardened, primarily due to a lot of the moisture of recent times having drained away. The cold had crisped up the grass slightly, covering the area in a sea of gentle whiteness, the morning darkness softened by the light of a three-quarter moon. The heat from a small fan heater sitting in a corner of the room kept the chill away. Outside the office, both men could hear horses being fed and watered and being put away for the rest of the day. Stable doors opened and closed. Buckets clanged and water ran from taps throughout. Jokes were being shared and laughter and giggles could be heard amongst the stable staff. Exercise and schooling were over. It was almost lunchtime. In the next hour, the stables would be quiet, horses and staff resting.

The table at which they sat groaned under piles of Racing Post newspapers all neatly stacked at one end. In addition, various pieces of racing equipment, including blinkers, ear covering's, *bits* and *bit rings*, even a part of a racing saddle were pushed to the other end of the table. All this *gear* were things that Telside was looking into for Cannon to see if they could use it as a replacement of Cannon's current or older pieces. Lighter *bits* made from new alloys, new coloured ear coverings made from newer materials were all items that any stable needed to keep abreast of, despite their expense. Any advantage within the rules of racing, that improved results, were always things that Cannon would gratefully look into, and if appropriate would use. Some horses needed blinkers to concentrate their mind on the job at hand. Others needed ear coverings, as the noise of a crowd would upset them. Others had *soft mouths* and the hard bits that they held in their mouths while racing were uncomfortable and sore, so a lighter softer bit could well make the difference between a horse trying or not trying, a horse winning or not winning, a happy owner or one that took his horses elsewhere. All these innovations were part of today's world of racing.

"I've done some analysis of Charles Flints' horses and I can understand now why Timms' is querying what's going on," said Cannon.
"Does it include his two of ours?" questioned Rich.
"To some degree, yes, but there is an anomaly,"
"And that is?"
"*RockGod*," replied Cannon, "look, let me show you."
Cannon opened a spreadsheet that he had printed out in his office before he had walked across to see Telside.
He pointed at a table that had four columns on it which was approximately twenty lines long. The columns were headed, *Horse name, Starting prices, Position finished, Stewards comments (if any)*.
"Look," said Cannon pointing at the column headed *Starting prices*, "nearly every horse, with the exception of *Youcantcatchme* started as the favourite or second favourite according to the official starting prices. And as you can see with the exception of *RockGod* every single horse belonging to Flint finished either last, fell or was pulled up and didn't finish the race."
"Well it does happen," said Telside playing devils' advocate.
"Yes that's true," answered Cannon, "but….." he hesitated.
"But what?"
"Take a look at the Stewards comments," went on Cannon, "what do you see?"
Telside scanned the list. "Lame!," he suddenly shouted out, "nearly all of the runners on the list that actually completed the race, finished up lame. How is that possible? Even our two runners according to this, finished up lame."
"That's right," went on Cannon. "What is the probability of every runner finishing lame?"
Telside thought for a second. "Hang on," he said, "what about *RockGod?* He also finished lame in the last race he ran in. He spread a shoe just before the final fence, but he still won. I remember that. It was at Sandown."
"And what does the Stewards report say?"
"It says exactly that," answered Rich.

"And if you look at nearly all the others, the same thing applies." he pointed at the list, running his finger down it and reading out the comments. "'Lost a shoe', 'Lame in off-fore', 'Pulled up lame'. Somethings clearly not right here," he said.

"So how come the Stewards or Timms' haven't connected the dots as you have?" asked Rich.

"I'm not sure," said Cannon, "maybe they are looking much wider than I am? Remember I am only looking at Flints' horses. Maybe Timms is looking at a bigger sample and perhaps they haven't been able to see what I'm seeing?"

"Umm, maybe," answered Rich, "maybe," he repeated, allowing the thought to drift away.

"So, what I need to do, is a little bit more investigating," went on Cannon, somewhat too eagerly for Rich. "I need to find out how and why both my horses ended up lame when, if you recall, the next day both of them were pretty much back to normal. Almost as if nothing had happened."

Telside looked at his boss, his friend. "Mike, is this heading where I think it's heading?" he asked knowingly.

Cannon looked at the ceiling as if thinking about what he was going to say. Eventually, he knew he needed to look Telside in the eye and tell his most trusted friend his thoughts on the matter.

"Rich," he said, "despite what you may think about me getting involved in something I don't know much about at this stage, I have to do it. You know I do." Telside stayed silent allowing Cannon to continue. "I have to do it because it's *my* name that's being besmirched here. It's *my* reputation on the line, *my* livelihood threatened. I just can't let it go," he declared, "I need to resolve this, for *my* own sanity. I can't...."

"Mike...Mike," interrupted Telside, "you don't have to convince *me*," he said, "we've been through so much together and I know you need to look into this and try and resolve it. So please, you don't have to go on, I get it and I'm with you on it, I'm okay and happy to step up as I did previously."

Cannon stopped for a few seconds, thinking about how to thank his friend. The silence was eventually broken by Telside.

"Just remember," he said raising an eyebrow, "the only person I think you need to convince, is Michelle."

Cannon nodded. "Already done Rich, that was the easy bit," he said smiling, "What I would like to ask though Rich is whether you would agree to back me up on this one? I mean, not just keeping the yard running as tightly as you do, but also help me with some of the investigative work?"

Without hesitation, Telside responded enthusiastically. "Mike, what's at stake here is both our livelihoods. We love doing what we do with these horses. We've been through a lot together and we've had some interesting moments along the road. We have the owners, but let's not forget these kids either, who depend on us," he said, nodding towards the sounds coming from outside the office. "If there is someone trying to destroy what we have, for whatever reason, then I'm all for jumping in and helping," he said. "Mike, this is *personal* now. As usual, you can count on me."

"Thanks, Rich," replied Cannon smiling, "I always knew I could."

CHAPTER 11

It was the flapping of the edge of the paper that caught her eye. The breeze wasn't too strong, but the chill it brought with it still made her walk with her head bowed. She had just come from the city centre and had gotten off the tube at Balham. Having turned into Boundaries Road she headed towards her apartment on Balham Park Road when the noticed the photograph.

It was a standard Police photo-kit picture. A grainy face with eyes closed, a monochrome picture with a boldly worded headline, *'Do you know this man?'*

She stopped, putting her portfolio down, resting against her knees. The protected base of the art carrying case sitting on the toes of her boots rather than on the damp pavement.

Staring at the picture and the contact number underneath the face, she felt numb. She knew him, but where was he? Was he in trouble? Was he injured? Was he in a hospital somewhere? Was this picture here on the lamp-post because the police needed to contact a next of kin or a relative of some sort? The poster was unclear as to its intent. Her mind spun as she thought of all the reasons. What options did she have?

She stood staring, not moving, oblivious to all around her. People walked by not noticing, nor caring. Her hair was wild, blown by the wind. Brightly coloured, with streaks of red, green and purple dispersed throughout her natural chestnut brown. No-one stopped as she kneeled down to catch her breath. Just another junkie staring into space!

The breeze that was previously uncomfortable now helped to cool her down. She was in shock. Her cheeks flushed, and her heart began pounding. She knew she had to get home before she fainted.

She knew the man in the picture, but where was he and why was he on a Police identikit picture? She needed to speak to Pete, but he hadn't been around for the last ten days.

She gathered up her portfolio. What was a good day previously, had now turned sour! She continued along the road until she turned into her street, made her way quickly into her flat, put down her portfolio and called the police. She also needed to find Pete.

The phone was ringing but he wouldn't answer it. He was watching the film. It was another sad-arse politician who would soon be in his pocket. It hadn't been difficult to set up the camera in the room. They always went there. It seemed Westminster was less important than spending every Wednesday afternoon with the woman, and it wasn't the man's wife either. The minister's secretary was doing more than taking notes for her boss. The film was clear. His and her faces could be frozen on the screen in high definition if needed.

Their lovemaking was loud, at times guttural, almost primeval. When each was satisfied, they lay back on the bed. Such personal films never failed to make the voyeur aroused. The power he was about to exude over the minister was better than the sex he had just watched.

Jack Williams wasn't a man to be messed with. He had hands like meat trays, butcher's hands and the size about him to match. A large man, but one light on his feet if he needed to be. A thief, a liar, extortionist, drug dealer, and murderer. More recently drugs and money laundering had become the most profitable part of his *business*. He commanded respect. Though he, in turn, had to provide it. He wasn't the only player. Some were even more ruthless than he was. He managed his business closely. Like anyone else, he had debts to pay. Sometimes that made him uncomfortable. Despite this when he didn't receive what he thought he deserved, he went out and got it. If his client didn't want to pay, Williams just took it anyway.

He had several 'clients' over the years who had tried to renege on their 'obligations'. Most eventually paid, some with 'impairments' to their being, others just 'disappeared'. He was hopeful that his latest 'client' would be able to offer something more useful than money. Contacts. Inside information. Time would tell. Despite his status, recent events were playing on his mind, not everything was going as well as he would like.

He looked at the mobile phone that he had previously ignored. His details were known to just a limited number of people and he liked to keep it that way. He changed phone numbers and used different providers every month. His 'colleagues' did all the work for him so that his name never appeared on any contract, or documentation of any kind. He saw who had called, decided that the caller could wait. He wanted to watch the film again.

CHAPTER 12

Cannon stopped his car in the parking area. Tony Campbell's stables just north of Stroud were just an hour's drive from those of Cannon. While they knew each other on the racecourse they were not friends or even socialized with each other, they were competitors

Alighting from the car, he was met by Campbell who offered him a strong but contented handshake.

Looking up at the weak sun, the grey wintry clouds caressing the sky like fingers on a fretboard during a lengthy guitar solo, quick, jagged and erratic Campbell suggested that both men should go inside the house. Once inside Campbell offered Cannon a drink.

"After all it is six pm somewhere," he chuckled.

Cannon politely declined but agreed to a coffee. His morning had been busy watching his horses go through their paces on the schooling and training grounds, then making the journey to see Campbell.

As they stood together in the kitchen, Cannon watched Campbell put the kettle on to make his drink. Campbell was a widower his wife having died a few years back from a pulmonary embolism. They had had no children, so at the time of his wife's death, Campbell had been alone. He had thrown himself into his horses, having some limited success. His most famous was in winning the Tingle Creek Chase at Sandown with a twenty to one outsider named *Willowbark*. Since then he had suffered the ups and downs of the "game" as he liked to call it.

Campbell was a short man, now in his mid-sixties. He had a full head of grey hair, grey moustache and despite being inside the house, he continued to wear his trademark flat cap. He was almost as wide as he was tall. His face was ruddy with light veins showing at his cheeks. He had green eyes, with a glint of mischievousness within them, but they were surrounded with puffy bags as if he didn't sleep very well. He also gave the impression of someone who was permanently cold. A former flat race jockey until weight became an issue for him over thirty years ago, for the past twenty-five years he had been a typical journeyman trainer. Making a living but not being fortunate enough to ever having a real champion horse in his yard.

They stood in Campbell's kitchen, surprisingly modern, with all the latest appliances, most of which Cannon surmised were seldom, if ever, used. As the kettle boiled, Cannon watched his host spoon instant coffee into a mug with a logo on it about being the *best boss*.

"Milk? Sugar?" asked Campbell.

"As it comes," replied Cannon, wanting to move on and talk to his host about the reason he was there.

Campbell led the way from the kitchen to a well-appointed lounge. It was decorated in what one would call a traditional style. Two large armchairs facing a fireplace. A three-seater couch sat alongside a wall facing a French window, partially covered by heavy velvet curtains tied back with roped cord thus allowing one to look out onto a small but neat garden. Logs in the fire glowed dully behind a glass fireguard, brass trimmings around the edges. On the walls, covered with pink carnation wallpaper set in an erratic pattern, were paintings of horse racing scenes. Cannon surmised that if they were originals, they were probably painted over a hundred years ago. The whole place seemed right out of a Bronte sister's novel. Cannon noting the juxtaposition with that of the kitchen.

"My wife's style," indicated Campbell, nodding towards the largest painting above the fireplace. It had pride of place. "Not mine to be honest though," he continued, chuckling to himself as he took a quick nip of the whisky he had poured earlier. "I'm more of a landscape man myself, watercolours."

Cannon smiled, allowing Campbell to get comfortable on his chair as they both took their seats. Cannon sat on the edge of his chair, trying to send signals from his body language that he was there to talk business.

"So, Mike, how can I help? You said something on the phone about an investigation you are undertaking. Sounds fascinating."

Cannon had called Campbell earlier that morning to check that he was not off to the races. He had mentioned to Campbell that he may be able to help add some colour to a theory that Cannon was beginning to form in his mind. He was hoping that Campbell would be able to provide some input.

"It relates to *Towelshifter* and *GrecianBoy*," said Cannon.

"What about them?" answered Campbell, "they are both having a rest at the moment. What with all this rain we've been having. After their last runs, I thought I might as well give them a break. Neither of them really likes the heavy ground, especially not *GrecianBoy*, he likes it to be much firmer."

Before Campbell began to talk about *Towelshifter*, Cannon interrupted him.

"Sorry Tony to jump in, but do you remember what happened in the last runs of both horses?"

"Of course, I do. What trainer worth his salt doesn't know what happened to his runners when they race? Especially when they both ended up favourite. If he's not on top of things, his owners would be all over him like a rash!"

"So, what *did* happen?" pressed Cannon.

Campbell eyed his visitor for a second. Cannon could imagine Campbell's mind wondering why he wanted to know about these two horses specifically.

"*Towelshifter's* bloody jockey made a mess of it, didn't he?! Got too close to

After the Fire

the hurdle on the first circuit at Worcester and the horse fell. Hit the bloody hurdle hard as well. The horse ended up lame didn't it?"

Cannon assumed the questions in Campbell's response were rhetorical so he ignored them, asking, "And *GrecianBoy*?"

Cannon knew that the 9-year-old gelding was a 'chaser'.

"Similar thing really," responded Campbell, 'though to be fair the jockey did say that the horse's action had changed a bit just a few strides before the fence that he fell at."

"Like he had lost a shoe or something?' asked Cannon.

"Yes, it was at the meeting at Bangor. The jockey said the horse seemed to stumble and hesitate just before the jump, and as a consequence was *looking for a stride* but couldn't get balanced again. He hit the fence and went down. Fortunately, both jockey and horse weren't injured despite the fall, but the horse ended up lame."

"Did the vet on course find anything else wrong with the horse?"

"No, he had a look at the horses' feet and saw that it looked like he had spread a shoe and that was that." answered Campbell, "of course, he looked over the rest of the horse but there was nothing obvious that he could find. Cheeky bugger just told me to get a better farrier next time. I told him that I had used the one on the course there before the race."

"And what did he say?"

"Damn all, just smiled and walked off. Anyway, why the interest Mike? You've got me curious." Campbell drained the last of his drink and placed the glass on a small table covered with a crocheted doily next to him.

Cannon gathered his thoughts, delaying his answer while he finished his coffee. He held onto the mug.

"Is the owner of both horses Charles Flint?"

"Yes,"

"Have you ever met him?"

Campbell thought for a second, then answered. "I have actually. Last season, about a year ago now. A tall man as I recall. Well educated. Met him at the races. Stratford, I think it was. He was up there for some cultural thing and we had one of his horses running. He didn't stay long, just said hello in the parade ring, then when the horses went onto the track he disappeared. Not even sure if he stayed to watch the race."

"How did the horse go?" asked Cannon.

"It was *Towelshifter*, he ran fifth of seven," replied Campbell, showing a resigned look on his face.

Cannon didn't want to pique Campbell's curiosity too much, so he decided to shift tack. Move the conversation in another direction. He now knew a little bit more about Flints' horses and was slowly building up a picture in his mind about Flint himself. He needed to know a bit more about how Leslie Timms' investigation was going.

After the Fire

"Have you had a visit from anyone from the BHA recently?" Cannon asked.

"No, have you?"

"Yes, just the other day. They were checking my infectious disease control measures," Cannon lied, making up a story to deflect the real reason for his visit, "I was told it was just a random audit that the BHA was undertaking. The equine flu outbreak last year up in Cheshire seemed to have spooked them a bit and so they seem to be in prevention mode"

"And how did you go?"

"Fortunately, the yard got a clean bill of health," answered Cannon. "I think they are doing the rounds. Could be over here soon I'd guess. Particularly if you're unlucky and they pick you out to be checked over earlier than others on their list," Cannon continued. Silence ensued between the two men as Campbell considered what he had heard.

"So why the interest in Charles Flint's horses then?" he asked unexpectedly. Cannon realized that Campbell was extremely sharp-minded, despite the early whisky. He had turned the conversation back to where Cannon had not wanted it to go. Cannon knew he had to choose his words carefully.

"Quite simple really," he answered, trying to hide the knot in his stomach as it tightened. He could think on the fly without a problem, but he was more used to telling and seeking the truth, not seeking the truth by lying. "I heard on the grapevine that *Mr..er.Flint* was considering moving his horses from me, as I haven't had the best of season's this year," he said, "and I think the visit from the BHA was due to someone spreading false rumours about my stables and how well I run it. I guess Mr. Flint may have used a bit of influence as well to see if this season's poor showing was as a result of any poor practices in my yard."

Cannon's face remained statue-like, but inside he was really churned up. He liked Campbell and he didn't want to lie to him. However, he felt he needed to keep his investigation private for now. He had discovered what he had needed to from Campbell, now he had to find the next piece in the puzzle.

"Ummm," thought Campbell, his hand rubbing across his chin as if he was thinking deeply.

After a few seconds Campbell raised himself up out of his chair saying, "Okay Mike, I believe you where thousands wouldn't," he smiled. "your reputation of being a good guy precedes you."

A glint in his eye told Cannon that his story may not have been fully accepted, but Campbell was prepared to go with it.

"Well, as you're here, come and have a look at the *cattle*," he chuckled. "I've got a couple of runners at Taunton tomorrow provided it's not rained off, so I would be interested to get your view on how they look."

Cannon's stomach churned. He knew that he had dodged a bullet and that his fellow trainer would be circumspect in not disclosing to anyone about

After the Fire

what he was investigating. Campbell had seen through Cannon's story but would be sensible and keep his mouth shut. After all, if whatever Cannon was looking into, was trying to find out what was behind one his horses falling, potentially injuring itself or its jockey, or worse still killing both of them, then Campbell was all for it.

As they walked out of the house through the back door and headed for the stables, Cannon said, "It would be good to see *GrecianBoy* if that's ok?"

Campbell just nodded, holding his cap tightly to his head with his left hand as the wind tried to whip it away.

"At least this will help dry out the tracks around here, hope it's the same down west," he nodded in the general direction of Taunton just over seventy miles away.

"Agreed," answered Cannon, his thoughts turning to *RockGod's* next outing. The eight-year-old gelding had won over three miles at Leopardstown in Ireland just after Christmas and his rating had risen to 162 so he was well set to qualify for the *National* and had been the mainstay of Cannon's financial survival. Without the horse, the income from its success and the fact that its profile maintained his reputation as a good trainer, despite the poor season, Cannon may well have been out of the game. It was only his passion, his commitment and perseverance to keep going, that he was still doing what he loved. His former life as a cop had been left behind a long time ago, but when his livelihood and family were at risk as they were now, he would stop at nothing to get to the truth. Some would say that Cannon never really left the force. The experiences he had endured during his time as a policeman, the things he saw, the way people lived, fought, died was imprinted in his mind, his dreams, his consciousness.

The two men walked across a pebbled yard. Members of Campbell's team struggled with the wind as they tried to hose down the area, trying to keep the area clean and tidy. Water sprayed in different directions as it was caught by the breeze, creating rainbows in the soft sunlight. Shadows on the ground from the stables created dark squares that gobbled the water from view as it dispersed in the air.

The stables themselves were neat and tidy, smelling of fresh straw and detergent. It was obvious that Campbell ran a disciplined yard. Everything had its place. The routine was obvious from the notices inside the building. As they walked between the stalls which numbered a dozen on either side, most occupied by sleepy, but alert animals, Campbell stopped suddenly at the third stall on the left-hand side as they walked.

"And this," he said, "is *GrecianBoy*". Cannon looked at the horse through the bars of the stall that sat halfway up the brickwork making up the front wall of the stable. The animal had turned away and had moved towards the back, his large rump the only part of the horse that Cannon could see. The bottom half of the stall door was locked however, the top half was open,

After the Fire

secured at the side by a latch. Despite the lighting inside the barn, the greyness outside made everything inside the stall seem dark and gloomy.

Campbell's hand moved to open the stall door. As he did so the horse turned its head towards the two men. Cannon noticed the horse seemed a little agitated, the eyes appearing dull. Spittle around the horses' mouth was a dead giveaway. Campbell who was talking about his staff as they entered the stall didn't seem to notice the horses' agitated state. Perhaps it was familiarity, perhaps it was the lighting, perhaps it was his senses being dulled by his whisky, but Campbell seemed totally oblivious of *GrecianBoy* beginning to lash out, kicking towards the two of them, his hind legs like spears. Deadly. The horses' first kick just missing Campbell and Cannon by centimeters as the hoof smashed into the stall wall.

As they tried to retreat out of the stall, the horse half turned, nostrils flared, teeth bared and kicked out again. Cannon screamed out to Campbell to be wary as he tried to drag him out through the stall door, but as he did so another spear grazed Cannon's thigh before hammering into Campbell's knee, splintering it into pieces. Campbell screamed out in agony, Cannon pulling him into the relative safety of the passageway between the two rows of stalls. *GrecianBoy* by now mad and delirious reared on his back legs, his front legs scraping the bars of his stable. Foam floated in the air, disturbed dust particles from the straw visible in the poor light. As the horse began to sweat up, lather covered his flanks, sweat dripped from his belly. Cannon slammed the stable door shut, locking it as he did so. He watched in horror as the horse whinnied and neighed in apparent confusion and pain. Cannon couldn't decide what was agitating the horse so severely but he could hear the screams of pain from Campbell. All the furore and noise had resulted in the staff outside and a couple from inside come running to see what was going on and how they could help. They swarmed around their Guvnor, trying to help the old man up from the concrete floor, his protestations about his broken leg clear from his verbal expletives.

Meanwhile, just as quickly as it had started, *GrecianBoy* stopped making any noise. The silence was palpable. The reason was obvious. One minute the horse was actively trying to kill the two men, the next it was dead. Heart attack? Poison? Colic? Other natural causes? Cannon wasn't sure, but he knew what he had seen. And from that, he knew something didn't seem right.

He turned to look at the injured man, who was now being attended to by one of his team. Cannon could see from the way the young woman concerned had taken charge of the situation that she was someone who had completed first aid training. It was obvious that she knew what she was doing.

"Has anyone phoned for an ambulance?" Cannon called out.

An affirmative response was given by one of the boys gathered around where Campbell lay, immobilized by the young woman. The boy, a young apprentice jockey, had been working outside, cleaning tack when Cannon had arrived at the yard. "And the Police!" the boy said.

Cannon responded with a *thank you*. His nerves were beginning to jangle with shock. His reaction to what had happened was not something he had ever really been able to control, despite all his experiences throughout the years in the force. One never did. It was a basic human reaction when one was close to death.

It may not have been obvious to most, but Cannon understood how horses react to things that bother them. It was a trait you notice over time, especially those that live and work with the animal over many years. The horse gives many signs as to how it feels. Fear, Surprise. All the signs are there. In the way a horse will hold its head, how it will flick its ears, or how it tries to bite or kick out. The same applies to injuries or illnesses. Some just require rest, being immobilized, others could require much more long term or stronger treatments. Either way, in time you can see and sense how an animal is feeling. He didn't know the horse and unfortunately, it was now too late for *GrecianBoy*. It had almost been too late for Campbell as well. Cannon didn't say anything but as he pondered what had just happened, he realized how close he and Campbell had come to being killed. He pondered whether they had come also close to being murdered?

CHAPTER 13

They were sitting in her studio, her apartment on the second floor. It was an old converted warehouse which years ago was used to store cotton that was being readied for export across the globe Along the sides of the walls stood various canvases of differing sizes. Some were finished paintings, others barely started, just smudges of paint that indicated the beginning of an idea then left alone for reasons known only to the artist. On shelves, on the floor and around two easels that had canvases upon them with half-finished paintings, abstract work, were bottles and jars, tubes of paint both closed and open, their innards spilling out onto various trays and blocks of woods like a recently gutted fish. The smell of ammonia, bleach, and glues filled the air, acrid.

Walsh found the place stifling and uncomfortable. Sedgefield sat passively holding his mobile phone in his hands ready to record the conversation. While Walsh went through the formalities of introducing both of them to the woman, Sedgefield scanned the room. Oblong glass windows, just above head height were streaked with grime from the rain and exhaust fumes from the passing traffic outside. They allowed small amounts of light into the room. Despite this, it was apparent that due to the almost continuous grey skies at this time of year it was necessary to leave on the bright florescent lights that hung from the heavy industrial beams spanning the ceiling. Without them, it would have been difficult to see, for an artist to work. The lights gave off significant heat adding to the policemen's discomfort.

At the opposite end of the room, a door which Sedgefield assumed was the bathroom, led off to the left. In the remaining space was a double bed, a kitchenette with a mini-fridge and a wooden dining table with four chairs sitting upon a well-worn Persian rug. A small television and sound system which appeared to be turned on to a local radio station stood on an upturned tea chest. *Very Bohemian*, thought Sedgefield.

"So, you say you know this man?" asked Walsh, handing over the photo of the face of the second body pulled from the Thames. The closed eyes of the man in the picture highlighting the lack of life.

The woman took the picture, staring at it before answering.

"Yes, I do," she answered, "he's my boyfriend. We live together as you can see," she nodded towards the double bed. "that's why I reported him missing. Is he ok? Is he hurt? It looks like he's unconscious. Is he in a hospital? Can I see him?" Her voice rose with each question.

The two detectives looked at each other realizing that this was a potential breakthrough in their investigation. Walsh ignored her questions for now.

After the Fire

"And how long has he been missing, before you reported it, Miss, um, Flint?" he asked, hesitating while he checked his notes to confirm her name.
"It's Ms. Inspector, I'm a Ms. *not*, a Miss," she replied somewhat forcefully. Walsh took note of the point she was making. In today's world of being PC and tolerant to all, he needed to be aware of people's sensitivities.
"I'm not married, never have been, never will be," she continued, "now could you please let me know what's happened? What's going on?"
"All in good time, Ms. Flint," said Walsh taking on board the woman's reaction to the use of the epithet he had labelled her with. In Walsh's assessment of her, he could already see she was someone with an alternative lifestyle. An artist, clearly independent and with a mind of her own. He liked that. She was approximately thirty to thirty-five years old, with chestnut hair, streaked with red, green and purple, tied back unnecessarily fiercely which pulled at the side of her face and caused wrinkles at the corners of her green eyes. Her skin was clear, a little pallid from the lack of sun, but Walsh could see that if she smiled, she could be quite attractive. She sat on the edge of what appeared to be a second-hand leather couch, cracks in the seats and backs clearly noticeable. Her hands were splattered with paint, visible across the knuckles. She held them together between her knees. She wore jeans and a dark blue shirt. Dressed to go out, but it seemed she had just returned from shopping in the city. On the arm of the couch lay a smock smeared with a rainbow of different colours, lying in a heap as if it had been hurriedly removed. Her working clothes. Walsh and Sedgefield were seated on rattan chairs opposite.
"Well Ms. Flint, is it okay if I call you Lucy?" he asked, again referring to his notes, and trying to be more engaging, given he was about to break the bad news.
"Yes you may Inspector, and to answer your previous question, the last time I saw Steve."
"Steve….?" interrupted Sedgefield.
"Yes, oh sorry," she answered somewhat apologetically. "Kaminski, Steve. Actually, it's Stefan Kaminksi, but I call him Steve. He's Polish, from a place called Torun. I last saw him about four or five days ago. Now can you please tell me what is going on?"
"Okay Lucy," replied Walsh, trying to show restraint and a level of compassion. "I'm sorry to tell you this, and I know it will be difficult for you, but unfortunately, your boyfriend, Steve, is dead."
"Oh my God," she wailed, falling back into her chair, tears beginning to run down her cheeks. "Oh my God," she repeated.
Walsh let the woman sob for a minute, allowing her to process what he had just told her. He watched her reaction, her body convulsing, hearing her say how? when? where? between her wails.
Walsh waited. It was a job he had done many times before. He didn't like it,

but it was a necessary evil. Part of the job. As the crying started to slow, he said, "Lucy, we don't yet know where he died, but we think we know how."

"How?" she replied, blowing her nose and wiping her eyes on a handkerchief that Sedgefield had offered her.
"We believe he drowned, but we are not sure yet where or how."
"Drowned?" she asked quizzically, her eyes red, her cheeks lined with grey tracks where her tears had run.
"Yes, but we will know a bit more once the autopsy results are made available."
"Drowned?" she repeated to herself, "I don't understand...."
The room was quiet for a few seconds before Walsh continued. He saw she was now more composed.
"You mentioned that you last saw Steve about four or five days ago. Can you be more precise?"
After a few moments Walsh got his answer, "It was definitely four days ago. Steve left for work on Sunday morning, that was the last time I saw him."
She began sobbing again.
"What did he do? For work?"
"He was an electronics engineer, by profession, but since he had emigrated to the UK about six years ago, he had struggled to find a suitable job for his qualifications, so he was working as a chef, while he did his Masters."
"And where did he work?"
"At *Lamberts* on Station Parade, not too far from here really. About a ten - minute walk or so."
"And his studies?"
"At Imperial College"
"Impressive," said Sedgefield, knowing how difficult it was to get into one of the top universities in London. He knew then that Steve must have had quite an intellect to study at Imperial College.
"Was it unusual for him, not to return home after he finished work?"
"Not really" she answered, "often he would go out for a drink after work, then if time didn't allow it because he had an early lecture or something, he would crash at a friend's place. Sometimes it would happen over consecutive nights."
"Did he do that in this instance?"
"Yes, he did. I received texts from him up until two days ago.".
"But you have no idea what his movements were after Sunday morning?"
"No, I haven't," she answered.
"Did you try to contact him since Tuesday?" he continued.
"Yes, several times but there was no answer, no reply to my calls or my texts."
"And that didn't raise any alarms?"

"No Inspector, as I mentioned before it wasn't unusual that he didn't come home every night."

Switching approach, but not wanting to let it be known that there were two investigations he was running that he believed were linked, Walsh asked. "Your boyfriend had a very distinctive tattoo on his forearm."

"Yes, he did."

"Do you have any idea what it means?"

"Not at all Inspector, we never really discussed it."

"Did you not find it unusual? Given you're an artist," replied Walsh.

"Not really. To me, it was just one of those things. Tattooing is a form of art I suppose," she replied almost dismissively, "but it's not something that I've really ever thought of. I prefer my art where people can see it," she pointed towards her canvases and other pieces that adorned the apartment walls.

Walsh could see her point. He let a few seconds pass in silence. He believed that he had all he needed, for now, before asking, "Could you provide us with *Steve's* mobile number please, along with any screenshots of the texts you sent him over the past few days? Also, we may need to examine your phone itself at some point."

"Sure, no problem," she replied, her composure now finally returning.

"And if I may ask, and I know this might be difficult, could I ask in the absence of any family members, if you would help us formally identify the body?"

Lucy Flint initially baulked at the suggestion, but finally relented after Walsh advised her that counselling was available to her should she need it.

"I know it is a difficult ask," he said, "but it's vital that we are able to properly identify the body. I'm sure you understand," he continued sympathetically. "It seems that you may be the closest person to him if there is no other next of kin. Do you know if he has any other family in the UK, or in Poland?"

"No," she answered, "and he never mentioned any family in Poland. As far as I know, both his parents have passed away, and he was an only child."

"Okay, thank you, Ms. Flint," Walsh replied.

After agreeing a time for Lucy to visit the mortuary to identify the body and receiving her commitment to her forwarding copies of the text messages that she had sent over the past few days, through to the police IT department number that Walsh gave her, he concluded their visit.

Once Walsh and Sedgefield were out in the street, both of them were happy to feel the watery sun on their faces and to breath the fresh air. It had been quite a while since the sun had made an extended stay. With the wind easing, grey and white puffs of stratus cloud slowly danced around the sky above them. Gaps of blue sky were now appearing regularly but erratically, as the sun burnt off the blanket of white that had enveloped the city over the past forty-eight hours. The sudden warmth seemed to lift their moods as they headed off towards their car which had been parked around the corner in Heslop Road.

As they closed their respective car doors, each turned to the other.

"What do you think Sir?" asked Sedgefield.

"Not sure to be honest. Seems straight forward enough, but let's follow up on those texts. Also, let's see if the IT team can find out where our boy was when those texts were sent. Hopefully BT or whoever can give us some detail about his movements from the phone signals. We also need to follow up with our Polish friends about that tattoo. Surely it means something?"

CHAPTER 14

"I believe the old boy is going to be alright," said Walter Offman, trainer of *Whisky-in-the-jar*, to Cannon.

They were standing in the parade ring at Worcester. The course situated on the banks of the River Severn. They were blessed with clear skies, sunshine bathing those who were willing to chance a trip to the racecourse for a special midweek meeting. At least racing was on. Many other courses, especially those further north, were still being affected by the recent poor weather. The wind had dropped overnight. An early morning frost had formed due to the clear skies, but by noon it had melted away like an ice cube on a warm pavement. Cannon had two runners at the meeting, *Whitehall Kid* and *Harvester*.

It was nearly forty-eight hours since Campbells' relatively lucky escape from the kick received from *GrecianBoy*.

"Yes, he was bloody lucky," answered Cannon, "well relatively. A little higher and it could have been his *crown jewels*" he continued, joking to try and minimize any questioning as to what happened to *GrecianBoy*.

"Any permanent damage then?"

"I understand he'll be on crutches for a while. I believe the operation on his knee was successful, but he'll need quite a bit of rehabilitation."

"And his horses?"

"Well Walter, I think he might be asking a couple of us to take a few of them off his hands for a while. I understand his owners are concerned about them not running. I think the bad weather this year has really limited the options for some horses as you know. We've all been under a bit of pressure in getting runs. Owners want to see their investment on the track, not just racking up bills for food and lodging."

"Yep, I agree," replied Offman.

Suddenly the parade ring began filling with bright colours. The jockeys for the upcoming race moved from the weighing room to join the connections of the horses for a quick meet and greet, talk over race tactics with the trainers and then to mount up. Cannon and Offman parted slightly, giving themselves an opportunity to talk with their respective owners.

The connections of *Whisky-in-the jar* admired their horse as he pranced around the ring, throwing his head up and down and giving his handler a hard time controlling him. It was obvious the horse wanted to get on with it.

Cannon only had his jockey, Simon McCorkindale, for company. The owner of *Whitehall Kid* unfortunately away on business.

"So just let him find his feet," he said to his jockey. "Don't rush to get to the front too soon. There's not much speed in this field and he can be a bit keen initially, so let's rather settle him down and get him to concentrate on his work."

McCorkindale had heard instructions like this many times before. He listened quietly, professionally to what Cannon had to say, then tapped his cap with his whip as he turned towards his mount, watching him parade quietly in the field of fifteen runners. A small bell clanged and the call for the jockeys to mount up was made. Fortunately for them both, the horse had stopped a few yards ahead of them. He stood still, ready and awaiting his jockey. Cannon walking a half step behind McCorkindale, took hold of the jockey's leg to give him a lift into the saddle. The owner's pale blue silks with a black 'C' on the front, a pale blue cap and the white jodhpurs of the jockey, reminded Cannon of Manchester City's colours. They would be easily identifiable when the race was on, but Cannon didn't expect them to cross the line first today. The horse was mid-table in the betting, about where Cannon thought he would be.

As the horse was about to trot away, jockey on board, ready to do another lap of the ring for the half dozen or so punters who remained leaning on the outside of the fence, Cannon repeated his earlier comments.

"Remember, keep him cold until the final three flights. He's doing well at home, I just don't think he will see out the two and a half miles though, the ground's still a bit too soft for him."

With those final words, the jockey took over. It was out of Cannon's hands now.

He watched from the owners and trainer's section of the stands. His binoculars scanned the book-makers boards then sought out the field of runners on the far side of the track. The field of horses bunched up together walking in circles, waiting to be called into line. As it was a hurdle race, not a chase, the fences were much smaller, but the pace was generally quicker than with the chasers. However, how quickly the horses raced depended upon the speed the jockeys wanted to push their charges. There were only one or two front runners in the race. Those horses that liked to lead, not be held back.

Whitehall Kid was a horse with a mind of his own. During his career sometimes he could spark up and decide he needed to get going quickly. Other times he would almost refuse to run. In recent weeks, due to Cannon's patient handling, he had settled down a little and was content to let the jockey decide where to place him while running in the race, at what pace to go and when to attack the lead.

The field was brought into line, the starter readied himself wanting to ensure a fair start. The horses bunched together, each jockey looking for any little advantage they could gain by having their mounts jump away cleanly. Cannon searched for his jockey's silks through the binoculars. He knew that there was no plunge on his horse in this race. At twenty to one *Whitehall Kid* was priced exactly where Cannon thought he should be.

As expected, the race turned out to be an absolute thriller. Three horses, almost line abreast attacked the last flight of hurdles. As the small crowd cheered, the favourite stumbled as it hit the jump with a loud crack, losing momentum. Both the other two horses jumped the fence cleanly, accelerating away towards the finish line a couple of hundred yards ahead. Neither of them was *Whitehall Kid* who was coming home fourth, so Cannon watched the duel between the two leaders as they battled it out towards the line. They met the finish line locked together with the winner being awarded the race after a long look at the photo of the finish. While the punters and connections awaited the judges' decision Cannon walked through the back of the stand and into the unsaddling enclosure to greet his horse and jockey.

"Not too bad a run," he said.

"He pulled a bit hard when we first set off," answered McCorkindale, "nearly pulled my bloody arms off."

"Ummm, I need to find a way to make him settle a bit more."

"Agreed," replied the jockey as he removed his saddle and weighing cloth from the horses back, ready for the weigh-in. Steam rose from the horse reflective of its exertions. "I think that he'll be better…."

Cannon's mobile phone was ringing, he noticed it was Rich Telside. He answered it while mouthing an apology to the jockey.

"Hi Rich, I'm just with…"

"Mike," interrupted Telside who was in the saddling area with his other runner of the day, "you had better get over here quickly. Someone has just tried to nobble *Harvester*!"

CHAPTER 15

"What happened?" asked Cannon.
He and Rich were standing with *Harvester* in the horses' box. They had withdrawn him for his race as a late scratching. The horse was standing on three feet, his near side hind leg raised a few inches above the ground, the racing shoe half hanging off, scraping on the concrete floor as the horse tried to put its' foot down.
"I'm not sure," answered Telside, "but it looks like someone has tried to take off *Harvesters*' shoe."
Cannon put his hand on the horse's shoulder to steady himself within the confines of the small stable. He bent down trying to get a closer look at the horses' foot.
"Did anyone see anything?" he asked.
"Not that I can gather."
"So where were you when this happened? And where was Albert?"
Albert was the groom who normally rode with the horse in the horse-box to the course. He looked after him before the race, grooming him, getting the necessary saddle ready and making sure the jockey's silks were available for the race.
"Albert called me over from the racecourse car park where I was getting the box ready for *Whitehall Kid* to be loaded after he had cooled down, as I would normally do," answered Rich. "He told me he'd just got a phone call from the hospital where his mum lives down in Eastbourne and that she'd had a heart attack. So, he asked me if it was okay for him to get away and get down there? He then asked if I could look after *Harvester* for him? Of course, I said yes. So, he called an Uber to take him to the train station. He left just before the start of the *'Kid's* race."
"So how come this all happened?" asked Cannon angrily, pointing at *Harvester's* leg that was still slightly off the ground. "And where the hell is that farrier?" he shouted out, to no one in particular. Frustration and tension pulsing through his entire body.
"Well after Albert had gone, I noticed *Harvester* wasn't as relaxed as he normally is, and I saw he seemed to be a bit edgy. So, I called the course vet and the course farrier to have a look at him. The vet seemed happy with him and when the farrier came, I asked him to check out the shoes as we had put new racing plates on earlier as you'd asked. While he was busy, I just needed to use the toilet quickly. I was only gone for a couple of minutes, but when I got back there was no one around and I noticed the problem straight away."

"And?" asked Cannon, his face reflecting the anger he felt inside.
"The guy who came to look at him wasn't the course farrier!"
"How do you know?" asked Cannon
"Because, the *real* one came to the stall a few minutes after I got back, asking what the trouble was."
"Bloody hell! So, this other so-called farrier was an impostor? Shit, I don't believe it!" Cannon exclaimed. "And why hasn't the real one sorted out the poor horse?" he shouted at Telside. "Poor bugger needs to be able to put his foot down as soon as possible. Where the hell is the bastard anyway? For Christ sake!" Cannon exclaimed, exasperated at the situation.
"He'll be back in a sec I'm sure," answered Telside.
Rich had only experienced Cannon's anger once before when a horse got loose on the downs during a training run, but he had never seen Cannon so animated. "He's had to go off and get some additional tools because whoever did this," Telside said, pointing back to Harvester's foot, "has made a right bloody mess of it."
Cannon shook his head while Rich explained, "John said the hoof looks okay but he won't be able to get the shoe off without his extra tools as the plate is all twisted and bent."
"Fuck!" exclaimed Cannon, "I need to get to the Stewards quickly. They need to know about this. We need to get course security onto it as well," he said his past life kicking in, his reaction robotic.
God! he thought to himself, as he realized how quickly he had reverted to old ways. Why was it that despite all the years since he had left the force, it appeared from his instant reactions that the force had never left him?

"Any CCTCV?"
"I've already asked one of the board members to check and let me know," replied Rich. It was obvious from Telsides' face and body language that he was feeling more than a little disappointed with himself and extremely annoyed at the perpetrator. "If I get hold of the bastard, I'll kill him!" he said.
Cannon wasn't sure what to think.
He had numerous questions in his head that he wanted answers to.
Why was *Harvester* targeted? By who and for what reason? What was so special about today, this meeting, this race?
They were standing at the horsebox that they had brought to transport *Harvester* and *Whitehall Kid* to the course. The horses were now safely locked away, both seemingly well. *Whitehall Kid* had now cooled down after his exertions and *Harvester,* was now more comfortable after being checked out by the course vet once his racing shoes had been replaced by the proper on-

course farrier.

"I've been in touch with the owner of *Harvester* and he understands what's happened, but he said that he may consider moving the horse to another trainer," said Cannon. "That's all we bloody need."

As he spoke, an announcement came over the course PA system asking Cannon to report to the Stewards office.

Having been through the drama with *Harvester* the last thing Cannon needed was a showdown with the Stewards of the course. He knew there would be an inquiry about what had happened, but what he didn't expect was to see Leslie Timms sitting at the Stewards boardroom table. The boardroom was situated at the top of the main stand, two floors up overlooking the course.

Cannon eyed him suspiciously, but kept a civil tongue in his head, saying his hello's and shaking hands with the man, while hiding his anger. Was this a setup?

"Looks like we have an issue here, Mr. Cannon," noted Timms, looking down at a piece of paper sitting on the table.

Cannon didn't rise to the obvious attempt to rattle him, to put him off guard.

"Nice to see you too, Leslie," he responded with a dead-pan tone. "To what do we owe you the pleasure?"

Before Timms could answer, the Chief Steward asked Cannon to seat himself down while a three-man panel gathered around the oak table. Timms took his seat and a lady Secretary sat to one side, waiting, ready to take minutes.

The Chief Steward, Gerald Glass, or GG as he was affectionately known was a retired ex-commercial pilot. Very precise in his language, someone who did not like scandal. Someone who ran things by the book, who liked to keep meetings short and to the point.

"Gentleman, this will not take long as we have a race meeting to manage," he stated, "however given what we have experienced this afternoon, it is important that we set in motion an inquiry to try and get to the bottom of this rather unsavoury incident."

Cannon noticed the use of the language, old fashioned he knew, but non-judgmental.

"Accordingly, I would like to suggest that Mr. Cannon gives us a brief overview of what he knows about the matter at hand and we can then make a decision about the next steps we should take." He nodded towards the trainer saying, "Mr. Cannon over to you."

Cannon relayed as much as he knew about what had happened to *Harvester*. The unknown farrier and the resulting need to scratch the horse from its' race. The whole summary took just a couple of minutes.

"Thank you for that Mr. Cannon," said Glass, before turning to Timms. "Mr. Timms, before I give you the floor, I want to advise Mr. Cannon

After the Fire

about the rules of racing, particularly in relation to manipulating the outcome of a race." He looked Cannon straight in the eye. Cannon almost reacted but bit his tongue. He knew he needed to endure the formalities but inside he was seething, he was desperate to have his say. Something was going on and he was caught in the middle of it all. Despite trying to extricate himself a little from the day-to-day activities of running his stable, it was *still* his livelihood, his passion and he needed to protect it, especially when he was under threat. So, unfortunately, he didn't think it was right to leave this type of matter or inquiry to Rich to handle. He needed to be in control. He was a racehorse trainer now first and foremost. His past was over. He had tried to leave it all behind yet somehow, he sensed he was being dragged back into something significant that could affect his future if he didn't address it. He surmised that whatever Timms would say in the meeting, it wouldn't be good. He stayed focused on Glass who was talking directly to Timms.

"From what you advised me earlier Mr. Timms, it would appear that there may have been an attempt today to manipulate the outcome of the race which Mr. Cannons' horse, *Harvester* would have been running in. Is that correct?"

"Yes, Mr. Glass," answered Timms, maintaining the formality of the meeting, "and because of this I wanted to advise Mr. Cannon here, that due to the information I have at my disposal, I will be recommending to the BHA Licensing Committee that Mr. Cannon's license be suspended with immediate effect, pending a more detailed investigation."

Cannon couldn't help himself his anger and frustration were no longer containable.

"What the fuck!" he shouted, raising himself from his chair.

"Mr. Cannon!" reacted Glass, "I'll remind you that that is a formal hearing of the Stewards of this racecourse. It is not a place for such language nor for such a show of contempt for the process we are following," he went on. "You will be given an opportunity to respond or rebut any charges relating to any allegations of wrong-doing made against you at the appropriate time and place."

Cannon reluctantly sat back onto his chair. He knew that to make a scene would be counter-productive. He needed to think about what was going on. He needed to consider what he knew. Was it just him who was being targeted and if so why? Were there others in the same predicament or was it something personal? Was Timms out to get him, destroy his business, his life? If so, why?

"Mr. Cannon," Glass said, "given the events of the day, I am going to end this meeting by advising you that we, the Stewards of this course, will be asking the local Economic and Specialist Crime unit, the Fraud squad, to investigate the information Mr. Timms has been able to provide us with. In addition, we will ask them to investigate what has taken place in relation to your horse. I can assure you that the incident will be thoroughly investigated in order to get to the bottom of it. Whatever the rights and wrongs, it is our job to protect the integrity of racing, specifically in relation to racing at this racecourse. Hearings, sanctions or otherwise will be handled by the appropriate authorities. The mandate of this body," he pointed to his fellow Stewards, "is to ensure that racing at this racecourse is undertaken in accordance with the rules of racing as set out by the BHA, nothing more."

"What is the so-called, information, provided by Mr. Timms may I ask?" interrupted Cannon as politely as he could, aware of his earlier indiscretion. "If due process is to work, and I am to receive any sanction, surely I need to know what for?"

"All in good time Mr. Cannon. As I said previously, the BHA will address that directly with you after receiving our report. Likewise, I'm sure the local police will want to talk with you as well. In the mean-time given you have no further runners today, I will close this meeting. We have a few more races to attend too. Good day."

And with that, the Stewards rose from the table. The meeting was over.

Cannon left the room first, heading down the stairs towards the course car park. As he reached the bottom of the first flight of stairs a voice called out to him. It was Timms. Cannon waited as Timms slowly descended towards him.

"Mike," he said. "It's nothing personal. I'm just doing my job" he went on.

Cannon looked Timms in the eye. Neither man wanting to be the first to blink.

"And I'm just doing mine," replied Cannon, his contempt and anger at the days' events and the implications of what he had just been through reflected on his face. His voice hardened. "Someone is trying to stop me doing my job. Trying to shut me down," he said, "and whoever that is I'm going to find out and when I do……," he allowed the implication of what he was thinking to drift off into the air. He knew full well that Timms had gotten the message.

Both men stood for a second, each thinking their own thoughts. Considering their positions. Timms turned, walking back from where he had come. Cannon watched him go, then made his way back to Rich.

He had to work out where to from here?

CHAPTER 16

"What do you mean he's disappeared?" he asked.
Perkel had received the envelope he was dreading. A similar-sized nondescript brown envelope like the previous three. It wasn't what he had expected. Inside it wasn't another piece of the larger picture of Flint and himself along with the underage girl taken at Flint's party, but rather several pictures of himself and his own lover. They had obviously been taken relatively recently. Edgar was overseas in the U.S. currently, but it was clear from Perkels' assessment of the surroundings and backgrounds in the pictures that they were taken while Edgar was in London between assignments. Perkel could tell the photos were taken at the Rosewood Hotel in High Holborn, not far from the Old Bailey. It was one of Perkels' favourite places to meet Edgar.
Edgar was a male model. Only nineteen but extremely beautiful in Perkels' eyes. Slim, narrow hips, long dark hair, almost androgynous. He could walk down a catwalk in both men's or women's clothing and still look good in either. In fact, he looked better in women's clothes according to Perkel. Better than Perkels' own wife would have looked in them.
In addition to the photographs, was the demand. The ubiquitous demand that Flint had predicted would be forthcoming. It was for this reason that he needed to speak with Flint. A quarter of a million pounds in ten days was something Perkel knew he could not raise.
"Where is he then?" he asked again, his voice rising, panic beginning to send shivers through his body.
"I'm not sure Mr. Perkel" came the reply. A female's voice on the speakerphone. "Mr. Flint hasn't been seen since Monday when he left the office around seven-thirty. He hasn't been answering his mobile phone either."
"Did he mention if he was expecting to go anywhere, meet anyone?"
"No, not at all. He had meetings with clients scheduled for yesterday and today. In fact, I had to cancel a luncheon engagement with a senior bank executive today due to Mr. Flint's disappearance."
"You've used the word *disappear* twice already Jean, how do you know he's not ill, sick, perhaps down with the flu? Have you tried calling his home?"
Jean Rice, Flint's PA/Secretary for more than twelve years initially considered letting her ire get the better of her, but she knew her job. She had a professional, not a personal relationship with Flint. She had already made the inquiries at Flints' house. She felt aggrieved that Perkel would

even question her on this.
"Yes, I have Mr. Perkel. I spoke with his housekeeper, Barbara. She told me his bed hadn't been slept in for the past two evenings. That he had left no more washing since Sunday evening, and that nothing had been moved in the kitchen plus no clothes had been taken from the wardrobes either."
Perkel began to feel more isolated, more frightened, more desperate than ever.
"Have you contacted the police?"
"Mr. Perkel," answered Jean, "no I haven't, I think it may be a bit premature to do that. It's been just over forty-eight hours that Mr. Flint has been away, so I intended to wait until tomorrow morning. Just in case."
"Just in case, what?"
"Well if he turns up in the morning, fresh as a daisy, it may be that there is a perfectly simple explanation,"
"Like what?"
"I don't know, but I've no wish to speculate either. I just don't want to look a fool should he come into the office and we've all gotten ourselves into a tiz over nothing," she answered.
Perkel sighed heavily to himself, before asking. "Perhaps a call to Lucy would help?"
"I'm not so sure Mr. Perkel. It's been a while I think since Mr. Flint and his daughter last spoke."
"But wouldn't she want to know?"
"Perhaps, but Mr. Flint always said that ever since he and his daughter had that last disagreement, he didn't want to have anything to do with her. So, with respect to his wishes, I haven't been in contact."
Perkel knew of the disagreement that Jean Rice referred to. It was one of those arguments that broke families apart. Flint had taken great pride in his daughter becoming a doctor. A specialist, a potential eye surgeon. However, it had never happened.
Somehow while at university, Lucy Flint had gotten herself involved in a crowd that was more into sitting around rather than studying. A group, according to Flint that was more into drinking, talking politics, the usual *radical* nonsense and less into doing anything worthwhile. Flint believed Lucy's focus moved from studying the eye to using it. She became infatuated with colour, the use of colour on the canvas. According to her father, Lucy threw away a privileged life, for the life of a struggling artist. She threw away the potential of a comfortable future and substituted it with a life of living from hand to mouth. Multiple live-in boyfriends and an unconventional, non-conformist, avant-garde lifestyle. It had resulted in a breakdown in their relationship. That was over twelve years ago now. Since then he had spoken with her only briefly over the phone, on two separate occasions. The last time, nearly three years ago. The conversation had

ended with things being said that shouldn't have been. It resulted in a total breakdown of the relationship.

"Okay Jean, if you hear from him, please let me know. Better still," Perkel went on, "please ask him to call me. Immediately."

"I will certainly do that," she answered, putting down the phone.

Perkel looked at the photographs again of Edgar and himself, before violently scattering them across his desk with a sweep of his arm. A soft wail escaped from his lips.

The covering letter along with the photographs was typed on an ordinary piece of A4 paper and had been delivered to his office by a courier service. The note was slipped inside a letterbox sized envelope, upon which his name was printed on the front. The envelope had no discernible markings. He stared at the words, the single page lying on his desk face up, the content mocking him.

The threats held within the words were unmistakable. Not just a matter of showing Perkels' wife his indiscretions, nor indeed the General Council of the Bar, but rather the threat of violence against himself, his family and Flint. Perkel wasn't a strong man in that regard. He abhorred violence, but the words on the page were clear. Clear and simple. No police involvement. No private investigations, just Two Hundred and Fifty Thousand Pounds to be paid into fifty separate bank accounts, commencing in ten days time and concluding within fourteen. If not, then the photographs would be shared and Perkel and Flint would, what was euphemistically called, *go missing*.

Details of which bank accounts the money was to be paid in would be delivered by courier, the following day.

CHAPTER 17

"So, Mr. Cannon," said Inspector Tom Phillips of the Worcester Police, "about the other day."
They were in the Inspectors office on Castle Street, on the other side of the racecourse, just a few hundred yards from the stables where *Harvester* had been attacked. It was late morning two days after the attack and it was now generally accepted that an attempt to injure the horse had indeed been made.
"Yes Inspector, *about the other day*," Cannon said, "I think it's pretty clear now what happened. What I'd like to know is why and by whom."
"You and me both, Mr. Cannon. or can I call you Mike?" replied the bespectacled policeman running his hand through his uncombed sandy coloured hair.
"Of course," replied Cannon. "I'm much happier with the informality."
He was seated behind a plain white desk that separated them. *IKEA* Cannon thought, reflecting briefly on how things had changed since he had left the force. Budget cuts everywhere! Despite the building and office, he was sitting in having been repainted only a few years ago the grubbiness of late nights working on multiple cases while consuming greasy hot chips, pizza, and canned beers were evident from the finger marks staining the walls of the room. The memories came flooding back. Some good, many bad. Cannon was glad to be out of it.
There was just enough space in the office for a couple of cheap chairs on the opposite side of the desk from where Tom Phillips sat. The backs of the chairs almost touching the walls.
Phillips was a relatively young man. Mid-thirties, well built. Cannon gave him a quick head-to-toe, noticing there was no ashtray or even smell or cigarettes in the office. *O.H. and S?* Cannon thought, realizing that Phillips appeared to be someone who took looking after himself seriously. It looked like he worked out, or was a jogger at the very least and likewise, it seemed he took his job seriously as well.
Cannon, however, being familiar with the investigation process wanted to get the meeting over and done with as soon as possible. He knew the get together was to be more of a discussion about what they thought had happened before he was required to give a formal statement. He also knew that it was necessary for the police to look at all possibilities, all angles. He also speculated that the police did not have resources to follow up the incident as quickly as he could himself and he was impatient to get on with it. However, procedures and processes had to be followed and Cannon

After the Fire

wanted the authorities on his side, especially if he needed them in the future, so he decided to bite his tongue and be as cooperative as possible. At least for now.

Given he himself had no idea why *Harvester* specifically had been targeted, he maintained the view that someone was trying to ruin him. Someone wanted him to fail. Wanted to take away all he had built since he had left his old life behind. Someone wanted to destroy his future.

Since the fire, he had needed to rebuild his yard and his life. The physical repairs as well as the emotional scars that he, Cassie, Michelle, and others still carried, but tried to hide, still affected him. Cassie leaving for university hadn't really helped, but he knew he needed to accept it. Despite this acceptance, her departure had inserted another hole into his life, a gap. It added to the sense of disruption. Their lives stop, starting like a manual car being driven by someone who could only drive an automatic one.

Throughout the past couple of years however, Michelle and he had worked hard. Along with Rich and the wider team they had persevered through the tough times, and now they had a horse that not only gave them hope for the *National* but also for the future. Indirectly *RockGod* had kept them afloat. Almost single-handedly the horse was the reason why many of the owners of his other charges had stayed with him, believed in him. They wanted to be associated with a potential *National*-winning trainer.

Someone, however, had other ideas.

As Rich and Cannon had arranged, Rich was away with one of the other horses, *TheMan*, up at Newcastle for a two and a half-mile chase. They had spent part of the previous day together discussing and checking the details of what had happened at Worcester as clearly as they could recall them. Cannon, therefore, was 100% happy in his own mind about what had occurred. What he didn't yet understand, was why?

"We've had a look at the footage from the CCTV cameras on the course," Phillips said, "but unfortunately it is a bit limited. We have however been able to get a couple of shots of the person we think is responsible for the attack on your horse,"

"Think?"

"Yes. Well we *believe* is responsible."

Phillips removed two printed photographs from a folder that sat in front of him and passed them across the desk for Cannon to look at. The images were clear, taken from a camera standing above the individual as they had walked past. The pictures showed the suspect from an angle that allowed one to easily see what the person was wearing. A dark duffle type coat, jeans, and a dark blue baseball cap. What the image didn't show however were the shoes worn by the suspect and unfortunately, the shadow of the cap obscured the persons face completely. It was easy to conclude the picture was of a burly man. They needed to be, thought Cannon, for them to try to remove the shoe or damage the foot of a race primed half-ton animal.

"Not much help is it," he said.

"Not directly," answered Phillips, "but it does give us something to work on."

Cannon remained quiet.

"We have been in touch with the course security team, to see if they have any other footage for us that could be of further use, but we've been told that they had a problem that day with their system."

"How convenient," interrupted Cannon sarcastically, his impatience beginning to get the better of him.

Phillips coughed and shifted in his chair. Uncomfortable. It wasn't what he was used to. He was dealing with a former cop who had been good at his job, but who had walked away from it all. Someone who had given up everything before it had gotten too much and before it had killed him or before he had killed himself. Those demons of Cannon's past that Phillips knew were still there, still sitting below the surface. Many who left the force did so because of what they saw, lived through. Phillips knew Cannon's background and the story of Cannon's experience with a previous colleague and how that had played out. It was not lost on him. It was something that had not been ignored by the racing authorities either.

"I agree," answered Phillips reluctantly. "Apparently there was an AV failure during the running of the previous race. I think that was during the race your horse, *Whitehall Kid* was involved in, wasn't it? I know it's not ideal, but we are pursuing other avenues, extending our inquiries to try and find out more."

"And where would that be Inspector? How? Have you or the racecourse authorities really got anything else to go on other than this?" he said pointing at the picture

"I.."

"To say I'm disappointed," went on Cannon, "is an understatement. My horse was targeted. It's as clear as day. But what I want to know is why? For what reason?"

"Mike, I know how you feel about this."

"No, you don't Inspector. This is something else. Something personal."

"This person of interest," Phillips pointed to the photographs now discarded by Cannon on the Inspector's desk, "any ideas?"

Retrieving one of the pictures for another quick look, then tossing it back towards Phillips and onto the folder, Cannon said, "None whatsoever, never seen him before. Not that you can see much of the face and the body shape doesn't ring any bells."

"Okay, thank you,"

"Is that it then?" asked Cannon, wanting to get back home, rising from the chair.

Phillips waited for a few seconds, noting Cannon's impatience. Slumping forward onto his desk, hands steepled together, he said, "Mike, I need you to work with me here. I know you are pissed off with me, but you need to be careful."

Cannon hesitated slightly, sitting back down. He realized that Phillips was genuine in what he was saying.

"While we only have these pictures to go on just yet," Phillips said, "I can assure you, we are putting resources into this case."

Conveying a sense of purpose, a commitment to finding the answer, Phillips said, "You're one of us Mike, and we protect our own."

"I appreciate the sentiment Tom, but I've left that world. I've moved on."

Phillips smiled ruefully. "Do we ever move on Mike? Really?"

Cannon did not respond. He kept his thoughts to himself.

"I'll be in touch as we progress the investigation," said Phillips trying to express a level of confidence that he didn't feel but tried nonetheless. "I've got a couple of my team looking through earlier footage of the day, what little there is, plus we'll be talking to as many of the stable staff, head lads, and others who were there on the day that we can. All of them should have been wearing some form of ID in order to gain access to relevant areas, but we think those on the applicable gates were less than diligent, unfortunately. That's something the racing club will need to look at. Finally, we're doing some door-knocking around the area to see if anyone saw anything, but that's a long shot."

"Umm," Cannon mused. "I get what you say, but I guess it's possible, that whoever it was, could have had some form of ID on them. In my view, I don't think things are taken that seriously when it comes to course security, especially a mid-week meeting, at this time of year. I think it's possible or even probable that this individual," he pointed again at the photographs, "had some ID on them which allowed them to gain access to my horse. Remember they even had tools of some sort with them, pretending to be a farrier!"

"True, and we haven't found them either."

"I'd suggest they are probably mixed up somewhere with the on-course farriers' tools."

"Don't worry Mike, we're be checking with him as well."

The two talked for a minute more, shook hands after having exchanged mobile numbers and then Cannon was escorted from the building.

As he got into his car, he noticed a few drops of rain hitting the windscreen. The sun was still shining, though low in the sky. The weather was slowly expected to improve over the coming week according to the reports he had heard as he had driven to the police station to see Phillips. Perhaps it was just a sun-shower he thought? As he started his car, his mobile began to

After the Fire

ring. He looked at the screen.

Timms!

Cannon contemplated ignoring it, but his conscience got in the way.

"Yes Leslie," he answered trying to sound engaging while feeling quite the opposite, "to what do I owe the pleasure?"

"Aah, Mr. Cannon, glad I could get hold of you," Timms said officiously, in line with the message he wanted to relay. "I just wanted to advise you that given recent events, the Disciplinary Committee of the BHA request you to attend a meeting here in the City, 75 High Holborn, at 10 am tomorrow. This meeting is to discuss with you why your Training License should not be immediately suspended. The suspension to occur pending further investigation into various anomalies in race results that I discussed with you at your premises a week or so ago."

"What the..? You can't...." interrupted Cannon, perplexed and angry at the speed the BHA was moving. What about innocent until proven guilty, he thought to himself. Timms ignored Cannons' protestations.

"For completeness, I just want to advise that a copy of what I've just advised you of, will be sent to you in the next few minutes by way of an email," Timms said. "Finally, if you are not aware, the Disciplinary Procedure does allow you to bring along anyone you wish to represent you in relation to this matter should you so need. We ask you to consider this seriously."

Cannon couldn't help himself his anger got the better of him, "You bastard Timms," he shouted into the phone.

Timms remained calm, saying, "We look forward to seeing you tomorrow Mr. Cannon. Goodbye."

The line went dead. Cannon threw the phone onto the passenger seat, it ricocheted onto the door, hit the glove box, finally landing on the floor.

"Fuck, fuck, fuck!" he shouted, venting his increasing frustration. He sat in the car oblivious of people in the police car park who watched him through the car windows as they walked by.

CHAPTER 18

"Any joy with those tattoos?" asked Walsh.

It had been two days since the visit to Lucy Flint. The team was assembled in the briefing room, as usual. 10 am.

"Nothing yet Sir, answered Windsor from IT, "and unfortunately nothing from the partial fingerprints either. It seems like our victim number one had no record here in the UK, at least not that we could find. We are still waiting to hear from our Polish colleagues though, perhaps they may have some luck? But at the moment we're at a bit of a loss," he said disconsolately, "We have no detail on him at all and yet he clearly must have entered the country somehow. Unfortunately for us, it could have been years ago. He could even have grown up here for all we know?" He looked at Walsh's face which was immobile, giving nothing away about what he was thinking. Windsor carried on regardless, "DNA samples haven't provided us any leads either and the forensic lab boys are even struggling to agree on where and when they think he went into the Thames. With all the river traffic nowadays, they keep telling me that what they conclude will be at *best* an estimate, given all the factors."

"Have they engaged Interpol anyway? Those tatts certainly seem Polish or at least Eastern European to me"

"Yes, we believe so."

Walsh was starting to feel concerned. He had two bodies on his hands but little progress. Other cases were beginning to pile up as well. His resources would soon be reduced if he didn't have anything to show for the man-hours spent on these cases. He knew they were connected. Somehow. Experience told him that.

"Wendy," he said to the Community Liaison Officer, "have you got anything to add?"

"Not really Sir, other than the little we did find out from the combination of the posters we issued and the door knocking that we undertook." She nodded towards Constable Fitch who was sitting to her right and with whom she had worked together, "It's probably due to the fact that communities in the Balham area and surrounds don't appear to be too co-operative when it comes to helping the police. Most people we tried to speak with, just wouldn't give us any time at all."

"Any reason why?"

"I think the obvious Sir," jumped in Fitch, keen to be seen as being as active as everyone else in the investigation. "That talking to the police is a big no-no."

"Nothing new there then, son. It seems like it's always been like that," answered Walsh, his eyes raised heavenwards, "ever since I can recall."

A couple of the team laughed.

Walsh ignored the sniggers. "Anyway, I'm not totally convinced of that Fitch because we did get a name and confirmation ID of one of the victims from a member of the public, Lucy Flint. She lives in that area so it's not been a total shut out, has it? You should all have those details," he continued. "if you have looked in this mornings' dispatches in your inboxes. If you haven't, I'll fill you in now."

He took a quick check to see if any of the team had caught up with the information already provided to them before carrying on his briefing.

"Ms. Flint formally identified the body as one Stefan Kaminski yesterday. Her boyfriend as it happens. So, there are at least *some* people Fitch, who are willing to work with us."

He watched Fitch and Carmichael quickly glance at each other. Clearly both embarrassed. Walsh ignored it. It wasn't a cardinal sin to have a view. It just needed to be supported by facts. Having made his point, he carried on, "We are in the process of trying to contact his next-of-kin in Poland, but in the meantime, we need to find out what happened to Kaminski. What his last movements were. Who did he see? Where did he go?"

Turning to Wendy, he opined, "From what you've told me just now, and the lack of any word on the street, it seems like as Community Liaison, it's not quite working for you is it, Constable Carmichael?"

Carmichael did not respond however she felt the heat of the question.

"To be fair, Sir," jumped in Fitch in an attempt to give his colleague some support, "from what I've been able to gather from the door-knocking we did, with the individuals and the small businesses in the area, I think there *is* something going on actually."

"What's that supposed to mean?" asked Walsh, getting annoyed.

Fitch took a few seconds to respond, almost gulping before answering the question.

"Well Sir, I have a couple of friends who live and work in the area. They are in the building trade, you know, doing extensions, small renovations, plumbing, electrics, that type of thing."

"I don't quite see the relevance here, but go on," said Walsh.

"What they have told me privately after a couple of beers, is that there is someone slowly muscling in on the area. Taking work from the market and putting a lot of small businesses like them, out of business."

After the Fire

"So? That's competition, isn't it? The Free-market?"
Fitch ignored Walsh's rebuttal and continued.
"I guess so Sir," he replied, "but from what my mates have told me, it seems like anyone who doesn't want to *play ball*, is ending up with their houses being watched or damaged, the odd car being torched and kids and wives being followed."
Walsh scratched his head. "Has any of this been reported do we know? Sedgefield?"
The Sergeant just shrugged. "Not sure Sir, but I'll contact the NCA, see if they are aware. It's not something that has stood out in our investigations to date"
"Sir," interrupted Fitch, trying to recover from the earlier put-down, "my mates said, it wasn't solely related to the building trade. Word was, that it included restaurants, dry cleaners and other small businesses."
"Drugs involved?" replied Walsh.
"Not from what they told me. Seems to be someone looking to fly under the radar, but people are scared Sir," went on Fitch, "scared to involve the police."
Walsh stayed silent for a few seconds. His mind trying to see if what Fitch was saying had relevance to the cases of Kaminski and the still-unidentified body number one. *Restaurants. Restaurants!* A thought suddenly dawned on him. Lucy Flint had said that Kaminski was working as a chef in the Balham area. Was there a connection? Was he a victim of someone trying to muscle in on the area? If so, why? As far as Walsh knew, Kaminski was a part-time chef and a Masters student. He wasn't an owner of any business. He had nothing to give or to lose.
Walsh walked over to the status board. The summarized details of their two cases, including photographs, notations, and linkages were contained on the touch screen. A menu to get more detail from within the summaries was laid out in blue on the right-hand side of the board. Walsh was now a little happier with the technology, especially given his office phone had been fixed, but he still preferred others to *drive* it for him.
"Do we have any CCTV footage of Station Parade in Balham and surrounds?" he asked Windsor.
Adrian tapped on the keyboard of his laptop. From Walsh's observations, it seemed like his IT guy was never without it. "From the database, it seems we have some. What date and time are we looking at?"
Walsh sighed. This could go nowhere he thought, but at least it was an angle worth pursuing. Given the lack of progress to date, it was one he was willing to follow.
"Sergeant, check on the web and find out what the working hours are for the restaurant that Kaminski worked at. That will be a starting point. That should give us some idea when he might have been in the area, either

during opening times or indeed afterwards."

"And how far back?" asked Windsor, "days I mean Sir."

"Make it ten days before the body was found. That will give us a starting point at least."

Turning to Sedgefield he noted, "Sergeant, I think we need to pay a visit to the restaurant where Kaminski was working. Maybe they can tell us if they or anyone else in the area have been subject to any harassment recently as Fitch and Carmichael are suggesting?" *Christ, I hope so* he thought to himself trying not to let the lack of progress he was feeling inside become noticeable.

Turning to face the team, he said, "I don't need to tell you that we need to get some meat on the bones of these cases soon. None of us want to fail, but we need results, and we need them soon. If not, the higher-ups will move and give the investigation to someone else and we don't want that do we?"

The assembled group nodded and murmured their understanding of Walsh's request.

"Sergeant, be in my office in ten minutes with the contact details and opening times of *Lamberts* on Station Parade in Balham," he requested. "We'll be paying them a visit shortly. I'm assuming they are open for lunch? So perhaps they can help us digest ours a little better?"

CHAPTER 19

Michelle was angry on behalf of Cannon.
They were sitting in their lounge room. The TV was off, and the used dishes from their evening meal were still on the table. It was just after ten pm. The curtains were still open and the half-moon shone through the windows. The last pieces of scaffolding from the renovations completed that afternoon by Pavel and his crew, as Cannon was driving back from Worcester, silhouetted onto the dining room walls. Michelle had advised Cannon that the remaining bits of metal would be gone the next day.
The sky was clear, and the temperature outside was sinking rapidly. A typical late Winter, early Spring weather pattern.
"But you've got horses to run!?" Michelle exclaimed. "Owners to satisfy. A team of good people who rely on you Mike, not to mention a family."
After Cannon had arrived home, he had immediately gone to the stables and had a conversation about the training outcomes of the day with Rich. He wanted to hear how *Whitehall Kid* had pulled up after his first training run post his race two days prior. Cannon had told Rich to give him light work, nothing too heavy. The horse usually recovered relatively quickly after a race. Others in the yard didn't, and needed more rest before resuming training.
"And *Harvester*?" he had asked.
"Sound as a bell," replied Rich. "It's as if nothing had happened to him".
"Thank God."
"*RockGod* and the others?"
"The *God* is jumping out of his skin I don't think he's ever been better."
Cannon had smiled but was unable to hide the frustration at the situation, the threat hanging over his head.
"What's up, Mike?"
Cannon relayed what had happened at Worcester Police Station and then the subsequent call with Timms.
"They can't do that Mike, it bloody outrageous!" Telside had shouted, his anger mirroring that of his friend.

"They can and they will," answered Cannon, "unless we can find answers to what's going on."

He had only told Michelle about the events of the morning after he had finally calmed down and retrieved his phone. He had called her from the car. They had agreed to discuss it when he got home.

Now sitting with Michelle, Cannon was at a loss for words. He had been through many a personal crisis before, but never one that involved his own integrity, his *raison d'etre*.

"Do they think that you were somehow involved in nobbling your own horses?" she asked.

"To be honest I have no idea what they are thinking. All I know is that since Timms' first visited, it seems he's had it in for me. For us. For everything we have worked for."

"But for what reason?" enquired Michelle. "I don't understand why."

"I have no idea either," he mused. Ever since his argument with Timms he had been racking his brains to work out what the connections were. Timms had talked about betting irregularities, but if the BHA really looked into them thoroughly, they would see that Cannon or even anyone in his stable had not profited in any way at all.

He was at a loss, confused. He knew he would just have to see what tomorrow would bring, but he would be ready for it.

"I think it's time for bed," he said, ready to get up from the couch, "though I doubt I'll get much sleep. It could be a long night."

Michelle instinctively reached over and took his hand. "Mike," she said softly, "no matter what happens tomorrow, just remember that I believe in you, love you, will always support you. We've worked too hard to put what we have at risk, surely they'll see that?"

"Thank you, Darling," he replied, kissing the top of her head, "I won't be giving up without a fight, you can be assured of that."

Michelle smiled. The kiss was one of his mannerisms that she loved about him.

"I'll sort out the dishes," she said, as he crossed the room to close the curtains.

"I guess it's perfect timing," he mentioned sarcastically, nodding towards the remaining few scaffolding poles lying against the house and on the floor outside the window. "We have the potential to lose everything, just when we finally get the house back in one piece again. I hope you haven't paid him yet?"

"Not everything," she said. "We still owe Mr. Wocjik, *Pavel*, about fifteen thousand for the roof, but we've paid him for everything else."

"Okay," he answered as he made his way to their bedroom, "just hold off for a week or so, he's already months overdue on the project."

Michelle turned towards the kitchen, dishes in her hands. Perhaps she would wait to see how tomorrow affected their future before shelling out any more cash. Money was getting tighter. Cannon was right, the builder would have to wait. She would see what she could do.

CHAPTER 20

"Then find him!" shouted Jack Williams. He hadn't been so angry for a while. Most of his business dealings had gone as expected. People saw sense. It was never a good thing trying to argue with him.

Now that the pressure on Flint and Perkel was being applied more vigourously, Williams knew that when the rubber hit the road, it was possible that either of his two victims could react in a way that was unexpected. Sometimes his victims tried to be clever. Some tried to engage the authorities. Some tried to use private investigators to find out who was behind the threats they were facing. It would seem that Flint had decided to run. This was the one thing that really angered Williams the most.

Sitting in his suite, on the eighth floor of the Riverside building, on Southbank overlooking London Bridge, he swiveled his chair away from his view of the river and faced the man who was the object of his frustration.

"Well, what are you waiting for?"

"Look, Jack. Trevor has his men out searching for him already. He's obviously gone to ground somewhere. Left Perkel to fend for himself, carry the can. But we'll find him. Perkel's not strong."

Williams considered this for a second, the anger still churning him up inside.

"Samuel," he replied, observing how his 2-I-C reacted when he used the formality of his name, rather than just *Sam*. This was something people around him understood. It was the sign that Jack was very upset. "You've been talking with Perkel all along about this matter. I'm relying on you to get this money. I've given my word that I will have it in time to meet my own obligations before the end of April."

"Understood Jack,"

"Is it?"

"Of course, why wouldn't it be?"

The tension between the men was palpable. Both knew that there were always bigger fish in the tank that they were swimming in. There were always those who wanted a piece of the action. The pie was large but others wanted to take some of Williams' crust, and they were already nibbling at the edges. Some even taking *bites*. Williams needed support, and it was those providing that support that he needed to pay, settle with. If he didn't, his backup could soon disappear.

"You know what I mean, Samuel.," answered Williams, his blood pressure slowly reverting to some form of normality. Turning the chair back towards the window, he said, "It's on your head. I'll leave it up to as to how, but find him. You've got seventy-two hours."

CHAPTER 21

Cannon sat down. The Disciplinary panel in front of him consisted of the Chair, the *Honourable*, Stafford Banterson, QC, and six other members of the broader Judicial Panel.

Off to the side sat Leslie Timms.

Cannon had arrived early to try and gauge the mood of the meeting. His train into Waterloo had fortunately been on time. He had then jumped into a taxi to take him the short ride to where he was *required* to be.

He had been offered tea by a lady Secretary who was to take the necessary minutes, but he had politely declined. Cannon wasn't in the mood. If his license was to be suspended, he was going to make sure he knew why.

If there was evidence of wrong-doing he wanted to see it. He knew from his *former life* that natural justice was his right. While the panel wasn't a court of law, there were still formalities to be followed and evidence to be provided. The Code of Conduct which trainers are subject too, and the sections under which Cannon was to be censured for, needed to be laid out before him and the wider Disciplinary panel, who would ultimately decide his fate. He assumed Timms would present the case against him

Banterson brought the meeting to order.

"Gentleman, and Lady," he said, acknowledging the Secretary, "can I have your attention please?" Looking at his watch he stated, "It is now five minutes past the hour of ten, and I would like to start the proceedings. Thank you."

The room went quiet, the odd cough into the hand of one of the panel members the only sound.

Cannon had been through many a review of procedures post-incident while in the Force. It was standard policy to do so when justified or not, there were complaints made against him or other members involved in an investigation. Disciplinary hearings were commonplace. He was used to defending his actions, he knew when he had pushed the boundaries. Knew that what he had done had blurred the edges, the means justifying the end. For such sessions, he had always been prepared. He had however never been through any such hearing as a racehorse trainer. The next half hour was a blur to him, it wasn't what he expected.

"As Chair of this Disciplinary meeting," stated Banterson addressing Cannon and the panel, "I am taking the rather unusual step of requesting that this conversation is to be off-the-record please."

Cannon was confused. *What was going on?*

"Mr. Chairman..." he said interrupting, trying to check if he had heard correctly, "I..."

Banterson put up his hand cutting Cannon off mid-sentence.

"Mr...Cannon, before we go any further, I understand you may be a little confused. Please let me explain."

Cannon was convinced he was going to be stitched up. His livelihood was on the line, he wasn't going to go down without a fight. He had psyched himself up for the argument. He knew he had done nothing wrong. It went against his nature but he bit his tongue. Reluctantly he acquiesced, nodded and acknowledged the Chairs' authority.

"Thank you, Mr. Cannon," responded Banterson. Turning to Timms, he gave him the floor.

"Mike," said Timms, standing up like a Barrister addressing the court, "the reason for this meeting is *not* what you may have expected it to be about, and for that, I personally apologize. Accordingly, let me get that on the table straight away."

Cannon just stared at Timms. His mind reeling.

"What this meeting is about, is frankly, to seek your help"

"*My* help?" asked Cannon.

"Yes, Mike. We need your assistance. We believe based on your background and experience as a former Detective, that you can help us."

"With what, may I ask?"

"You may recall a few weeks ago, I came to see you about some strange results in a number of races and what we suspected was going on."

"Yes, it's been bothering me ever since," replied Cannon. "Frankly I've been thinking about nothing else. Plus, what happened at Worcester the other day has just exacerbated the issue."

"I understand," said Timms.

"Do you?"

Timms ignored the inference. Continuing, "I know we have brought you here under what you may consider false pretenses, but it has been necessary," he said. "Mr. Banterson and the rest of the panel have also given up their valuable personal time to be here, but we felt it appropriate to do so, to show you how seriously we are taking the matter at hand."

"And that is?" asked Cannon, his patience beginning to wear thin.

"We believe that there is someone, an individual, a group, actively interfering in the proper running of some, possibly many, races. We believe that this person or group is unfairly profiting from this, and it is putting the entire integrity of the sport at risk."

"Do you have any idea who this *person or group* is?"

"No, unfortunately despite our best efforts we don't"

"None whatsoever?"

"The only linkage we have is to that of Mr. Charles Flint."

"And that's why you came to see me the other day? To see if I was also involved?"

"Yes, and unfortunately I think we got off on the wrong foot."

"I'll say," replied Cannon, "you really pissed me off."

"Mr. Cannon!" chimed in Banterson, "we have ladies present,"

"Sorry Sir," he responded. The lady Secretary just smiled.

Timms continued with his explanation. "We needed to test whether you were aware of our concerns. From your reaction, we had a view, but as the BHA we needed to proceed with caution. What happened at Worcester convinced us of your innocence and hence why we are here."

"For my help?" reiterated Cannon.

"Yes,"

Cannon considered what he had heard.

"So, what convinced you about my innocence may I ask? If I'm to help you, I need to know that you trust me. How can I be assured of that?"

"We now know that what happened at Worcester had nothing to do with you."

"Go on,"

"As I'm sure you'll understand Mike, without going into all the detail, we've been able to establish that someone, the bogus farrier who attacked your horse *Harvester*, was able to obtain access to the course at the far end of the track, a couple of days prior to the meeting."

"And what, somehow remained unnoticed all that time? For two days?" responded Cannon almost incredulously.

"Yes." Timms replied, "the course Security has now been able to provide details of someone climbing the wall that abuts the allotments on Pitchcroft Lane and got into the course at around about that time. However, given it was a couple of days before the meeting and at night, it was thought that it was someone trespassing who was later scared off. You may not know, but that part of the track is so far away from the main grandstand and the on-course stables that given there were no signs of damage or break-ins anywhere the next day, Security thought nothing more of it."

"And?"

"Now we think that the individual somehow managed to hide away on course somewhere…"

"Where, in the stable block?" said Cannon.

"Possibly."

"But you don't know?"

"No, we don't," admitted Timms, reluctantly.

"So, getting access to my, or any other horse, if they wanted to, was pretty easy?"

"Yes, we think the person had plenty of time to dress appropriately and fake the necessary badges needed to get to where they wanted to go."

After the Fire

"Bloody hell!" said Cannon, unable to contain himself.

Banterson, just glared, not convinced the meeting was a good idea now. Admitting to such failures was not what he wanted discussing openly.

"And as we know," continued Cannon sarcastically, "there was no CCTV footage of any use either".

It was not necessary for anyone to say anything at all, Cannon knew he was right. Had been all along. His suspicions were proven.

"So, what do you want from me?" he asked.

"As I mentioned before, the common theme running through what we know so far is Charles Flint and his horses."

"You think he has something to do with it?"

"To be honest, we have no idea. But we'd like you to find out."

While Cannon had already made his mind up about investigating what was going on, he had kept those thoughts to himself. He had a personal agenda because he believed that there was a personal element to what was going on. He just didn't know why.

"Do you have any idea how these scams are being done? Executed?" he asked.

"None whatsoever. We just know something very clever is being perpetrated and we need to find out, why, by whom and to stop it, obviously."

Cannon thought he would throw a curveball into the conversation. He still wasn't totally convinced why they needed him specifically.

"Why haven't you got the police involved? Fraud squad? It should be right up their alley."

The comments from the Chair clarified Cannons' question.

"Mr. Cannon, on behalf of myself and the rest of my colleagues around the table," he said, nodding left and right towards the others in the room who had remained silent throughout the conversation, "I can assure you that we did give it serious consideration regarding engagement of the Police. However, after careful thought, and input from Mr. Timms here, we decided it best to keep the matter in-house, so to speak. At least for now."

"And that's where I come in?"

"Yes, Mr. Cannon, it is."

Timms took up the conversation again. "Mike, not only is your background known to us, as you would expect but also, we know that if we are to get to the bottom of what is going on, then who else would be willing to help, other than someone directly affected?"

"An insider, a victim, like me?"

"Precisely."

"And what's in it for me?" asked Cannon.

"Unfortunately, we can't guarantee anything other than we will provide your family and your stables with additional security and necessary support as you need it. Given we don't know who we are dealing with, we can only provide a watch-and-act-brief for now. What agreement we come to in this room needs to stay within these four walls. We can't let it be known by anyone that you are working for us on this matter."

Cannon thought about this for a while. He considered what he could be letting himself in for. He had vowed to himself that once he had left the police force, then he was out of it for good. No longer putting himself, or his family at risk. Unfortunately, he had failed in keeping that commitment.

"Does Charles Flint know that he is under investigation?" asked Cannon.

Timms made a quick glance towards Banterson. It did not escape Cannon's attention.

"No, we don't think so," answered Timms.

Cannon wasn't sure if it was true or not, but he kept his thoughts to himself, eventually asking the question that had been concerning him for a while.

"If I help you," he said, "as far as the general public are concerned, as well as my owners, everything should seem as normal, right?'

"Yes, absolutely."

"Which means then that the horses I train for Charles Flint should continue to be allowed to race. Correct?"

"Until we establish whether there is a reason for those horses not to race, then, of course, they can run," replied Banterson. "That includes your horses or those owned by Mr. Flint trained by any other trainer."

"And if you find reasons not to allow them to run?"

"Then we will suspend them immediately."

Cannon was uncomfortable and said so.

"Mr....Banterson, Sir. I have two of Flints' horses under my care. One of them, *RockGod* has qualified for the *National*. He is the best horse I have and I'm not ashamed to say this, but he is the reason why I have been able to stay afloat as a trainer. His success has helped me keep a reasonable number of horses in training and kept those owners with me," he said. "If I lose the right or ability to keep him with me, or Mr. Flint decides to take him elsewhere, then that could seriously jeopardize my future. I need, no want, assurances from you, that no matter what happens, the horse is allowed to run in the *National* next month."

A silence descended over the meeting for a few seconds. Eventually, it was decided that Cannon leave the room while the panel considered his request. Cannon waited outside, pacing. His mind filled with a million thoughts. Getting involved as he was being asked to do, was bringing back ghosts of the past. Did he really need to see them again? Did he really have a choice? He had endured much while he served in the Force. Did he really want to go back there, albeit surreptitiously, under-cover?

The door to the room he had vacated stood like a barrier to his future. He could hear the murmurs of the debate going on, on the other side. After what seemed an age, the sound of the door opening banished the clouds swirling in his head.

"Apologies for the length of time we have kept you outside Mr. Cannon," said Timms, "however we believe we have a solution."
"I'm all ears," he said.
Banterson folded his hands, cleared his throat before addressing Cannon. "Mr. Cannon. We, this panel, as I'm sure you understand, have an obligation to ensure that the Rules of Racing are upheld at all times."
Cannon nodded his acknowledgment as Banterson continued, "And that includes making sure that trainers, officials, owners, committee members, jockeys, and the general public do not in any way attempt to influence the outcomes of Racing. The integrity of the sport is paramount."
"Understood," replied Cannon.
"Accordingly, while the rules are clear, this panel, this committee does have certain powers as we indicated at the outset of this meeting. However, this *get together* is actually off the record and hence we have no reason to use such authority. What that means is, given the circumstances, this meeting did *not* take place. We did not discuss anything at all. This gathering *never* happened," Banterson stated while smiling to himself.
A private joke thought Cannon. He noticed the Secretary close her notepad.
"Which means?" asked Cannon.
"Which means," replied Banterson, "that there is no issue in relation to your standing. Your horses can continue to run in whichever race they have qualified for, including the *National*."
"While I investigate Flint?"
"Yes, while you continue with that *work* on our collective behalf, Mike," said Timms flippantly. Almost as if undercover investigative work was a walk in the park.
"And what if I say no?" he asked.
It was clear the panel had not considered Cannon's reply as an eventuality. They had made an assumption that their position had made his involvement a *fait accompli*.
Timms responded. "May I speak on behalf of the panel, Mr.Banterson?" he asked nodding towards the Chair.
"Go ahead, Mr. Timms."
"Thank you."
Turning to Cannon, Timms said, "Mike, I think we understand where you are coming from, and in the spirit of openness, I think it right that I share with you everything we can so that you know where we all stand."
Cannon sat quietly allowing Timms to continue.
"Firstly, let me say that we really do appreciate it that you are willing, at

least *considering*, to get directly involved in this investigation. We realize also that this will be an impost on you, your family and your business. We are not immune to this".

Cannon nodded. His face remained still, giving nothing away. Hiding his thoughts.
"However," Timms continued, "I'm sure you realize that if we had the necessary trained resources available here at the BHA, we would undertake the investigation internally and we would not be seeking your involvement. Unfortunately, we do not. In addition, as far as we are concerned it is still too early to engage the police as we need much more information, more evidence in relation to this matter."
"You've asked them?"
"Yes, Mike we have, but like us, they have limited resources themselves, as I am sure you know."
Cannon nodded. He knew there were always issues with resources. Financial crime, or fraud, always took a back seat to murder, terrorism, protection of assets. Crimes in sport, of whatever type, while noted, often became the remit of the sporting authorities to resolve first, before the police would ever get involved.
"And that's why we need your help."
Cannon felt a shiver run up his spine. It wasn't the cold, but that old feeling that he had tried many times to shake. Somehow it kept on returning. A feeling in his gut. Excitement. Fear. The feeling of being alive, yet one of disturbing the ghosts of the past. He knew the more he tried to run, the quicker the ghosts became. He had tried to reconcile with them over the years. Tried to forget, but somehow, they refused to stay where he thought they were buried.
"Tell me all you know," he said.

CHAPTER 22

"Good morning Mr. Tupage, and thank you for your time," he said. "I'm Sergeant Sedgefield, Andrew Sedgefield, and this is Inspector Walsh."
Walsh and Tupage shook hands. They were sitting in a small office at the back of *Lamberts* restaurant. It was just before eleven a.m.
In the background, Walsh could hear voices. People were working in the kitchen, getting ready for the lunch trade.
Orders about food preparation were being barked and replies of *'yes, Chef!'* could be heard. Sounds of large pots clanging and cutlery scraping shiny surfaces evident. *Just like on the TV cooking shows,* thought Walsh.
"As I mentioned on the phone, Mr. Tupage," continued Sedgefield, "we wanted to talk to you about one of your staff, a Mr. Kaminski. Steven or Stefan Kaminski."
"What about him?" asked Tupage, "he's not in trouble is he?"
"No Sir, he's not," replied Walsh.
"That's good, he's due back tomorrow. After his break."
"His break?" enquired Walsh.
"Yes, he was going back home for a week to see his family."
"And that was too…?" enquired Sedgefield.
"Poland. Katowice."
Sedgefield looked at his notes as Walsh continued his questioning.
"So how long has Mr. Kaminski worked here?"
Tupage put a finger to his lips, thinking, obviously trying to recall from memory how long his staff member had worked at the restaurant.
Walsh looked the man up and down while he waited for the answer.
Tupage was a short man. Almost as wide as he was tall. He had dark curly hair that seemed plastered to his head. A small head, *too small for his body*, thought Walsh. He had a goatee beard around an oval-shaped mouth, green eyes and a veined nose. One of those complexions that others unfortunately imagined belonged to that of a *drinker*. He wore a dark suit, a crisp white shirt, and tanned coloured shoes. They knew he was both the owner and maître-d of the restaurant.
Eventually, Tupage stood up and turned to a four-drawer filing cabinet standing in the corner of the office. He pulled out a beige file, saying, "I keep all the Personnel records here," indicating the cabinet. Placing a single file on the desk between the policemen and himself, he opened it. Attached to the top page, a small photograph of the head and shoulders of a man.

"Now let me see," he said. "Ah, here we are. He joined us in September, just over eighteen months ago."
"And you said he was away currently? What, on leave?" asked Sedgefield.
"Yes, that's right. He hadn't taken a day off since he started with us."
"And you believe he was back in Poland?"
"Well, that's where he said he was going. It's not really my job to pry, is it? Look what's going on Inspector?" Curiosity getting the better of the man.
Walsh decided that it was best to be upfront with Tupage.
"Unfortunately, Sir, Steven is dead."
"Dead? Oh my God!" he exclaimed, the news clearly disturbing him. He began to shake. "What? How? Was it an accident?" he said. "I think I need a drink."
Walsh nodded to Sedgefield, who quickly left the office, to return thirty seconds later with a glass of water.
Tupage gulped it down, placing the empty glass on the table afterward, thanking the Sergeant as he did so.
Walsh noticed the sounds from the kitchen had subsided. Sedgefield's' request for the glass of water had caused some form of an inquisitive stir.
"I'm sorry Inspector," Tupage said, "it's just that the staff are very close. We work as a team to make this place successful. Losing one of them like this is, well, deeply upsetting."
"I can imagine," answered Walsh.
"I'll need to let the rest of the staff know as soon as I can. It won't be easy for them. Stefan was well-liked."
"I understand," replied Walsh. "How many people work here?"
"We have two Services per day, except Sunday when we just have the one, but between all the different roles and shifts we do, it's about thirty-five people overall. Including the front-of-house staff."
"Front-of-house?" asked Walsh.
"Waiting staff, Greeters, that type of role." Sedgefield made some notes.
Walsh continued, "We may need to talk with the staff at some stage about Stefan and their movements over the past two or three weeks, however, I need to ask you a few more questions if I may? Given you are the owner."
"Of course."
"Thank you, Sir. I'll try not to take too long."
Walsh could see that Tupage was thinking about Kaminski, that he wasn't really concentrating on his questions. To try and soften the blow he asked.
"If it would help Mr. Tupage, we can always conduct this interview down at the Police Station, perhaps later today or tomorrow?"
"No, no, let's do it now," replied the restaurateur clearly distressed. "I'm sorry Inspector, I'm just a bit overwhelmed by it all."
Walsh made a quick decision, choosing to jump to the important questions he needed answers too before he lost Tupage totally.

After the Fire

"Sir, could you tell us if there have been any threats made to you in recent times?"

"Threats?"

"Yes."

"What type of threats?" replied Tupage, "has this got anything to do with Stefan?"

Walsh could sense that Tupage was getting more and more uncomfortable, agitated.

"We have reason to believe," went on Walsh, "that there may be people moving into the area that are looking to take over businesses or indeed close down some of those already existing, those already established in order to gain a foothold for themselves. For various *personal* reasons and using inappropriate means, shall we say."

"What like extortion, protection rackets, that type of thing?"

"Well you may have been watching too much TV, Mr. Tupage, but yes, *that* type of thing."

Tupage thought for a second before asking. "Was Stefan killed by these people?"

Walsh and Sedgefield shared a glance.

"We don't yet know if it is relevant and we haven't formally released any details as to how Mr. Kaminski died, Sir. Nor have we yet concluded that his death has anything to do with anyone else. We are just investigating several lines of inquiry."

"So how did he die then?"

Walsh relented, deciding to let Tupage know. "Sadly, Mr. Kaminski drowned, but we are not sure where or how just yet. His body was found in the Thames a week or so ago."

"Drowned?"

"Yes."

"How terrible," murmured Tupage to himself.

Sedgefield who had been studying his notes asked, "Mr. Tupage, you mentioned earlier that Stefan, as far as you were aware, had gone to visit family. Is that correct?"

"Yes, that's what he told me, and several of the other staff as well."

"Earlier you mentioned Katowice, in Poland"

"Yes, that's right."

"Is that where he is from?"

"Yes, see here."

Tupage turned the file on his desk around, so that it faced his visitors. The file no longer upside down to the two policemen.

He pointed at the paperwork, at the appropriate line with his finger. "See here gentleman," he said, "it clearly states in his own handwriting. Place of Birth, *Katowice*."

Walsh and Sedgefield looked at the form, then at each other. Both looked confused.

They knew that from their conversation with Lucy Flint, Stefan Kaminski, her boyfriend, was from Torun in Poland, not Katowice. In addition, she had told them that he had no family there, that his parents had passed away. They looked at each other once again, both thinking the same thing. Something was very wrong. The photograph attached to the Personnel record was not what they expected. The person in the photograph was *not* the body they had in the mortuary. The picture was not that of Stefan Kaminski.

CHAPTER 23

"Jean Rice," she said into the phone.
"Could I speak with Mr. Flint please?" asked Cannon.
"Who may I say is calling?" she asked in an officious manner.
"My name is Mike Cannon. I am one of Mr. Flints' trainers. One of his racehorse trainers," he added for clarity.
"I'm afraid Mr. Flint is unavailable at the moment."
Cannon could tell from experience that the tone of the voice at the end of the phone meant that he had hit a brick wall. A secretary or assistant who was there to screen calls, to protect her boss.
"Will he be available soon," he asked as politely as he could, "or can I have his mobile number and I can call him directly?"
"I'm sorry Mr.. umm, Cannon," she answered, clearly intending on putting him off, "but I can't provide you with Mr. Flints' private details without his permission. Unfortunately, as I have already indicated, he is unavailable currently, so I am also unable to ask him at this point in time."
"What if I told you it is urgent?"
"Irrespective."
She had been fending off callers for nearly a week now. It was getting to her. She had managed to keep people away, disclosing nothing, however, the pressure was getting to her. She had been polite despite some of the callers being incredibly persistent. Even Henry Perkel had been fobbed off when he called.
Cannon was beginning to get angry. He wasn't in the mood for all the verbal dancing he needed to do.
"Look, I need to speak to Mr. Flint as soon as possible," he went on, "could you give me *any* indication of his availability please?"
"I'm sorry but Mr. Flint is away from the office," she answered. She had been fielding the calls for nearly four days now. Thank God the weekend was nearly here. She couldn't keep the pretense up for too much longer.
Where is he? she thought.
"Unfortunately, I can't give you any more detail than I have already," she continued.
Cannon knew when he was in a battle. He had been there many times before. Investigations had often hit snags or been sent down rabbit holes. He thought he'd try the charm offensive. At least have one last try.
"Look, I'm really sorry to be a nuisance and I do understand your position, but it's vital that I speak with him or at least get a message to him. It's

about his horses, particularly *RockGod,*" he said, "I am hoping to confirm with Mr. Flint whether he still wishes to run the horse in the Grand National." It was a ruse but Cannon hoped it would work. "Is there anyone else I can speak to? A family friend or a business partner? Anyone who may be able to pass on a message?" he pleaded.

She thought about Cannon's request for a second. The mention of the Grand National was something she knew Flint was very keen to participate in. He had mentioned it many times to her, how he had a horse that could potentially run in the race. Maybe, she thought, if she gave Cannon the one number she had, then perhaps Flint himself would eventually get in touch, let her know his circumstances, where he was?

She hadn't wanted to follow it up herself for fear that he would be upset with her. She had always been dutiful to him. She prided herself on following his instructions, on being there for him. She knew it could never be said, but she was in love with him. Her boss of over a decade.

She started to waver. What if Flint was hurt somewhere? What if he actually *did* need help? She had been to his home, knocked on his door to no answer, no one home. She hadn't told Perkel this when he called over the past couple of days, but now she was beginning to think that she had done the wrong thing by being overprotective.

"Mr. Cannon," she said eventually, "it's probably more than my job is worth to do this, but given Mr. Flints' absence and your obvious need to speak with him, I do not think I will be betraying Mr. Flints' trust if I provide you a phone number that may be of use to you. However, I must insist that if I do give you this information, you need to know that *you did not get it from me.*"

"Understood," he replied.

The line went quiet for a short while. He could hear her breathing into her headset microphone as she began tapping keys on a keyboard.

Eventually, she said, "Mr. Cannon. I was told by Mr. Flint never to give out this number unless there was an absolute need to do so. Again, I ask you to be circumspect with it."

"You can rest assured I will be."

"Okay, thank you."

She hesitated momentarily, still unsure if she was doing the right thing. The details that I am going to give you are those of Mr. Flints' estranged daughter," she said, "he told me to give them out only if there was no other way that he could be contacted. If there was an emergency. Mr. Cannon, it seems like this is such a time."

"Emergency?" enquired Cannon, "has something happened?"

She had put up a front long enough. The inquiries that clients, bankers, and others had made over the past few days had hit their mark. She had fought them off one at a time, but each inquiry had taken her closer to the edge.

She had acted professionally. She had pushed back the tide for as long as possible, however, each inquiry had added to the stress, the burden of lying continuously had eventually gotten to her. Cannon was the fortunate recipient of that dam bursting.

"I'm not sure Mr. Cannon but I'd like to help you if I can." She hesitated for a moment. Cannon could sense her thinking it through. Trying to decide what to do. Eventually, after what seemed like an eternity, she relented. "Mr. Cannon, I am going to give you a phone number. Mr. Flint told me never to give it out unless it was a last resort. He gave me strict instructions," she repeated, indicating the seriousness with which she viewed the matter. "It's a mobile number. Please be aware that Mr. Flint and his daughter are not on the best of speaking terms. Unfortunately, I am not privy as to why, but as she is the only family member of his that I am aware of, and I am sure that despite their differences Mr. Flint would want her to know if something had happened to him."

"*Has* something happened to him?"

"I'm not sure, nor suggesting something has occurred either one way or the other, but he has been uncontactable now over the past few days which is most unlike him."

Cannon didn't know what to think. He just knew that Flint had always been elusive.

"Have you contacted the police?"

She laughed down the phone. A nervous laugh.

"Mr. Cannon, I'm sure you would appreciate what the police would say to me if I told them my boss was absent from work for a few days?"

Cannon knew all too well, but he surmised from her concern that there was something unusual about Flints' absence. Just the way she spoke, he guessed his disappearance was out of character.

"Yes, I understand what you mean," he replied. *Little did she know*, he thought. "Have you given the number to anyone else?" he asked.

"Not even to his lawyer, one of his closest friends."

"Any reason why not?"

She considered it for a moment before saying, "I don't really know. I think it didn't seem necessary. Most of his business associates already have his mobile details, they have no need to contact his daughter, whereas you do."

"Wouldn't it easier to give me his number then, rather than me having to speak with his daughter. Perhaps upset her, when it would unnecessary to do so?"

"Ahh, Mr. Cannon, you nearly caught me out there," she said.

"And why," he interrupted, "have *you* not tried to speak with her directly? Asked her where he might be?"

"Mr. Cannon," she responded, her tone changing as if he had offended her, "as I said before, I did not want to cause unnecessary concern for his daughter. I've tried to be pragmatic so far, given the circumstances. Your request and need to speak with Mr. Flint do require me to act. Because of that, I am relenting. Perhaps it is against my better judgment, but I will live with that if I need to."

Cannon sighed inwardly and indicated his understanding. She gave him the number and he thanked her, wished her well. If he found out anything, he would let her know. As he put down the phone, he wasn't sure what to think. It all seemed very odd. He was beginning to make a few connections in his head but were they the right ones? He picked up the phone and called the number he had been given.

CHAPTER 24

Henry Perkels' body had lain on the floor, slumped against the wall leading down to the parking area at the back of the Drury Lane Travelodge hotel. It was clear that he had been strangled. The blue tie around his neck had cut into the flesh where it had been twisted by his killer.

He had been found by a young couple who were guests at the hotel. They had been out on an all-nighter and were trying to use the wheelchair ramp entrance on the Shorts Gardens side of the building when they saw the body lying on the ground. Initially, they had thought that he was just another drunk who had passed out in the driveway. When they took a closer look, however, the light from the torch on their phone soon indicated that the man was dead. His eyes open, but seeing nothing, a swollen blue tongue lolling out of his mouth. The girl had screamed with revulsion. Her panic and fear soon negating the alcohol she had consumed during the evening at a local dance club. Instantly sober she had turned to her partner and buried her face deep into his shoulder as she sobbed. The sight of death had sent her into shock.

The police were called by the hotel's night receptionist who was almost ready to go off duty when the couple had charged into the reception area.

Walsh had received the call just after six am. It was now just before seven.

The area had already been cordoned off, the blue and white tape around the immediate site of where the body lay. Yellow and black tape was used to block off the road that ran adjacent to the building. Constables stood guard at both ends of the street keeping onlookers back. Even this early in the morning there were small crowds gathering.

The weather had been kind, the brief overnight shower had passed. It was still cool though. March winds were softer this morning, blowing the clouds away from London, towards the East, leaving the sky with the potential to deliver a sunny day. Dawn was breaking, slowly and incrementally providing additional light on the scene to supplement those already set up by the forensics team. A crime scene analyst and a crime scene technician were already on site when had Walsh arrived. A constable who was first on the scene after the 999 phone call, stood to one side, keeping out of the way. Walsh nodded to the senior officer.

"So, what have we here?" he asked. He knew it was going to be a long day. Another body adding to his workload. Another file to open. Resources to be stretched yet again. He thought they were making some progress on the cases he was working on. The Kaminski case appeared to be gaining traction until the shock he and Sedgefield had received at *Lambert's*

After the Fire

restaurant. The outcome was a step back, not a step forward. What they had learnt from Tupage meant another meeting was needed with Lucy Flint. She was due into the station at midday and Walsh and Sedgefield had still not touched base on what questions they needed to ask her. The only obvious one being who was the person in the photograph?

Would she know?

Why did he have the name Stefan Kaminski, work at the place she said her boyfriend worked at, and yet was clearly not *the* Stefan Kaminski she had identified?

Walsh took a deep breath and sighed. He listened to crime scene analyst Bill Portman's commentary in answer to his question.

"Male, mid-fifties, well dressed, obviously strangled, but not your average mugging that went bad," he said. "This poor soul has been tortured. Particularly badly beaten around the legs. The way he is lying seems to suggest that broken could be broken. I also think he's been subject to electric shocks. Whoever did this," he pointed at the body, "is vicious, ruthless."

Walsh knew Bill well. They had worked on many cases together over the years.

"Any idea as to the time of death?"

Portman knew that he was not able to give an exact time, just an estimate. Over the years though he had become pretty good at getting close. Based on the state of the body and temperature readings they had already taken, he looked at his watch and said, "No rigor at this stage. Temp still high, body relatively warm to the touch, so I would say about two hours ago. Around five o'clock this morning Inspector."

"Thanks, Bill," he replied, thinking that the first thing they needed to check was local CCTV. Walsh looked up noticing cameras on Dudley Court, the flats next to the hotel parking entrance. He also saw cameras on buildings further up the street.

If the victim had been murdered in the street, there would be some vision of the perpetrators, he thought.

"Do we know who he is?" he asked.

Portman called over to Susan Doyle, the analyst, asking if there was any identification on the body.

She held up a wallet in her gloved hands, reading out Perkels' name and address from the driving license. The likeness from the photograph with the body, unmistakable.

"Thanks," said Walsh.

Knowing that he could not do much more, he asked whether an ambulance had been called, then indicated that he would leave the forensics team to their job gathering all the necessary evidence they could from the scene. Once back at his office he would organize a team to begin working on the case. He took one last look around. From experience, he already knew that the body had been dumped and that the poor bastard had been killed elsewhere. Taking his phone from his jacket pocket he dialed the usual number.

"Sergeant," he said, "guess what. We have another murder to add to the caseload. Call the team together. I want everyone available at 9 am sharp!"

CHAPTER 25

"Thank you for seeing me, Ms. Flint, I really appreciate you giving me some of your time," he said.

She smelt of paint thinners and glues and Cannon noticed how firm her grasp felt when she shook his hand.

"Comes from holding a brush for so long," she replied, noticing how he reacted to her touch.

They were now sitting in the *Brother Marcus* Brunch restaurant not far from the Balham railway station from where he had walked. It was the closest place and the easiest form of public transport for him to use in order to meet her She had walked from her studio apartment to the café. The early morning dullness had cleared and the midday sun had permeated through the clouds. It was a typical early Spring day across the London boroughs. A weak sun and mid-teens temperature. No rain expected, for which Cannon was thankful.

He had stayed at the Travelodge on Drury Lane the previous evening, as it was one of the cheaper and more reasonable hotels close to High Holborn where he had met with the BHA. He hadn't noticed the police activity at the back of the hotel as he walked the 10 minutes to catch his train.

He always wanted to be the first to arrive at a place that he had never been to before, so he made sure he was there in plenty of time to meet her. Old habits die hard, even if they were from a long time passed and a lifetime ago.

He had called Rich while he waited for her.

The morning gallops had gone well, and all the horses had eaten up after their exercises. Cannon had read the Racing Post whilst on the train. He had bought it from a kiosk at Leicester Square station. He noticed that *RockGod* had been priced at 16 to 1, the fifth favourite for the *National*. The pressure and expectation were beginning to mount. He wasn't sure how news about *RockGod's* form was getting to the paper, but someone was aware of how well the horse was going.

He had entered the horse into one last run before the great race in Liverpool, a three-and-a-half-mile chase, at Newbury, in a week's time.

After his call with Flint's secretary, he had contacted Timms and let him know what he had found out. He had then called Flint's daughter. She had been surprised at his call but had reluctantly agreed to meet with him after he had introduced himself as the trainer of two of her Father's racehorses and explaining the reason, he needed to speak with her.

On the phone, she had explained to him that she was unaware of her fathers' whereabouts and wasn't sure that she could help him. He had indicated to her that he understood that she and her father were estranged, but he was hopeful that she could help him find some way to contact him. He advised her that as *RockGod* had been entered into the Grand National he needed to verify with her father his willingness to pay the entrance fee for the horse to run in the race and hence needed her help in trying to contact him.

She had been polite on the phone when he had called her, not even asking how he had come by her phone number, but had expressed total ignorance about her Father's racing interests and indeed she made it very clear of own total lack of interest of horse racing in general.

After she had sat down Cannon had ordered the coffee and cakes that were then delivered to their table. The pastries remained untouched as she drank the warm liquid, cupping the mug in both hands.

"They do good coffee here," she said, putting the mug back down onto the table.

Sipping his own drink, he nodded his agreement. Much better than that offered by the many chains that were found on every street corner nowadays he thought.

"So, how can I help you Mr. Cannon?" she asked smiling. Her body language suggested that she was open, genuine. As he was about to reply, she added "I'm sorry but before you answer that question, let me repeat what I said last night. If it's solely my fathers' movements you want to know about, then it will be a very short meeting."

"You've lost touch with him?"

She laughed inwardly, the expression on her face however gave away what she was thinking.

"You could say that," she answered. "Let's just say, we don't talk anymore."

Cannon let the moment pass. He realized that there was more to the story. He didn't want to push things too far. The relationship between Charles Flint and his daughter was none of his business. He just wanted to find his client.

"I understand," he said.

Cannon realized immediately from her reaction that he had reached a cul-de-sac. Lucy Flint was not able or indeed willing to help him. It had been a long shot. The fact that she had agreed to meet him was somewhat puzzling. It was quite apparent though that she couldn't, or perhaps wouldn't, provide any more information about her father.

He decided to have one last go at getting anything useful from her at all.

"Forgive me for asking," he said, "and I will totally understand if you don't want to share anything with me, but may I ask why you and your father no longer speak?"

She smiled enigmatically. Picking up her mug, she finished the remains of her drink.

"You're right Mr. Cannon," she said, "I don't want to share it with you."

"So why did you agree to meet me?" he asked.

Still holding the mug in her hands, she looked deeply into it as if it would tell her what to say in answer to his question.

While he waited, Cannon looked into her face, the strangely coloured hair, red and purple, now hanging freely framed her head. He couldn't guess what she was going to say, but what she did say surprised him.

"Mr. Cannon,"

"Mike please," he interrupted. It seemed he needed to do this all the time. Formality did not make for good bedfellows when you are trying to get information. He hoped that using his Christian name would make him more accessible to her.

"Okay, *Mike*," she answered, her voice strong and clear, "I'll put it this way. I'm an artist, I find expression in the things that I paint. My paintings are like those of the impressionist movement. They are extensions of myself. How I see things, not necessarily how the world sees itself, or how people see themselves."

Cannon noticed the passion in her voice, the depth of feeling in her words. He listened intently as she continued. "My Father and I lost touch years ago and I have no desire to see him again or hear anything at all about him," she said, "however if I can help *you* personally then I will."

"Why would you do that? Given what you just articulated so clearly" he asked.

"Why?" she replied, echoing him. "I do it because it's who *I am*. I help people. In whatever way, I can."

He wasn't sure what she meant. He looked quizzically at her.

"Twenty-five percent of my earnings I give away to charity," she went on, "It is something I have done for years."

"Very noble," he replied, trying not to sound too sarcastic.

"Yes," she answered, "but I don't want praise or thanks, I just want to remain in the background. Help where I can. Practice what I do and show my art."

"But isn't showing your art putting yourself front and centre, bearing your soul to the public? Letting them in?"

She ignored his questions, her eyes on his. Cannon felt that she was looking right through him.

"I'll give you a number, a name, someone who is close to my father. He will have his details, where to find him. Once I've given you that information, I intend to get up from this table and walk out of here. After that, I don't want to see you ever again."

Cannon was taken aback by the strength and tone of her comments. *She is a contradiction*, he thought.

Lucy Flint took a pen from a small satchel that she had been carrying when she had arrived and wrote on the paper napkin that lay under the still uneaten pastry. Once she had done so, she stood up, passing the napkin to Cannon and left the table walking straight out of the front door of the café and into the street. Cannon studied the name written upon the paper. *Henry Perkel*, alongside an office address and a mobile phone number.

CHAPTER 26

Jack Williams was livid.
"What the fuck do you mean, you *had* to?" he shouted.
"Look, Jack, we had no choice. He didn't have the money. He refused to tell us where Flint was and he tried to run."
"Run?! Run?! Where the hell too, Sam?"
Williams' enforcer Sam Teal was a big man. He knew his own strength because it had been tested many times. Ex-army, SAS, he was in his early forties but acted like a man much younger. He worked out daily, took vitamins and protein shakes to increase muscle mass, and prided himself on the size of his biceps and thighs. He had shaved off his hair and loved to use baby oil when he was working out in his gym. He liked to have his skin shine. A vain man, who bordered on the psychotic.
"Anywhere Jack. He could have disappeared anywhere, just like Flint has if we hadn't been careful."
"But he didn't, did he Sam?" answered Williams, "he was scared, too scared to do anything."
Teal knew when to and when not to argue with Williams. He had seen a number of people over the years trying to do so. Many of them were no longer living. Others had a physical infirmity. He decided to keep his mouth shut for a while. See how things developed. Teal had confidence in himself but for now, decided that discretion was the better part of valour.
"So, what happened?" asked Williams.
Teal checked himself before answering. He needed to ensure that his story came across clearly and that Williams accepted it. He would not share all the details, the full story, he would leave out the part of him smashing Perkels' knees with hammers so that the kneecaps splintered. He would tell Williams just enough to keep him sweet. It had been easy to get to the fire escape. Teal and his *associate* Paul, had walked into the Perkel's office

building at lunchtime. A few days earlier they had stolen, copied then falsified the necessary security access cards. No one had challenged them. They had worn dirty brown overalls, caps low down on their heads covering most of their faces and they had carried buckets and mops. They looked like typical maintenance men or cleaners. They had ridden a lift to the 2nd floor of the building, then walked back down the fire escape steps to the underground parking area. They then disposed of their disguises by putting them at the back of the void underneath the bottom set of stairs. They had waited there in the darkness, sitting on the buckets for hours until Perkel appeared, keeping silent as other workers walked down the final flight of stairs leading to the underground car park.

Recognizing their target was simple.

Teal enjoyed the memory of seeing the shock on their victim's face. He had walked out of the shadows just as Perkel was about to open the fire door into the parking area.

"We *met* Perkel as he was leaving work and took him for a short ride to that lock-up we have in Stratford to remind him of our *expectations*," said Teal casually.

It had been 7:45 pm, by 11 pm Perkel was in so much pain he had passed out, by 5 am he was dead.

"Don't be sarcastic Sam. Just get on with it. Did you find out anything about Flint or not?"

"No," answered Teal, "nothing at all. The bastard said he didn't know where Flint was. Said he didn't have the money either."

"And?"

"As you'd expect. He tried to bargain his way out of it," Teal replied, believing his actions, his *means*, justified the ends. "After a little encouragement, he tried to tell me that he *did* have access to the money we wanted, that he hadn't spoken to the police, and that he would pay us what we wanted. Immediately."

"And so, what happened?" asked Williams, rubbing a hand across his face, not believing what he was hearing, what he *knew* was coming.

Williams really needed the money from Perkel and Flint. They were soft targets as far as he was concerned and he had always believed that as such, they would easily pay up. He had extorted money many times from many people. It was what he did. It allowed him to meet his own commitments. To pay off those who he owed, which in turn gave him license to operate.

There was a pecking order in his line of business. He wasn't at the top of it, but he wasn't at the bottom either. He operated within the boundaries, paid his dues and had the protection he needed. However, things had gone wrong recently.

Flints' horses had been the source of a good income stream, but Williams was aware that there was a limit to how long that would continue. It was

After the Fire

good while it lasted, and it had been for at least two years now, but Williams didn't believe in flogging a dead horse, for too long. He knew things would come to an end at some point. Now was the best time to cash in his cards. He just needed a final payout from Flint and from Perkel. He was already moving on to other opportunities.

"Well we asked a few more questions about him and Flint," continued Teal enjoying his storytelling, "and all we got was '*I don't know*'. So, we put a bit more pressure on him over the next couple of hours but eventually, my patience just ran out," he said.

Williams knew what he meant.

"After a while and a little bit more persuasion he said he would be able to get us the money straight away, that he would raid a few trust accounts he had access to if we would just let him go. He said we could go with him if we wanted, back to his office. But it was just a ruse. We had been careful to hide our appearance when we went into the building originally but he knew there was CCTV in the lifts, in the foyer, and he knew that security would be asking questions if we went along with him at 10 o'clock at night. So, I told him that. He said that I was just being paranoid. I gave him a few reminders about his current position," Teal went on, smiling at his own joke. "Eventually he said that instead of us going to his office, we could go to his house. He had access to the funds through electronic banking, but that the passwords to the Trust Accounts were in his folders and files there. He said that he couldn't remember all the details so that was why he needed to go to his place as it was where he kept all the information he needed."

Williams stayed silent, listening. Waiting for Teal to finish his explanation.

"He told to me that he once he had all the information, he could make the transfers. But, remember Jack, we asked him to make payments to multiple accounts to avoid the transactions being reported to HMRC right?"

Teal paused, letting Williams know that he wasn't as dumb as some people may think. Williams nodded an understanding and asked Teal to continue.

"When we left the lock-up to walk to the car parked about fifty yards up the road, Paul went to get his key from his jacket pocket and as he did so that bastard Perkel, kicked out at me, and tried to run. Unfortunately for him, he tried to run past Paul, but he wasn't was quick enough and Paul stuck out a leg and tripped the little *shit*. He hit the ground, knocking himself unconscious for a few seconds. I picked him up and took him back into the lock-up, tied him to a chair. Fortunately, there was no one around."

"So, you took him back inside the lock-up where you killed him?"

"I tried to be nice," replied Teal, 'I really did, but after an hour or so of his continuous whining and us not getting anywhere, I lost patience with him. I grabbed him by his throat, then held him up by his tie and unfortunately held on a bit too long," he said, sniggering. Williams just stared.

"Sorry," Teal continued, without any hint of feeling or sympathy, a

sardonic smile spreading across his face.
The bald head and open mouth, incisors showing, reminded Williams of a snake.
"And you dumped his body, where?"
"Somewhere different this time."
"Let me guess," replied Williams, frustration, and anger sitting just below the surface.
"No need boss, I'm happy to tell you," replied Teal.

CHAPTER 27

"Mr. Perkel has not been in today," she indicated to Cannon.
He was standing in the lobby of Perkel's offices having arrived unannounced. He had entered the reception area through a set of automated glass doors which included upon them a logo and an etching of *Perkel and Partners* in fine Antiqua script.
Cannon tried to be nice, but his patience was wearing thin.
He had called Michelle earlier, just before 8 am. She had been on her way to school. She had let Cannon know that *Pavel* Wojcik, the builder, was at the house removing the last of the scaffolding from the property and he had reminded her of the money they owed. She had told Cannon that she had fobbed him off with a promise of payment in the next couple of weeks.
Cannon knew that Michelle had never been able to lie and reading between the lines concluded that she had likely suggested to Wojcik that they would settle all monies owed to him in the coming days, not weeks.
What had made matters worse and was not helping Cannons' mood was a text that had arrived just as he was leaving his hotel on his way to Perkel's office. It was from Cassie.
She had said that the dress she was hoping to buy for 100 pounds had been sold to someone else and that an alternate dress she was looking at was 160 pounds. She had requested the difference from him. He had replied that he would consider it, but he knew that he would ultimately acquiesce He always did and Cassie knew that. His generosity towards his daughter always bothered him as to why he couldn't say no when he needed to. He had replied that he would let her know later in the week.
"Is he expected in though?" asked Cannon to the receptionist, indicating by his tone that he already knew the answer to his own question.
"I'm not at liberty to say," she replied. She was an extremely well-spoken woman, dressed immaculately in a dark blue suit, blonde curly hair cut short, just like Meg Ryan in the 1998 film, *'You've got mail'*.

After the Fire

"Does Mr. Perkel have a secretary?" he asked.

"Yes, he does Sir," she replied, "If you can confirm you have an appointment with him, for me? Your name please?"

"Unfortunately, I don't have an appointment," he replied. "My name is Cannon, Mike Cannon, and I really do need to see Mr. Perkel. Urgently."

The receptionist noted Cannons' plea then asked him to take a seat in the reception area. She told him that she would see what she could do.

While he sat on a couch pretending to read the Economist magazine that was fortunately only a week old, he noticed a considerable amount of hushed conversations happening around him. He became aware of the odd sideways glances at him from a number of people who were being taken into offices made of see-through glass paneling. The receptionist who he had spoken with had left for a minute or two leaving the desk unattended. Now sitting back in her chair, she gave him a false smile and advised him that someone would be along to see him shortly.

Eventually after what to Cannon felt like an age, but was less than fifteen minutes, a man approached him from his left and introduced himself. "Richard Fleetwood," he said.

He shook hands with man, who was about five foot seven tall. Cannon noticed how well tanned the man was considering the time of year. He wore a dark grey suit, blue shirt, and a deep blue tie, his shoes were immaculately polished. He had the archetypal middle age greying of the temples, an extremely attractive man. "Just arrived back from holiday," he said, "my first day back at the office. *Agadir*," he continued, "hence the tan."

Cannon just nodded.

"Please follow me, Mr. Cannon."

The two men walked down a short passage before Fleetwood opened a door, "my office," he said.

They sat at a large table, huge floor to ceiling windows gave them a view of the *'Gherkin'* building, with the *Shard* in the distance. Buses, taxis and the normal everyday life of London could be seen below. Fleetwood sat back in a high-back chair behind his desk, crossing his legs as he did so. Cannon waited for him to speak, noticing the man running a hand along the creases of his trousers.

"I'm so sorry to have kept you waiting, Mr. Cannon, but we just needed to make a phone call before I could speak to you?"

"Phone call?"

"Yes, a phone call," Fleetwood replied, looking as if he needed to repeat the words so that Cannon would understand better the second time.

"To whom?" he inquired. "If I may ask?" he added, trying to sound contrite.

Fleetwood seemed uncomfortable. He seemed to be choosing his words carefully. Eventually, he said, "Mr. Cannon, I'm a partner in this law firm, along with several others, including Mr. Perkel, who is the *senior* partner. So when we are requested by the authorities to pass on any information we have that may be useful to them under such circumstances, we will certainly do so…"

"Sorry, Mr. Fleetwood, er Richard," Cannon interjected, getting annoyed at the merry verbal dance he was being led, "please excuse me for being a little forward, but I'm confused here. Could you be specific please and cut out the bullshit? What circumstances are you talking about?"

Fleetwood was taken aback by what he saw as Cannon's rudeness. He sat open-mouthed for a second. Cannon assailed him further. "I came here to see Mr. Perkel as I desperately need to find one of his clients, one Charles Flint. And before you start talking about privacy and client confidentiality, I want to advise you that I have been requested to do so by the BHA, the British Horseracing Authority, who have indentured me accordingly."

Cannon realized that he had revealed too much about his purpose, his reason to speak with Perkel, to Fleetwood, but he had decided that it was a risk worth taking. He needed to find Flint and the only way he knew how to was through Perkel.

"Mr. Perkels' dead." A deadpan response. A simple comment said without emotion.

"What?!"

"The phone call I was referring to."

"What about it?"

"It was to the police," replied Fleetwood, "they asked us to let them know if anyone enquired about Mr. Perkel."

"But I could have been anyone. A client. Anyone."

"That's true," replied Fleetwood, "but most of Mr. Perkel's clients would have had appointments. They would have been expected. You arrived unannounced, asking to see him. The police asked us to check with them first if that happened."

To see if whoever came to see him without a formal appointment, was aware of anything that could tie them back to who may have wanted him dead, thought Cannon. His mind quickly reverting to his past life. Any information that the police could get would be useful, especially if they had very little to go on.

"And what did you advise them?"

"That you were at our offices, asking about Mr. Perkel."

"And what did they tell you to do?"

"Just to get your details and to pass them on accordingly."

"To who?" asked Cannon.

"An Inspector Walsh."

After the Fire

CHAPTER 28

Charles Flint looked out through the window towards the Isle of Arran. Like Robert the Bruce who purportedly hid in a cave on the island, Flint had been hiding away in the northwest of Scotland, hopeful of evading his past. He had registered under a false name. Paid cash for his stay. He had left no trail behind him for anyone to follow.
The sky and the sea merged in a swirl of dirty grey. Whitecaps rose on the water and then fell away again as the wind from the north whipped them skywards in a salty spray.
The Waterside Hotel in West Kilbride had been an excellent choice. After the conversation with Perkel in the Punch Tavern, Flint knew that he had to get away, escape, consider his options.
He had always been a coward. He had always been arrogant. It wasn't something he would ever acknowledge, however. Only weak people did that, he thought.
He lifted the glass of whisky to his lips, taking a sip, enjoying the taste of peat as the liquid warmed his throat.
Looking out again towards the west he watched a small fishing vessel push its way through the waves.

Jack Williams put the phone down, his hand shaking as he did so.
The phone call he had just concluded had ended badly. To maintain what he had, he needed to keep the peace, to keep *them* sweet. If not, they would move in and take everything he had. So far, he had given them all that *they* had asked for. Now they wanted more. He had expected it. He had made a deal with them. One final *large* and they would back off. Without it though, all bets were off.
"Fuck," he said out loud, "we need that money!"
He pushed an intercom button on a unit next to him.
"Yes, Jack?" answered Teal.
"We need to make sure *that* horse runs in the National," he said, "it's our way out of this mess," he continued.
He had a plan. He needed *RockGod* to run, but definitely *not* to win.

CHAPTER 29

"So, tell me, Mike," said Walsh, "why the interest?"
"In Perkel?"
"Yes."
"There isn't one."
They were sitting in Walsh's office. No recordings as far as Cannon could tell. He was just helping with inquiries. Cannon knew what that meant, but hoped that he could learn from Walsh and Co. much more than they could learn from him.
Walsh smiled.
Cannon had presented himself at the Police station. After he had finished with Fleetwood, he had made the call to Walsh, introducing himself as a trainer of racehorses. He did not mention anything about the BHA.
They had agreed to meet later in the day after Cannon had advised Walsh that he had spoken with Fleetwood and that he, Cannon, had been told of Perkel's death. He had not relayed anything about his past, but it was clear upon his arrival that Walsh knew his background, about him being an ex-cop.
"So, if no interest, why were you looking to speak with him?"
"I was trying to find out if he knew where one of his clients was?"
"Why?"
"Because he owed me money," Cannon lied.
Walsh stayed silent for a few seconds hoping Cannon would continue, providing any more information that he may have, that Walsh didn't. Anything perhaps that would or could provide a reason why Perkel was killed. Cannon sat tight-lipped. It was a game of reading between the lines.
"And?"
"And what?"
"Obviously you got nothing from Perkel. Could anyone else give you what you needed?"
"No."
Walsh considered Cannon's answer.
"How did you know to contact Perkel about your missing client?" he asked.
"Why is that important Inspector?"
Walsh sighed. The stress of what was on his plate was beginning to show itself in his level of frustration. The team could see it, they could feel it. Walsh seemed angry all the time now. Age and workload were beginning to take their toll. He and the team needed a breakthrough from somewhere. He tried another tack.
"Mike, I'm going to share with you something that I normally wouldn't do

with any member of the public, but I'll make an exception in this case."
"Go on," Cannon said.
"I know your background, Mike. You were a good cop. And I know why you walked away from it all. Don't blame you," he went on. "thinking about doing the same myself."
Cannon just smiled. He knew this trick. Pretend to be friends, be amiable, get as much information from them as you can, but only give back what they already know.
"Should I take out my violin?" he said eventually. "You don't know anything about me," he said. "I left the force because of what my wife went through, what my daughter went through, what *I* went through. What it was doing to me. I saw things in the job I didn't want to see anymore. My wife was dying of cancer and I wasn't there for her when it mattered. That was enough in itself."
Realizing he had let his guard down, he stopped speaking, castigating himself internally. He could have talked about so much more. He had been told to do so by the police psychologist. He had ignored that advice.
Walsh was a little taken by surprise by Cannon's show of indignation towards him.
"Just trying to show some empathy, Mike."
Cannon took a hold of himself. Got a grip. He understood that he shouldn't have let his emotion and his own frustration get the better of him.
"Sorry Inspector," he replied, trying to sound sincere, but still wary of what he may be questioned about. "All came a bit of a shock this morning. I didn't expect to be talking to the police in relation to a man's death. It's all a bit surreal, to be honest."
"Duly noted," replied Walsh.
"What was it then that you wanted to share," asked Cannon, "that you *normally* wouldn't do?" he smiled, trying the change the mood, create a better atmosphere between himself and Walsh.
"The man you wanted to speak with. Henry Perkel."
"Yes?"
"He was murdered. Tortured actually," Walsh advised, looking Cannon in the eyes, looking for any reaction.
"Shit!"
"Interesting reaction, Mike. How well did you know him?"
"I didn't."
"So that being the case, I'll ask you again. Why the interest?"
"As I said earlier, I am looking for someone he knew. An owner of mine. I was told that Perkel knew how to find him."
"By who?"
"My owner's daughter."
"And who is this owner?"

"Charles Flint. His daughter *Lucy* gave me Perkel's details."

Sedgefield pushed the button to begin the recording process. They wanted the interview with her to conclude with a signed statement. Modern police procedures now meant the process included a recording that could be transcribed, then signed. It was no longer necessary for an individual to write a statement themselves. But to ensure the statement was genuine, a recording needed to be made to prove that there was no coercion in what the individual included in the statement.

Walsh presented her with a copy of the photo of Stefan Kaminski that they had taken from Tupage at *Lambert's*, passing it across the desk that they sat either side of.

Lucy Flint looked at the picture, her face expressionless.

Walsh and Sedgefield briefly looked at each other, passing a quizzical glance between them as they waited for her to react.

"Look what is this all about? I thought you wanted to talk about Stefan?"

"We did," replied Walsh, "but we now have some conflicting details that we need your help with."

"Sorry, I'm confused," she replied.

Walsh rubbed his temples. If she was confused, then God help the rest of us, he thought.

"Okay," he said, "let's start at the beginning. When we interviewed you last time in your studio, we did so, following our appeal to the community of Balham and surrounds for the identity of a deceased person. Is that correct?"

"Yes," she replied, "as I told you previously, I saw the photograph on the poster and contacted the police."

"And you told us that the person in the photograph was your boyfriend, Stefan Kamimski from Torun in Poland. Is that also correct?"

Lucy Flint nodded her acknowledgment.

"For the recording, could you please confirm your agreement verbally?" he asked. She did as asked.

"Finally, you told us that your boyfriend had worked part-time as a chef at *Lamberts* Restaurant. Is that also correct?"

"Yes."

"Thank you for confirming those details Ms. Flint," stated Walsh. He wanted to ensure that the recording would be uncontestable if required in any future proceedings.

"So, now we come to the photograph before you." he went on, "and for the benefit of the recording," he said, leaning slightly forward to ensure his voice was clear, "I am showing Ms. Flint the photograph noted as exhibit A

that we received from the owner of *Lambert's* restaurant, a Mr. Tupage. Mr. Tupage has confirmed in a separate discussion that the picture we are showing to you Ms. Flint is that of *one* Stefan Kaminski."
Walsh pointed at the photograph.
"Is this Stefan Kaminski?" he asked her.
"No inspector, it is not," she replied.
"So, if not Stefan Kaminski. Who is it?" he asked.
"I have no idea."
"You have never seen this man before?"
"No,"
"Yet he worked at *Lambert's* and went by the same name as your boyfriend."
"And as you can see, this photograph is not of the man whose body I identified. This picture is not of my boyfriend!" she answered.
"And this is why we needed to talk with you again, Ms. Flint," jumped in Sedgefield. "If this is not anyone you know, yet it is a picture of someone calling themselves Stefan Kaminski, who was working at the same restaurant that you claim your boyfriend was working at, then hopefully you can see our problem?" he asked.
"I'm not sure I do."
"Let me spell it out for you then, Ms. Flint," Walsh said, taking back control of the conversation from Sedgefield. "We have a body with a name. The name you told us, Stefan Kaminski, your boyfriend you said. But we now know of another person, the one in that photograph in front of you, who could be very much alive, with the same name, working at the very same place as *you* claim your boyfriend worked at. Do you see our dilemma?"
"I guess so," she answered, "but I can't add anything further. All I know is what I told you previously."
Walsh wasn't convinced.
"So, does it not strike you as odd that we have two people, both apparently with the same name, apparently working at the same place?"
"It looks that way, but again I can only tell you what I was told."
"You never doubted it?"
"Doubt what?"
"That your boyfriend didn't work where he claimed too?"
"Why would I do that?"
"Well, perhaps he didn't cook as well as he might? Being a chef," replied Walsh expressing doubt about her story in his tone of voice.
Lucy Flint sighed. Her face showing that she was getting tired of the innuendo, the doubts about her integrity.
"Look, I wasn't interested in his cooking," she said. "If you really want to know. He was good in bed and that was all I wanted from him."
Her comment almost sucked the air out of the room. Both policemen

coughed into their hands. They knew Lucy Flint was *out there*, she was an artist, someone who expressed themselves differently to many others. She hadn't embarrassed them as they were both too experienced for that, however, her forthrightness was totally unexpected.

Walsh made to restore the natural order. He was in charge. He had cases to solve. He needed to move on.

Not wanting to waste any more time with her on the issue, he asked, "Tell me about your meeting with Mike Cannon."

She seemed surprised that Walsh would know anything about her meeting with Cannon.

"Why? What relevance is that to Stefan's death?"

"None. *As far as we know*," he replied.

"Well then," she said, beginning to stand up, "unless there is anything else, I think we are done. Don't you, *Inspector?*"

He let her put on her coat, then pick up the satchel that had been sitting on an empty chair next to her.

"I'll let the sergeant here show you out. But before you go, Ms. Flint and for the record," he pointed towards the recording buttons, "I'd just like to advise you that the person whose details you gave to Mr. Cannon. One Henry Perkel was found dead yesterday morning. Beaten, tortured and his body dumped."

"My God," she said, sitting back down in her chair.

"Yes, my God indeed, Ms. Flint."

She sat silently for a few seconds. She seemed to be looking off into space. Gathering her thoughts. Walsh and Sedgefield remained still. They knew she would speak again if they let the silence linger.

"He came to ask if I knew where my father was."

"Who did?"

"Cannon."

"And?"

"I told him I didn't know," she whispered. "I told him I didn't want to know. That he should speak with the only person who I thought would know."

"Where your father could be?"

"Yes."

"Why Perkel?"

"He was a longstanding friend of my father. The only number I was ever given as a contact."

"Go on," Walsh encouraged.

She took a deep breath before saying, "My father and I don't get on. It's been a long time since I last spoke to him. He gave me Perkel's name and number if I ever needed to contact him. I never bothered," she said. "Can I go now, please? I have nothing further to say."

Walsh looked at Sedgefield, then nodded. They let her leave offering her a lift back to her home. She declined.
After she had left the premises, Walsh walked back into his office, calling to Sedgefield to join him.

"Get the team together in the next half hour," he asked, "we need to find out who the *real* Kaminski is now. Somehow these murders," he said, referring to the body that Lucy Flint had named as Stefan Kaminski, "and Perkel are linked, but I'm buggered if I know how. The only thing we have in common so far is Cannon and Charles Flint. We need to find him!"

CHAPTER 30

RockGod looked magnificent. His coat gleamed despite the weak Spring sunshine. Just over sixteen hands to his withers he appeared to be much larger than some of the other five competitors. He danced on his toes as he was led around the parade ring at Sandown Park racecourse. Just over three weeks until the *National* it was his last run before the big race. Basically, a chance to blow out the cobwebs after the limited opportunities available to him, given the winter rains. Cannon had not wanted to run the horse at the recent Cheltenham festival, an obvious place to take on the best, as he knew if he did, the horse would not be able to recover in time to face the grueling fences of Aintree. While the Gold Cup was the most prestigious trophy to win, and the Cheltenham meeting the most popular, the day of the *National* was the most-watched and loved horse race of the nations' casual punters.
Ever since *Redrum* in 1973 and the great battle with the giant and gallant Australian horse *Crisp,* through to Redrums' third win in 1977, the *National* had found its place again in the hearts of the country. Sporting features like Royal Ascot, the Boat race between Oxford and Cambridge and the *Ashes.*
Cannon knew he needed the exposure. He hoped the *National* would bring it. A big ask, he knew, but he had just the right horse to do it.
RockGod continued to jog around the ring. He was a very strong favourite, six to four on. The distance three and a half miles over the chase course. More than twice around the circuit. He was ready.
To ensure there were no hiccups or potential issues, Cannon had suggested to Rich that they bring their own farrier along to fit the racing shoes on the horse once they had settled him in the holding barns. Geoff Stones had agreed to go to the races with *RockGod.* It was an expensive move by Cannon as Geoff had to turn down other work at other stables in order to be there, but Cannon thought it worth it.
"Looks really well, doesn't he?" Cannon said.
"Never looked better Mike," replied Rich.
They were standing in the middle of the parade ring. Their coats were done up tightly to keep the cold breeze at bay. It was now blowing from the East, swirling as it did so and whipping away the hats of those women brave enough to wear one. The stands that stood on three sides of the ring were almost empty, though a few brave punters sat in their seats hunched up like

squashed gnomes. Others leaned against the parade ring-fencing, coats, and scarves wrapped around them. Most of those attending the meeting at the track had sensibly retired to the bars and restaurants or the betting hall to keep warm. They would venture out to the stands once the horses were on the track. The large video screen towards the members, jockeys and weighing rooms showed each of the runners in turn. The odds for each runner barely changing every time they popped onto the screen. Most punters were expecting a *RockGod* win. The second favourite, *Smite'm* was at odds of seven-to-one, all the rest were at double-figure odds.
"What about the opposition?"
"Nothing to fear Mike. Most haven't raced successfully over the distance, certainly not this season anyway."
"Yes, you are right, but *Smite'm* and *For a Pound* have won some reasonable races in the past. Either of them could be a danger. We need *RockGod* to jump well," Cannon replied.
As they spoke a bell clanged in the distance, the signal for the jockeys to enter the ring.
Various huddles formed within the parade ring. Jockeys, trainers, owners curling up into loose circles making introductions and discussing race tactics.
Cannon and Telside were joined by their regular jockey, Simon McCorkindale. He was wearing Flints' racing colours, black cap, red shirt with a white chevron. Nice and clean now, but would not be that way for very long. The going had been described as 'dead' but when Telside and he had walked the track earlier in the day, it was clear that it was still rain-affected and was soggy underfoot in places. The race would be a slog, especially coming up the hill at the end. The three of them stood quietly together for a few seconds, there were no other connections associated with the horse attending the meeting, not like some of the others. In one group it looked like there were twenty people standing around their jockey. Must be a large syndicate mused Cannon. He spoke with his jockey.
"Simon, small field. What do you think?"
McCorkindale ever the professional, answered as Cannon expected he would.
"Will ride it as it comes Mike. There is no real speed in the race. Tracks holding up well. Heavy though in places, especially near the dam."
The racecourse was well known for its dam or lake jump just at the start of the straight at the bottom of the hill.
"Okay," replied Cannon, "my view is to try and get him settled as soon as you can. Keep a tight hold until the last three furlongs. Let him find his feet but stay at the back out of trouble. Most of these," he pointed towards the runners walking around the ring, each being led by their work riders or stable minders, "will be struggling over the last half mile," he continued.

After the Fire

"You should be able to pass them at will once in the final straight."
The jockey acknowledged Cannon's comments with a smile. A call came from the ring to mount up and the trio walked across the grass to where *RockGod* was waiting. Cannon gave McCorkindale a leg up and the horse reacted. He knew he was at the track to race. He flared his nostrils then began jig-jogging. The jockey undid the reins that had been tied together, moved his whip to his right hand and sat serenely as they continued around the ring. It was clear that the horse was fit and ready to run. The jockey felt the power within the animal as he sat astride him, legs hanging loose down by the horse's flanks. As he put his feet into the stirrups after adjusting them to suit him, he looked across at Cannon and Telside smiling as he did so. This is a winner he thought.

The two men, one of them well built, bald and muscled under his oversized windbreaker stood just inside the stand, looking out at the runners through glass windows. His companion was of similar build and wore a beanie like a number of others that were in attendance. Both wore jeans, and runners They were protected there from the wind and the cold outside. They looked innocuous, non-descript and they did not attract attention to themselves. They looked at the six horses in the parade ring. They knew which one would win.

Cannon raised his binoculars as the starter dropped his flag and the race began. He watched as the line of horses took off, gaining momentum as the race began.
RockGod initially fought his jockey for his head. He wanted to get to the front of the field. Show the other horses who was boss. McCorkindale pulled the reins together, the bit in horse's mouth hit hard against the back of the horse mouth. *RockGod* gripped the bit then changed his *action*, his racing rhythm, allowing himself to relax as three of his competitors moved ahead of him by a few lengths. They headed towards the first fence.
All the horses cleared the obstacle, though the outsider in the race hit the barrier hard, losing a few lengths to the others. Over the next few fences, and up the hill past the stands and down the side of the track, the race order did not change. Three horses raced together tiring each other out about fifteen yards ahead of the favourite. *Smite'm* raced a length behind *RockGod* and tailed off, roughly fifty to a hundred yards behind was the outsider in the race.
The order of the running didn't change over the next mile and a half with the exception of the last-placed runner being pulled up two miles into the race. This left a five-horse, field.
As they moved into the last turn before the straight, *Smite'm* moved ahead

of *RockGod* who was still travelling extremely well, jumping superbly. The race was now on. The pace quickened. The jockeys were beginning to earn their fees. They began pushing their mounts to accelerate. As they turned into the straight for the final time, a wall of three horses spread across the track, almost a line abreast in front of *Smite'm* and *RockGod*. McCorkindale decided it was best to go wide and onto the outside of the course in order to get around them. They raced towards the third last fence, *RockGod* closing the gap on the others with every stride. His legs stretching out, eating up the turf. His ears pinned back as he began his final assault towards the finishing line seven hundred yards ahead. Twenty yards before the obstacle, the dam fence, it happened!

Two of the horses ahead of him suddenly veered left, towards the outside of the track. As they did so they knocked over a third horse that was running next to them. The jockey of the third horse hit the turf. He was ten yards ahead of *Smite'm* as he did so. Instinctively the fallen jockey grasped his head with his hands. All thoughts of his body ignored until any broken bones or fractures could be tested for later.

Smite'm had nowhere to go, he crashed into the felled jockey somersaulting as he did so, sending his own jockey into the fence ahead. The jockeys of the two horses that had suddenly each veered left tried to correct themselves, each leaning right. It was not enough, momentum and being unbalanced took both horses into the obstacle. In a sickening moment, both jockeys and horse felt the feel of the hard plastic and birch of the fence. A ton of muscle gyrated in the air as both horses plummeted over the fence hitting the ground with head and neck.

McCorkindale couldn't believe what had seen ahead of him. He steered *RockGod* further to the left ensuring open turf ahead of him. He jumped the fence with ease, keeping his mind on the job but conscious of the carnage all around him as he did so. In less than two seconds he had been in a race of five, now it was down to a race of one. The disaster at the third last was unusual and the on-course commentary reflected it. For a second the commentator was almost speechless after what he had witnessed. He had been describing a race one minute and then an instant later the field of horses had been decimated.

The small crowd drew a collective breath. While falls were spectacular at times, mass falls were unusual. Punters liked the events, the challenges, the race, but didn't want horse or jockeys hurt.

RockGod continued up the hill. McCorkindale slowing the horse down to a steady canter, allowing him just enough speed to clear the final two fences without mishap.

As they crossed the line, a cheer went up from the small crowd. The favourite had won but given the circumstances, it hadn't been a great race in the end. Six runners, one pulled up and four others falling at the same fence.

Cannon turned to Telside as they walked through the stand towards the winner's enclosure.

"At least it wasn't too hard a race for him, but I hope everyone is okay," he said, showing his concern.

"True. A good outcome actually," replied Rich. "I wonder what the hell happened down there?" indicating the fence where the events they had just witnessed had unfolded.

"No idea, but it was a bloody mess, whatever it was."

The two men watching from the non-members stand knew exactly what had happened. It had worked perfectly.

Charles Flint smiled as he watched *RockGod* pass the finish line.

The hotel had a racing channel and he had made sure that he was able to watch the race.

It was time for him to get back to London. He believed he now knew how to get out of the mess he was in.

The *Grand National* was the key.

CHAPTER 31

"Do we have anything at all from the CCTV reviews?" asked Sedgefield.
"And what about those tattoo's?" shouted Walsh from his office.
The team had been reassembled and Walsh had made it clear that he needed outcomes, results.
"Adrian?" asked Sedgefield, "anything at all from IT? Carmichael, Fitch, anything else from your community inquiries?"
Adrian Windsor answered first. "Sergeant, what we have been able to discover from the CCTV around the area of *Lambert's* restaurant, was that our body number two, the one identified as Stefan Kaminski by Lucy Flint, never, *ever*," he said for emphasis, "went into *Lamberts*. From the footage we have checked, we have seen that the man did move around the area at times, but certainly didn't go to the restaurant."
"In addition," shouted Fitch, in an almost celebratory voice, "I've just got off the phone to Tupage, and he just advised me that *his* Kaminski has just returned to work as expected after his holiday."
"Shit!" exclaimed Sedgefield, "if that's true then we're almost back to the beginning. Square one." He was trying to figure out the implications in his own mind, given what he had just heard. Thinking out loud he said, "If our body number 2 is not who we thought he was, and the person who identified him believed him to be someone he's not, then we have another problem. Who the hell is he then?"
The team was silent. Progress was not only slow, but it was basically stagnant. Given how things were going, it wouldn't be long before Walsh would be hauled over the coals. Currently, he had three bodies, three cases, but no solid leads in solving any of them. Despite requests from Interpol on the tattoos, there was just radio silence. Surely Brexit and its implications hadn't resulted in the who's who of Europe, East or West, hating everything about the UK?
"Anything from the CCTV in relation to the Perkel murder then?" asked Walsh as he came out of his office.
"Nothing so far Sir," answered Sedgefield.
The Sergeant walked over to where Windsor, sitting at his desk was talking into the microphone of his headset. There was no telephone to be seen. *Softphones*! Standing beside him, hand on the IT specialists' shoulder as if both of them looking at a computer screen would immediately produce results, he asked, "Anything?"
Windsor apologized to whoever he was speaking with, pushed a button on

the right-hand side of his earpiece and terminated the call.
"I was just speaking with my forensics colleague upstairs," he said. "They've been reviewing all the footage so far. The software has been able to track a vehicle of interest in and out of the area and my mate has just told me that they have been able to edit the recordings for us. They'll be sending me the file in MPEG4 format shortly."
Walsh, Sedgefield and the rest of the team were all ears. They needed a break. All eyes were on Windsor. He relayed what was had just been advised.
"They told me that what can be seen from the vision is a grey van pulling up behind the hotel. Two men getting out of it, opening the back doors and just dumping the body. They didn't seem to rush. They acted casually. It was five am, still dark and very few people around the entire area. Once they dumped the body, they got back into the van and drove off. Just as if it's a normal thing to do." His tone was filled with admiration as to the audacity of the actions of the men. He had his arms wide open, like a priest. He relayed in words and animated actions what many in the team were thinking. How could the men concerned be so bloody blatant?
"What about vision leading up to that point. Where they came from, where they went to?" asked the Sergeant.
"Due to some of the five hundred thousand cameras around the city," he said, acknowledging the network of assets available to the police, "we've been able to track them, at least for a while." He sounded disappointed. "We lost them once they headed beyond Ilford, though it seems like we were able to pick them up again near Southend-on-sea, and then again in Colchester. We think they were heading to Harwich and possibly onto the continent after that."
"And any idea who these guys are? Any clear vision?" enquired Walsh.
"Umm," responded Windsor, "this is where we have a problem."
"God preserve us!" complained Sedgefield, raising his eyes heavenwards. "What's the problem now?" He was exasperated. Everything seemed to be an issue currently.
"Well believe it or not Sir, the van was being used by Uber drivers."
"What the fuck? An Uber!"
Sedgefield looked around the office catching Wendy Carmichael's eye. She didn't say anything. Political correctness and watching one's language were now expected as part of HR policy, but real life got in the way. Sedgefield's outburst didn't worry her. She heard worse things every time she walked in the street, rode the tube or watched TV.
Windsor looked embarrassed at what he was about to say, knowing it wasn't something the team was hoping to hear.
"Yes Sir, the van in question was being used as an Uber, but…"
"But what?" interjected Walsh, wanting to get to the point. His impatience

getting the better of him.

"It was stolen."

"When? Was it ever reported?"

Windsor was starting to feel intimidated. He put his hands up, almost in defense of himself. What he was relaying to the team was only what he had been advised on his call. He looked at his notes.

"Sir," he said, feeling he needed to unfairly explain himself. "The van was apparently stolen over a week ago, but only reported as missing a few days later. It appears the owner, a Mr. Dabang Singh, who lives in Southall, used the van as an Uber vehicle during the day but allowed it to be used by his brother-in-law, one Sangat Soor, as a panel or freight van at night. Basically, delivering parcels or doing courier work overnight. Apparently, the brother-in-law used to take out some of the seats," he added, shrugging his shoulders.

"And?"

"Well Sergeant, this is our first problem. Mr. Singh has apparently advised that he left the vehicle the night it was stolen, outside his brother-in-law's house. He claimed the arrangement wasn't unusual and that it was quite common for him just to park the van there. This was because Mr. Soor could often be home late from another job that he holds down."

"Bloody hell," interrupted Walsh, "how many jobs do these guys have?"

Windsor decided it was best and expedient to ignore Walsh's outburst.

"When Mr. Soor arrived home," Windsor continued, "the van was gone. *Apparently.*"

"Apparently?"

"Yes, Sergeant. It seems Mr. Soor and his brother-in-law have engaged in making false insurance claims in relation to cars being stolen in the past and because of that, we are not sure if what they told us so far, is true or not."

Walsh shook his head. "I assume statements or affidavits have been taken or lodged re the theft?"

"Yes Sir

"Let me get this straight," asked Walsh, "despite the vehicle having been stolen over a week ago, and there was no sighting of it up until the night of the murder, the thieves still left the car registration plates on? And it was only reported missing days after the event?"

"Appears so."

"Sounds a bit dodgy and amateurish to me. Surely if it was on the road at some point, there was the risk of it being picked up as stolen?"

"I agree with you Sir, but seems like it wasn't."

"Sergeant," Walsh said, turning to Sedgefield, "have someone pay a visit to Messrs. Singh and Soor and find out a bit more if they can."

Turning back to Windsor he asked. "And no sightings until the night of the body being dumped?"

"Apparently not Sir,"
Thinking about this for a few seconds but keen to move on, he asked, "Okay, what else?"
As Windsor checked his notepad, Fitch jumped into the conversation.
He had been quiet up to that point, listening to the exchange between Walsh, Sedgefield, and Windsor. Wanting to show he was part of the investigation he said, "We have contacted the National Crime Squad in Holland, the *Dienst Nationale Recherche,* to be on the lookout for the suspects off the ferry."
"Hang on," interjected Walsh, "I thought Windsor here said we didn't have any vision of those in the van?"
Windsor flushed. "I didn't say that, Sir."
"Well, do we, or don't we?" Walsh asked, his voice rising.
Fitch took over, giving Windsor some air cover from Walsh.
"We have *some* detail and we've managed to piece together some data that we believe could be of use."
"Go on,"
"The CCTV footage from the back of the Travelodge showed the two men in the van to be wearing dark overalls, gloves, balaclavas, and heavy boots. Both men are pretty stocky, well built from how they fill out their clothing, both about one metre seventy, to one metre seventy-five."
"Guys, who work out? Ex-army maybe?"
"Possibly Sir, but the vision gave us nothing in relation to their features. Whether they were white, black, bearded whatever."
"So, what else?"
Fitch smirked slightly, lips together creating a thin line across his face. "Well Sir, this is where we've had a bit of luck. When we picked them up around Colchester, they made a quick stop at a drive-through McDonald's. They still had the overalls on, gloves, etc, but had replaced their balaclava's for caps. The one in the passenger seat had undone a few buttons of his overalls and we were able to see that he had a soccer jersey on underneath."
"And, what was it a Chelsea or Man. United shirt?"
"No," answered Fitch, "Legia Warsaw!"
Walsh felt an immediate mood change in the room as if the revelation had caused a spark to be ignited within the team. Another link with Poland.
Fitch continued. "We've really struggled to find clear vision of the two men anywhere, given the sort of disguises they used and especially given the complete covering of hands and faces. It has made it almost impossible. *However,*" he said, a touch of triumphalism in his voice, "we did get a further shot of them both around the ferry terminal. It seems they *walked* into the terminal wearing different coats, gloves, etcetera. As there was no sign of them driving into the car park, we think they may have dumped the van close by and walked the last bit."

Before Walsh or Sedgefield could ask, Fitch, said, "we've contacted the local area command to see if they can find it, but it's possible that it has been torched or run off a cliff."

"What do the ferry people say?" ask Sedgefield.

"They have the vision of them getting on board the 11 pm ferry to the Hook."

"And have they been able to supply us that footage?"

"Yes, Sir. Again, it's not great vision. The suspects have been clever in shielding most of their faces, disguising nearly all of their features. The coats, scarves, gloves, dark trousers have been used to prevent any distinguishing features they may have from being seen or photographed."

"They definitely know what they are doing," suggested Sedgefield.

Walsh was still irritated, bemused somewhat. Despite all the talk, he felt the conversation had left things flapping in the wind. As if the break they needed was just out of reach.

"This football jersey then. What's so unusual about it?"

"It's bright green, Sir. Quite uncommon. None of the British clubs have such a distinctive colour. Not very common in most parts of Europe either."

"So?"

"From our initial inquiries with our colleagues in Holland, we asked them to see if they were able to get any better vision of the men arriving at the Hook."

"And did they?"

"Yes, Sir, they did. They passed it on immediately to Interpol which has already issued a *red notice* as required by law to search for the men and seek extradition. It seems like the green football jersey stood out when the men disembarked from the ferry the next morning. and surprisingly they were easily identifiable. Seems like they thought that after a night on the ferry, they were less concerned about their profile. Their pictures have been circulated already but the Dutch authorities are in the process of digitally enhancing them for better identification against their databases. It is expected that in the next 12 hours or so, every police force across Europe will have the pictures. Hopefully one of them will be able to verify who they are."

"Then someone needs to be able to find them," stated Walsh, knowing the ins and outs of extradition of criminals to the UK from Europe was never easy. And that assumed the men were ever caught.

"Okay, good work," he said, not wanting to sound too negative. While there was progress, there were other cases to be going on with. The Polish connection was interesting. It reminded him, he still needed to speak with the real Kaminski, now back at *Lambert's*.

He still had other things that he needed to chase up as well.

"Now what about those tattoo's…?" he said.

CHAPTER 32

"I don't know what happened," Cannon stated to Timms.
He was speaking on his mobile phone from his house.
Michelle was marking some homework at the dining room table, Cannon sat in his office.
Darkness had enveloped the house like a blanket hours before Cannon and Rich had arrived home from Sandown. It was a clear night. Ice had started to form on the outside of the window. The temperature dropping quickly due to a cloudless sky. His computer was on and the reflection of the screen on the dark window brightened the room.
"It seemed very strange to us, watching the race video several times over," said Timms.
"I agree,"
"But do you have a view?"
Cannon considered what he was about to say carefully. He didn't want his perspective to influence how Timms or anyone else came to a conclusion about the events at Sandown. Not least because Cannon benefitted from the outcome.
"Yes, I do," Cannon eventually admitted. "Like you, I've watched the race a number of times now, but the only thing I can conclude is that it was likely jockey error. Poor judgment on tiring horses."
"You can't be serious surely? asked Timms.
"Well, it mirrors what the race stewards concluded after discussion with the jockeys."
"True."
"So why do you think any different then?" Cannon asked.
Timms didn't respond immediately. He and Cannon were trying to find answers to the same thing, the same puzzle. However, they had different agendas.
"Mike, when you've been involved in racing as long as I have, and have seen what is done in an attempt to make a quick buck, you won't be surprised at anything some people can get up too."
Cannon didn't wish to rain on Timms' parade and so bit his tongue. He had

seen human nature at its very worse. His time in the force had scarred him mentally. His new life was a release but perhaps not surprisingly whenever he thought he was free from the memories, the angst, and the pain, it would show itself again. Despite being out of that world for so long, human greed, apathy, dishonesty and the unscrupulous nature of man was never far away. Was it applicable in this case, the event at Sandown?

"I understand," he answered eventually. "So, what did *you* see that I or others didn't?"

"Nothing at all," answered Timms. "I just have a gut feeling about it."

"Okay, that's fair enough. You are entitled to that view. I just think that while it was unusual, a fall of multiple runners at one time at the same fence is not completely uncommon."

Cannon could sense the smile on Timms' face, hear it in his voice when he replied, "I think it's easy to say that Mike, especially when you're the beneficiary."

Cannon didn't rise to the bait. He stayed silent, waited patiently for Timms to continue. After a few seconds, Timm's said. "Nice horse *RockGod*, might be worth a bet in the *National*."

Cannon sighed inwardly. Was this a ploy? Did he really mean it or was this Timms' way of getting closer to him? Cannon still wasn't sure. He wasn't convinced yet about who was on *his* side.

"How did he pull up?"

"No problems at all, and since we got home, he's eaten up everything. We'll see how his legs feel in the morning, but so far so good."

"That's excellent."

"Yes, it is. Pity the owner wasn't there to see him run."

After they had said their goodbyes, Cannon left his study and walked towards his lounge. Passing the dining room, he stuck his head around the door and peered into the room asking Michelle if she wanted a drink?

"Tea," would be nice, she said.

"Okay," he said, "just be a couple of minutes."

As he walked into the kitchen, the home phone began ringing. Cannon looked at his watch, it was a quarter to ten.

Unlikely to be an owner. Most of them called closer to the weekend, generally on a Friday. Those who had a runner and could make the meeting liked to check in with Cannon before they made arrangements to travel, especially to *distant* courses. They had the usual questions about whether their horse could win? What odds could they expect? A multitude of things that Cannon didn't always have answers too. He could only tell them the obvious. The horse was well. The course suited or the weather didn't. The majority of them had been extremely supportive and for that, he was eternally grateful.

"Hello?" he enquired as he put the phone on speaker.
"Hi, dad!" the excited voice of Cassie.
Cannon heard Michelle call from the dining room asking him to say her hello's to Cassie for her and to pass on her love. Putting the call on speaker had ensured Cassie's voice pierced the silence.
"How are you?" Cassie asked before he could say anything.
"I'm fine," he replied, "a little tired. It's been a long day. Will be off to bed soon."
"Yeah, sorry I'm calling so late, but I needed to ask you something."
Cannon took a deep breath. Not sure what to expect. Life at university was an amazing opportunity, although he himself had never had that privilege. From his recent experience with Cassie however, he also knew that it was expensive to live away from home, especially for the parents. He braced himself for what she was about to ask. He decided to test the waters.
"Don't tell me," he said, trying to keep his voice lighthearted, "your calling because you need some.. *money*?"
The line was quiet for a second as Cassie considered how best to answer his question. He hadn't even queried her about how her studying was going. She wasn't sure if she should tell him or not. Maybe another time, she decided.
"Well, yes and no," she replied, in a vague answer to his question.
"Umm, not sure if that's good or bad."
"Well, actually it's both."
He was somewhat confused and bemused. The sparring around money and how much she seemed to need was not yet a source of friction, but the joke was starting to fade a bit.
"Go on," he said, as he sat down on the couch. It was easier to sit next to the phone than stand over it. The TV had been left on but was muted, neither he nor Michelle had been watching. A crime drama was showing and was shortly about to finish another episode in time for the news at ten o'clock. Cannon looked at the screen but wasn't taking anything in.
"I've been following what's been happening with *RockGod*," Cassie said, "and I wanted to check if it was okay to come to the *National* with you?"
Cannon sat up in his chair, his curiosity piqued. Cassie had hardly shown much interest in how the stable was doing since she had finished school. In fact, even while still living at home she rarely paid much attention to what was happening in the stables. Too busy on her social media accounts, talking to her friends and *liking* stuff he had always thought.
"So, if you are fine with it, Dad," she continued, "I'd like to come along."
"You said there was a good bit and a bad bit. Not sure yet which is which?" he joked.
She reflected on the tone of his voice before answering. Cannon could tell she was taking a few deep breaths as if gathering herself. Finally, she blurted

out, "Well dad, the good bit is you get to see me. The bad bit is that I'll need you to pay for the privilege."
Cannon laughed out loud just as Michelle came into the room. He had taken too long in getting to the tea and she realized that while he was on the phone, she would need to make it for both of them if he still wanted any. She made a sign of a cup to the lips which he acknowledged with a nod of the head.
Cassie noted the brief silence, "Dad? she asked, "are you still there?"
"Yes, I'm here. Michelle was just offering to make me some tea," he said, smiling.
"Hi Cassie," Michelle called out as she left the room.
"Oh, Hi," her voice from the speaker lost on Michelle who was already in the kitchen.
"So, dad. What do you think?"
What did he think? After his call with Timms, it seemed like everyone was seeking his opinion. He had lots to think about. A few things were forming in his mind, but the dots were not yet connecting.
Eventually, after letting her hang on the line for a few seconds, he said, "I think…Brexit is a bit of a mess…."
"Dad!" Cassie exclaimed, realizing he was teasing her.
"Okay, okay, okay," he replied, "just joking."
He heard her laughing. It was a nice sound.
"Alright, being serious," he went on, "I think if you want to meet us there the day the meeting starts which is on Thursday, that would be great. I have entered another runner, *Visitation,* in a race on that day so I need to be there for the start of the festival. That will give us Friday to spend some time together before the *National* on Saturday so yes, I think that would work. Plus, it's only a couple of hours from York to Liverpool on the train and its reasonably cheap if you book now."
"Dad?" she asked trying to interrupt him, but he was on a roll, not listening.
"I've already booked a place using Airbnb as well. It's just outside Chester and has a couple of bedrooms, so should be good." He was about to ask her the dreaded question about how much she needed when she said.
"Would you mind if we only come on Friday, as we have lectures to attend and assignments to hand in on Thursday?"
The inflection in her voice when she said *we,* shook Cannon from his reverie. He was suddenly all ears.
"We?" he asked.
"Yes, *Blake* and I."
Cannon was dumbstruck for a moment. While Cassie was now eighteen and living away in student accommodation, she was still his little girl. Still his baby. After what had happened to her only two short years ago when she was taken by a vengeful madman as a hostage, he was overly protective of

her. He knew it, but couldn't help himself. Her going away to university meant she was growing up. He didn't like it. The thought of serious boyfriends so early in her university life was anathema to him. While he knew it would happen, he wasn't prepared for it yet. And besides, what kind of name was *Blake* anyway?
"And who is Blake, may I ask? Is he one of your classmates?"
"Dad," she said, trying to get a word in, wondering if it was a good idea to try and explain things to him.
"What's he studying?" Cannon asked.
"Dad!" she shouted down the line, so loud in fact that Michelle could hear her in the kitchen.
"What?" he answered. His mind all over the place. Airbnb. Shared bedroom. He wasn't ready for it. Even though he knew that while she was away at uni, she could be up to anything. The thought of his little girl and this Blake guy was getting to him.
"Dad," she said gently, trying to get his attention.
"Yes, I'm listening," he replied, unconvincingly, his heart rate racing "Fill me in," he asked, resigned to the inevitable.
"Dad, Blake is a *girl*. A fellow student. She's from Dorking, in Surrey."
The silence from Cannon was deafening. He felt embarrassed. He had assumed everything, despite knowing nothing and had made a fool of himself. "Are you still there?" she asked.
He tried to sound normal, without showing how relieved he was. He knew it was a normal reaction to how life changed as parents and children got older. As days and months became years and decades. As children became adults and adults became seniors. Despite knowing all this, he still wasn't ready to accept it.
"Yes, I'm here darling."
"Good. I know its late, so can I take it as read?"
He knew she was good. Her timing had been impeccable. She had nabbed him while he was unaware. Her negotiation tactics were perfect. She had caught him and reeled him in. He admired her for it.
"I guess so," he said. He had nowhere to go. He couldn't say no anyway. He wanted to see her. Where better than at Aintree?
They discussed the cost of travel, what other monies she needed for clothes and spending and confirmed that he would add both Blake and Cassie to his table for the traditional dinner of *National* participants on the eve of the race itself. He tried to be pragmatic about what she needed and why.
Michelle sat and listened after she had brought him his drink, encouraging him to be a father as well as a responsible trainer looking after his costs. Running the stables was a business, but she pointed out that it was also his life. Cassie was part of his life, just as Michelle was. He needed to embrace all of it. Cassie being away should not mean that she was out of his

thoughts. He needed to get the balance right. Cannon understood that Michelle was correct. He knew that taking *RockGod* to the *National* was possibly the first and last time he would ever get such an opportunity. Who knew? Some trainers lived a lifetime and never got themselves a horse good enough to get into the race. Now that he had one, he needed to find Flint before the horse was disqualified from running in the event.

CHAPTER 33

The view from their table on level 33 of the Shard was blighted at times by the low-level cloud scudding across the sky. St. Paul's Cathedral was illuminated, standing out against the black of night, surrounded by coloured lights including those of the various bridges stretching across the Thames. The wind from the west indicated a front was moving across the capital and had already passed over the south and west coasts before moving towards Europe. It was a dry change, the cloud holding no threat of rain. While other diners marveled at the sight from their vantage point, it didn't bother the two men seated at a table against the window. They were in deep conversation and had been all night. The meal was long finished, their minders sitting behind each of the men. Neither invited to eat.

The bottle of cognac between the two was still half full. It was unlikely to be finished, the remains of the bottle would be left on the table. Ignored. It was a sign of their confidence, their success, their inherent power.

Holding up a glass and swirling around the golden liquid inside, the glint of the subtle lighting of the restaurant highlighting the small vortex within, the man finished the drink in a single mouthful. Placing the glass back on the table he wiped his mouth with a napkin and said.

"I don't like Chinese food. I suggest we try something else next time."

Jack Williams maintained a stony face. He clenched his teeth, trying not to show how he felt inside. His stomach churned. The man opposite, the man whom he had invited here, had just told him in a not so subtle way who was who in the pecking order. Had put Jack firmly in his place. Jack didn't like it but held his tongue. His best defense was to keep quiet and work out a strategy later. Getting back control of *his* area of London would require some thought. Now was not the time.

Zymon Madzia was *visiting*. His area of control now extended beyond Croatia and his original birthplace Poland. He had *influence* in many parts of Europe and was building a good base in the UK. Unfortunately for Jack Williams, it included the area that Jack previously *owned*.

The two men were meeting for only the second time. Jack owed Madzia for two million pounds worth of drugs that had been provided to him by Madzia's network. Unfortunately, the shipment had been intercepted when it came through Calais. The risk of delivery had already passed to Williams by then. His own men had gone to Frankfurt to collect the container after it had arrived by ship. Jack knew people in the logistics and distribution world. He was able to *convince* them to have his men collect it and drive it back into the UK through Dover. Unfortunately, they never got near it. Someone had tipped off the local authorities.

Normally such a simple supply transaction would not require them to meet, especially not in public. But given the money owed by Jack, he had engineered the meeting in order to strike a deal.

Williams was getting older. Despite his standing with his peers, age was catching up with him. He hadn't let anybody know about how he felt, but he knew that he wanted an easier life.

Over dinner, they had agreed that Madzia would take more of a stake in Jacks' business. Jack wanted to *semi-retire*. He had access to some important people that he had influence over. The deal would allow for a reduction in the monies owed, and to square the ledger, Jack would repay the balance before the end of May.

He hadn't told the Croat how he would get the money. His current options had limits. He could only squeeze the lemon so much before it ran out of juice. Some of those he continued to extort money and favours from were beginning to run dry. Other's had sought solace elsewhere and needed to be found. One such individual was Charles Flint. It wasn't the man himself that Jack wanted. He would address that later. It was the opportunity he presented with his horses. One, in particular, *RockGod* and his entry in the *National*.

CHAPTER 34

"I've already told you this before, Officer, I don't know this man."
Stefan Kaminski pointed at the picture of Lucy Flints' boyfriend that Walsh had a placed onto the desk in front of where he sat. Walsh noted that he spoke perfect English.
They were back at *Lambert's*. Tupage had allowed them to use his office, but he wasn't happy about their timing. It was nearly lunchtime and bookings had been good. Kaminski was needed in the kitchen.
Walsh looked at Sedgefield who was sitting to the left of Kaminski in the cramped office environment.
"But he went by your name, and he even claimed this restaurant as his place of work," replied Walsh, "any reason why he would do that?"
Kaminski made a deep sighing sound. He had just returned from Katowice and had walked into a police inquiry of which he knew nothing about. Dressed in a uniform befitting the quality establishment *Lamberts* was, a blue and white apron over his chef whites, he appeared much younger than the original photograph Walsh and Sedgefield had originally been shown by Tupage. Since that picture had been taken, he had bleached his hair leaving a blond streak along one side of his head. He was in his mid-twenties. His passport confirming his date of birth. He was tall, around six feet and wiry. His face showed signs of old acne pockmarks that were slowly fading. He had green eyes and a long thin face. When he spoke, he showed a full set of well-maintained teeth. For a chef, Walsh found this surprising, but he guessed that as a chef he made the food but didn't particularly eat much of it. He was obviously nervous about the police asking questions about himself and his background, where he was from and what he had been doing in recent weeks. Walsh suspected that he was just a victim of circumstance. Of identity theft more than likely.
"The man in the photograph was also Polish, apparently from Torun."
"As I said officer, I do not know this man."
"And you are from Katowice, yes?" continued Walsh.
"Yes,"
"And you say you never met him,"
"Never."
"Not even at a pub? A party?" asked Sedgefield.
"No."
"Do you live around here?" asked Walsh, knowing full well that he did.
"Yes, there are a large number of Polish people living in this area."
"You live alone?"

Kaminski smiled. "On my earnings?" he laughed. "No, I live with friends. In a *share-house,* I think you say in English."
"How many?"
"Five others."
"And what do they do?" asked Walsh.
While Kaminski was collecting his thoughts about those with whom he shared a house, Walsh knew most of the details already. However, he needed more. Before they had made arrangements to meet with the chef, they had checked out who had the lease for the property where he lived. There were four names on the lease. Kaminski himself was one. Noting there were six people in total staying at the premises, Walsh was keen to know who the other two were.
"A couple of them are students with part-time jobs, others have different work," he said. "One is a motor mechanic, one works at Heathrow in baggage handling, one works for a builder and there is me."
"Can I get the names of everyone, please?"
"Of course," replied Kaminski.
Once they had all the details Walsh was satisfied that somehow the mysterious boyfriend of Lucy Flint, the late and now unknown *Kaminski* was not really who she believed him to be. Somehow, he had acquired a name, acquired a back story, had given her details about himself that were totally untrue. The obvious question was why? Who was he and what was he really up to?
"Can I go now?" asked the young chef.
"Yes," replied Walsh, "and thank you for your time and your honesty. We hope it won't be necessary to talk with you again, but if it is, we will try to do so at a more practical time. Hopefully, Mr. Tupage has been able to find someone to fill in for you in the kitchen?"
The young chef smiled, standing as he did so. He was keen to get back to work and reached for the door handle.
As he made to open the door, Walsh said, "just one more thing, Mr. Kaminski, if I may?"
Kaminski turned back towards the Inspector.
"Can you tell me what you think this means?" he asked, pulling a photograph of the tattoo taken from the *dead* Kaminski's arm. Lucy Flint's late boyfriend. The image was now much clearer after the technical team had been able to enhance the original digital picture.
"It's Polish, I understand."
"It's not Polish," came the reply.
"Are you sure?" asked Walsh.
"Of course, I am, Officer."
That might explain why there had been no response yet from our European colleagues, Walsh thought. Maybe they were asking the wrong question and

maybe it was being relayed via Interpol to the wrong force? Besides, it wasn't terror-related and most resources across all police forces in Europe seemed to be on terror watch all the time now.
"So, what do you think it is?"
"I'm not sure," came the reply, "maybe Slovakian, Croatian, Czech?"
God, that's all we need, another level of complexity, Walsh thought.
"Do you have any idea at all as to what it could mean?"
"None whatsoever. I'm sorry but I can't help you," Kaminski replied. Looking at the disappointed faces of the two policemen, he asked, "Can I go now, please?"
Walsh nodded. He was more confused than ever.

As they drove back to the station, Walsh called ahead to see if there was any progress in finding Charles Flint. The response was still negative. He was still amazed how in this day and age, with all the electronic wizardry available to them, that a man such as Flint with such a high profile, could disappear so easily? He needed Flint to be found and found soon. Walsh knew he needed to up the ante with his team. He had three bodies, no suspects in custody as yet and just a glimmer of hope that his European counterparts would up their game and provide some assistance. Unfortunately, that was more a hope than a promise.

CHAPTER 35

Charles Flint called Jean Rice from his taxi. He had flown down to London from Glasgow the previous evening. He had used a private charter flight into London City Airport. Staying 'offline' and inconspicuous was his plan. Having booked himself into the Doubletree Hilton at the Royal Victoria Dock under a non-de-plume, he had planned to travel into the city and go home before going into his office. Perkel had not been in touch since the argument., Flint believed Perkel would blink first and contact him, whining, looking for help and seeking a way out of the mess that had led them both to being blackmailed. He wondered however why Perkel hadn't tried to contact him during the time he had been up in Scotland. *The little shit, let him stew*, he thought.

He had not tried to contact Perkel either. He believed in looking after himself in the first instance, but he *had* expected some attempt to be made to get hold of him, even if he wasn't going to answer the call.

He now believed that Perkel was just being bloody-minded and wanted to get one over on him as payback to what was said at the Punch Tavern, the last time they met. He believed that the silence was a game. An attempt to make him uneasy. To make him feel that Perkel had capitulated and had gone to the police rather than try and find a way out from those trying to extort money from them. He began to feel a pang of concern. He was unnerved slightly. Perkel's apparent show of steel was out-of-character as far as Flint was concerned. Did the police now know anything at all? He needed to speak with Perkel, his own curiosity, his narcissism and desire for control were beginning to eat away at him.

"Hello Jean," he said nonchalantly as if he had never been away, "good morning. How are you?" he asked.

"Charles!" she exclaimed, "where are you? Where have you been? Everyone is looking for you."

Flint ignored her questions, his mind wondering if she included the police in her definition of *everyone*?

"I'm on my way to the office but I need to stop off at home first. Sorry I've been out of touch. Poor reception you know," he added, trying to sound calm. "Just wanted to ask if you could set up a time for a call with Henry, Henry Perkel, for me, please? I've had some trouble trying to get hold of him," he lied.

"Of course, Charles. Mr. Perkel has been trying to get hold of you as well," she said.

"Oh, when was that?"

"A few days ago."

"And what did you tell him?"
"I told him that I was a bit worried about you, as you had vanished suddenly without providing any details as to your movements. I had to cancel some very important meetings at short notice which I found most unprofessional," she said.
Flint knew how passionate she was about her role and having to take the actions she did would have made her very uncomfortable. He considered it for a split second then ignored her concern. It was her job, he thought.
"…and your housekeeper told us that you hadn't been home for a few days," she continued, "I was really worried!"
"Thank you so much," he replied, without any real sincerity in his voice, "your concern though was unnecessary."
"Well perhaps next time you would be so kind as….," she exclaimed before he interrupted her.
"Jean! Jean! Perkel! Can you arrange a time please?"
"Of course," she answered, accepting his admonishment. She began to write in her diary, a copy of Flint's own, the details of the meeting he was suggesting. Time and place.
As she wrote, she noticed an earlier note she had made when Cannon had been in contact. The note that indicated that Cannon had wanted to speak with Flint about *RockGod*. Once she had taken down all the details from Flint about a catch-up appointment with Perkel, she said. "Oh, by the way, Mr. Flint, a Mr. Mike Cannon also tried to get hold of you, a day or so ago. He needed to speak with you about one of the racehorses you have with him."
"Thank you," he replied forcibly," I will give him a call later, but first Henry Perkel. Can you please set up a time with him asap Jean?!"

Two hours later, Flint walked into his office having passed Jean Rice who was looking ashen-faced sitting at her desk just outside his door. Initially, Flint did not notice. As he unpacked his briefcase onto his desk, she came through the door carrying a tray with a teapot, milk, sugar and Flints' personal cup and saucer. He noticed she had been crying,
"Are you okay Jean?" he asked.
"I'm sorry Mr. Flint, but I've just had an awful shock."
"In what way?" he asked
"About your friend, Mr. Perkel."
"What about him?"
"I tried to set up that appointment, that call you asked for."
"Yes,"
"Well, when I spoke with his secretary,"
"Yes," he repeated, trying not to show any expression of anxiety on his face

but hoping she would get to the point soon.

"She advised me that Mr. Perkel was dead! Can you believe it? It is such a shock. I am so sorry for you Mr. Flint," she said, "I know he was a good friend of yours."

Flint sank into his chair. He sat like a statue. Still, silent, stunned.

Jean carried on telling her story, not noticing Flints' demeanour.

"Mr. Perkel's secretary also said that the police were investigating what had happened and that they may be in touch with you as well."

Flint's mind began to race. Perkel dead! Was this because they hadn't paid up, hadn't buckled to the demands of their blackmailer? It didn't make sense. Blackmailers normally didn't become killers. To them, it was all about the money. At least that was Flints' hope.

Also, why did the police want to talk to him, he thought?

What was so unusual about Perkel's death that the police would need to talk with him about it?

"Did she say how he died? Was it a car accident? Something else?" he asked, trying to find some logic to all that was happening. "A medical episode maybe?" he suggested, knowing that Perkel was overweight and had in recent years been cautioned by his personal doctor about his heart health. He was trying to eliminate why the authorities were linking him to Perkel. He was reaching for answers but grasping at straws.

"I have no idea," she went on, "but it is terribly sad. He did seem extremely stressed when he originally tried to get hold of you. I hope that didn't contribute to the whole affair?"

"I'm sure it didn't," he said, trying to work out in his own mind what Perkels' death now meant to his own situation. Was it worse or better? He needed to get on the front foot. Find out what the police knew or didn't know.

Also was there likely to be a move now by the blackmailer towards himself? Would whoever it was who had the photographs, now begin to pressure *him* for the money?

And what would happen to the photographs now?

Would they be sent to the police or the press?

Did the police already have them?

Flints' minding was looking for options, a way out.

"Oh, and I know it's less important given the circumstances but before I forget, please remember to call Mr. Cannon," she went on.

"I will," he said, "I haven't called him yet. Is it urgent?"

"It may be," she replied, "he called a number of times and because you weren't available, and I was very worried about you, I gave him your daughters' number as a contact. I hope that was okay?" she asked, "I thought maybe Lucy would have some idea of your movements even if nobody else did."

Flint was extremely annoyed with her. He kept a lid on it, however.
He needed to concentrate. Work out what Perkels' death meant. He needed to know the bigger picture.

"Jean," he responded in answer to her question, "yes, it's alright, don't worry. I doubt Mr. Cannon would have got any help from Lucy, but I'll give him a call shortly and see what he wanted to talk about. I think it is in relation to *RockGod* because the horse has qualified to run in the Grand National and I need to pay a fee of some sorts to enter him formally," he said, trying to tone down the seriousness of the conversation about Perkel, "thank you for reminding me anyway."

Jean Rice nodded. As she turned to leave the office, Flint picked up the phone.

CHAPTER 36

Cannon concluded the call. He put his phone back into his pocket. He had agreed to meet with Flint the following day. If, as he hoped, Flint agreed to pay the fee for *RockGod* to run in the *National* then they needed to conclude all the formalities as soon as possible.
That included confirming jockeys and finalizing the training plan.
He raised his binoculars to his eyes, training them on the horizon to his right. The sun had risen in the east to his left. He watched as the second string went through their paces, each horse running towards the sun, ultimately becoming a silhouette as they ran away from him, the steam from their nostrils and bodies flaring then disappearing into the cold of mid-morning.
There was a crispness to the day. Spring was just about to raise its head, nodding a goodbye to the end of winter.
Cannon needed to call Timms to let him know of the meeting with Flint and to get confirmation that there was nothing in the way of *RockGod* running at Aintree. He would do that later as he also wanted confirmation that no matter what happened as he investigated further, the BHA would not pull something out of the hat and suspend the horse at the last minute. In addition, he needed to see Lucy Flint again. The relationship between her and her father had been playing on his mind ever since they had met. He needed to find out more.
Thank God for Rich, Cannon thought. If it wasn't for him, the stable would grind to a halt.
"Looking good, hey Mike?" asked Rich.
"Absolutely," Cannon replied, "looks like some of these are running into form, and they are certainly jumping much better. Pity, it is the back end of the season but I'm sure a couple of them may have a few summer runs."
"That'll be good."
"Both for us and the owners," Cannon noted.
As they watched, the horses turned towards them in the distance, the sun reflecting off buckles, rings, and bits. The brief glint seemed a slight metaphor in Cannon's mind, of a spark, a link in the chain that he was trying to unravel.
He turned to his assistant. "Let's hope we have a good day at Stratford today. I'm expecting *TheMan* and *Visitation* to have reasonable runs. Up at Newcastle last time, I think it was too wet for the *TheMan*, but today should suit him much better with the drying out of the track. *Visitation* I'm not so

sure about though, but at least his owner's representative who I spoke to last night doesn't seem too fussed. I think they are just enjoying being part of it."

"Yes, it's a big syndicate. Most just in it for the fun, which is great," Rich replied.

"Wish we had more of them," Cannon remarked. "The more people who get involved and see how we care for the horses and how much time we spend looking after them, the better."

"Couldn't agree more, Mike," answered Rich, his lifelong love and passion for the sport evident in every fibre of his being. He could talk for hours about each and every horse he had ever had the privilege of training and looking after. Every one of them was like a child to him.

The two men stood as the returning horses completed their work. The riders urging their mounts into and over the obstacles, ensuring they rose at the right time, on the right step and were not reaching or spreading themselves in order to clear the fences.

Cannon felt good, what he had seen of the work pleased him. This was confirmed as each rider gave feedback to Rich and himself.

As the horses circled in their *cooldown*, Cannon said his goodbyes to his team, wishing Rich well for the day and headed back to his office. He needed to make those calls. Michelle would have left for work. It was getting close to exam time and she had papers to prepare. The house would be empty now. He never liked that, but he was glad that the builders had finished and gone. The noise of the repairs, the hammering, the shouting was now a thing of the past. Thank God, he thought. At least I can do my race placements and training plans in peace.

The call from Cannon had annoyed her. She hadn't expected it as she had told him quite firmly that she didn't want to see him again. Had he not heard, she thought.

Lucy Flint was working on a new theme. Around her on the floor of her studio were jars of water each with different shades of colour. She stood in front of an easel, upon it a blank canvas. In her hand she held a paintbrush, it was moist with the paint from a sky-blue jar. She looked quizzically at the nothingness in front of her, seeking inspiration. Watercolour was a new medium for her. She knew the science behind the different paint types and how they transposed themselves onto the canvas.

As she stood, stock-still, water dripped onto the floorboards. Her mind was unsettled. She had still not heard from Pete, despite desperately trying to get hold of him. Now she had Cannon calling her again, and the police wanted to see her too. Angrily she threw the brush at the easel, it hit the top left-hand side of the canvas creating a blue bob. A watery streak ran down the canvas towards the floor eventually dripping onto the floor. She looked at the effect, the mess she had created. For a second she admired what she saw then launched herself at the easel, swiping it away across the floor with her flailing arms. The jars of various coloured water were scattered across the room as she kicked out at them. She screamed as she did so. Her frustration evident in the violence of the curses that tore from her very being.

CHAPTER 37

Charles Flint had made himself available to the police. He had a method in his madness. He needed to find out if Perkel had been to the authorities about the blackmail threat and potentially made it worse for them both. After speaking with Cannon and setting up the lunch meeting with him for the next day he had asked Jean to call Walsh. The Inspector was quite incredulous to receive the call. He was also impressed with himself that he had been able to use the computer on his desk, to use the *smartphone* software, which allowed him to answer the call when Flint had been put through to him.

Flints' call had also aroused his suspicion. The man had been away, uncontactable. Now suddenly he reappears. They needed to find out where he had been and why?

As they sat in an interview room, Walsh along with Sedgefield, Flint on his own, Walsh noticed how calm Flint seemed, how self-important and arrogant he appeared. Flint was dressed formally in a business suit. He sat crossed-legged on the chair, pushed back away from the table that separated him from the two police officers.

Sedgefield had activated the digital recording device after Walsh had advised Flint that the interview would be recorded and that Flint was entitled to a transcript of the recording, should he so desire. Flint had waived the offer away. His gesture was indicative of how Walsh had assessed the man. The Inspector began the conversation.

"So, Mr. Flint. thank you for very much your time, for making yourself available," he began, "as I mentioned previously this is just an interview and hopefully you can help us with our inquiries. We just wanted to speak with you about Henry Perkel. A friend of yours we believe?"

As he waited for Flint to respond Walsh looked him up and down, looking for signs of discomfort or nervousness. He saw nothing. Flint sat calmly, no expression on his face.

"Yes, a very dear friend."

"And are you aware that he was killed a couple of days ago?"

"I'm aware of his passing yes, my secretary told me, after she had tried to contact him to set up an appointment."

"And why was that?" asked Walsh.

Flint was a little confused by the question. He tried to work out if Walsh was playing mind games. Virtual intellectual chess. Did he know something but wasn't saying? He took the easy route.

"I'm sorry," he said, "I'm not sure what you mean."

"What was the meeting about. The *appointment?*" emphasized Walsh.

"Oh, sorry Inspector," Flint said, raising a smile in an attempt to disarm the situation and slow the churning in his gut, "I didn't quite understand what you meant."

Walsh was sure Flint was playing for time Trying to settle his nerves. Walsh went with it. He had other cards to play yet.

"It was just an ordinary business conversation. He is, sorry *was* my lawyer you know."

"So, nothing in particular then?"

"Nothing relevant to what you may want to ask me about Inspector."

"Are you sure, Mr. Flint?" Walsh's tone was intended to imply that the police knew more than Flint was giving up, but Flint kept his powder dry. He wouldn't concede or acknowledge anything that he may be accused of. Even with a legal representative by his side, he would always deny everything.

"Of course, Inspector. I'm not sure what you are implying but I can assure you that I know nothing about Mr. Perkels' death. I don't even know how he died. Perhaps you could tell me?" he asked.

Sedgefield noted the slight smirk on Flints' face after he had posed the question. He was convinced that Flint knew that whoever asked the questions, controlled the conversation.

"I won't go into details Mr. Flint, but needless to say, he was murdered."

"Murdered?" Flint repeated. "Do you have any suspects?"

"At this point, I'm only at liberty to say that we have some leads we are following up on Mr. Flint," replied Walsh, feeling less confident than he was portraying.

"Please Inspector, call me Charles," Flint replied, starting to feel more comfortable, more in control. "I think we can dispense with the formality of titles don't you think?"

"Okay…Charles," responded Walsh slightly awkwardly, "it's fine with me, though I should advise you that while you are not under caution, this is still a police inquiry and formality or not, nothing changes."

"I understand that, Inspector."

Walsh decided to take a different tack. "Tell me about your daughter," he said.

"I'm not sure what to say. What is it that you want to know?"

"Your relationship for a start."

"What about it?" Flint bristled slightly. While he was still answering their questions with another question, he knew that he would have to say something eventually. He couldn't work out though the linkage, in relation to his daughter and the murder of Perkel.

"How would you describe it, the relationship with Lucy?"

"So, you have met her?" Another question.

"Yes."

"And what did she say," he replied, "in response to your own question about our relationship? I assume you asked her about me?"

"Look, Mr. Fli…er, Charles, let's stop playing games, I am trying to solve a murder here," muttered Walsh, aware of how the temperature was beginning to reach boiling point in connection with the three cases he and his team were trying to solve. Through clenched teeth and trying not to let his annoyance overflow into anger at Flint's arrogance, he said. "I need your help. If you are not prepared to do provide it, then we may need to be a little more formal and get you to give a proper statement about the matters we are investigating. Would you prefer that we go that route?"

"I'm sorry Inspector, I didn't mean any harm," answered Flint, raising his hands in a defensive posture and uncrossing his legs as he did so, "I'm just not sure where all this is heading."

Walsh looked at Sedgefield sitting quietly to his right, then took a deep breath. "Let me ask the question again then…Charles," It was clear from the pause each time that he spoke that Walsh wasn't happy with using Christian names when he was interviewing people. "Tell me about the relationship between you and your daughter."

"It's *strained*, I believe is the correct word."

"And why would that be?"

"It's a long story but I'll make it easy for you Inspector, seeing as you want to get to the bottom of things quickly," he said sarcastically. "The relationship has broken down due to my daughter's career choices."

"As in?"

"Simply put, we vehemently disagreed about her decision to become an artist, when she had both the means, capacity, and intellect to become a surgeon and she threw it away to become what, a, a, bohemian!"

Both policemen noticed how Flint's face showed the disgust he felt inside as he described the circumstances around the relationship breakdown with his daughter.

"And now you don't talk?"

"We haven't for a few years now."

"Yet she shared Mr. Perkel's phone number with your racehorse trainer, Mike Cannon when he was looking for you?" asked Sedgefield.

"Well, apparently Cannon did try to contact me directly a short while back.

After the Fire

My secretary, Jean Rice, told me that she put him on to Lucy thinking she would be the best person who would be most aware of how to get hold of me given I was out of the office," he said. "Jean's a lovely lady and she knew of the problems between Lucy and me, but she was worried about my whereabouts and decided that Lucy may know. She didn't," he emphasized.
"Anyway, what does Cannon have to do with Perkel's murder?
"We're not sure," replied Walsh, "but it seems that shortly after Cannon tried to contact Perkel, he was dead."
"Woah, Woah," interjected Flint, feeling quite uneasy. "I'm meeting with Mr. Cannon tomorrow at *his* request. Are you suggesting that I'm in danger? That somehow Mike Cannon is involved in Perkel's killing?"
"No, not at all, but we understand that you owe him some money. Is that why he wanted to get in touch with you?" asked Sedgefield, "at least that's what Mr. Cannon told *us*."
Both policemen were trying to change Flints' focus of attention. By each asking questions, they were trying to see if his guard would slip. To see if he would contradict himself in any way. They suspected that somehow, he had something to do with Perkel's death, but were not sure to what extent. Sometimes gut feeling was a good indicator. Once supported by evidence, the various pieces of information would fit together. The jigsaw solved. At the moment though they still were missing some of the elements.
Flint smiled. He knew now that the photographs had not surfaced anywhere. That the police did not know about them. Somehow, at least for the present, the police were focused on other matters. He decided to throw them a bone that they could go and chase. A bone that meant he would have time to enact his plan to save his own skin.
"I don't owe Mr. Cannon anything. All my expenses with him are paid on time, every time. If he told you that, then he is incorrect. I suggest you take that up with him again, as it is clearly false. I heard a while ago that Mr. Cannon's stable had been having a lean time of things, and that my horse *RockGod* was essentially keeping him afloat, but I can't believe that money issues would lead to anyone being killed."
Flint folded his arms across his chest and crossed his legs again. He had thrown them a big bone and he knew it. The question was, had they taken the bait. Did they think Cannon had something to do with Perkel's murder? He wasn't sure, as Walsh and Sedgefield hadn't reacted, but he was already signaling by his body language that he believed the conversation was over. That he had provided them enough information. A lead, albeit a false one.
Walsh surprised him with a comment from left field.
"Do you know that your daughter's boyfriend was killed recently?"
Flint sat quietly. His rested his right hand on his knee, palm upwards like an upside-down claw. He looked at the nails, then blew on them as if removing a piece of dead skin.

Slowly, cautiously, not sure why the question was asked of him, he answered, responding with another series of questions of his own.

"Her boyfriend? What type was this one? Another loser I suspect." He leaned forward in his chair to emphasize the point he wanted to make. "Inspector, I believe Lucy's had many *boyfriends* as you call them over the past few years. Sometimes even more than one at the same time. So, forgive me for no longer being surprised at what happens in her life. Quite frankly I don't care. I have no interest at all." Flint sat back in his chair, disdain for the subject showing on his face.

Walsh didn't react. He wanted to push Flint a little further. To see what was behind the mask. What type of man he was really dealing with? Had he *no* feelings at all towards his own daughter?

Eventually, Walsh said, "His name was Stefan Kaminski. A Polish citizen, we believe."

"A Polak?" replied Flint disdainfully, "someone claiming benefits I suspect. Are you going to tell me how he was he killed? Did he die from all the paint fumes in their apartment?" he joked.

Walsh said nothing, did not rise to the bait. Calmly and after due consideration of who he was dealing with, he responded with compassion in his voice. "He was a student apparently. A Masters student, in Electronics. Not your average Joe at all," he said. He wanted to make the point that Flint's prejudice was noted. "We've verified his enrollment with Imperial College," he continued, then after letting Flint digest his comments, added, "he drowned."

There was silence in the room for a few seconds. A lot had been said. In Flints' mind, he was only concerned with himself. Lucy's problems were of her own making.

"I'm sorry if I appear dispassionate about Lucy's *late* boyfriend," he stated, "but as I said earlier, our relationship broke down some years ago and we haven't really spoken since. She is an adult and has her own life to lead. As do I, I might add."

Walsh knew what Flint was insinuating in the choice of words he was using. There was no more to say on the subject as far as he was concerned. Subject closed. Flint decided to make his move. Now was the opportunity. He stood up saying with a significant dose of sarcasm. "Delightful as this has been gentleman, I think it is time for me to go now. So, unless you need me any longer or have any further news or questions for me, I would like to excuse myself, please. I have work to do."

Walsh nodded and Sedgefield spoke for the record that the meeting was over, noting the time the interview concluded, then turned off the recording.

"Thank you, Mr. Flint," Walsh said, standing up and holding out his hand, "we appreciate your input. We will continue with our inquiries and will be in touch if necessary. We do have your mobile number on record now I believe."

Flint nodded and obliged the Inspector by taking Walsh's hand in his own.

"No problem," he replied, "always happy to assist the police." He didn't really feel that way but wanted the pretense to continue. He needed to resolve his own *problem* before the police got wind of it.

"Good to hear, Mr. Flint. I'm sure we will take you up on your offer, and be in touch as needed."

Flint stared into Walsh's eyes trying to see if there was anything behind the comment, Walsh stared back, giving nothing away. Flint blinked first.

CHAPTER 38

Cannon sipped the tea he had been offered. He decided that it wasn't for him and placed it carefully on the small table standing next to his chair. He wasn't sure if Lucy Flint noticed his initial reaction to its taste, but decided he would rather accept a withering stare if one came than to try and finish the drink. Green tea of any sort wasn't his preferred drink. Peppermint tea even less so.

He looked around her studio. He was lucky that she had finally agreed to see him again. He had met with her Father the previous day, a meeting that was short and somewhat unsatisfying, but at least he had finally secured a commitment to race *RockGod* in the *National*. Cannon decided not to mention the meeting with Lucy's father to her.

He had noted when they met that Charles Flint was distracted, not surprising with a friend of his having been recently murdered Cannon thought. Cannon also suspected something else was going on in Flint's mind. He wasn't sure what, but Cannon's intuition, his sixth sense, prescience, leant towards Flint being involved in something more sinister, something more disturbing than what Timms had asked Cannon to look into. Flint had agreed too readily to his horse running at Aintree. He had accepted Cannon's proposal without condition, had asked no questions about who would ride, whether the horse needed any more runs prior to the race, basically expressing little more than a passing interest. Strange, Cannon had noted, given it was the biggest race of the year. He knew Flint didn't normally engage much, but Cannon did expect more excitement, more emotion, from the man. Even Cannon's invitation to him to attend the pre-race function along with Cannon and his family hadn't seemed to extract anything other than a "yes, I will be there," comment.

"Too hot?"

She pointed to the cup. Cannon was shaken out of his reverie by her question.

"Oh, sorry, yes, it is a bit," he replied, his cheeks flushing slightly. In the past when he was in the force, he had learnt how to control his emotion, the physical elements that can give away what a person was thinking. He realized that he was slowly losing that skill, that he was signaling to her that he was thinking about something else.

He needed to concentrate.

The light from the skylight indicated that the clouds outside still persisted in blocking out the sun that was battling its way back to Spring. The lights that she had turned on in the room gave the effect of being inside an operating theatre. Bright, and focused. Cannon noticed a few spots of paint on the floor and a curve of blue where it seemed something may have spilt or had been flung. Apart from the light, the smell that he had initially encountered, experienced, when he had first entered the flat seemed to have gotten stronger. Turpentine, glues, bleach came to mind.

"Thanks for seeing me again," he said, trying to sound contrite, "I will try not to take up too much of your time."

"Thank you," she replied, "I do have a full day ahead. I have a piece of work I need to complete asap for a possible new client of mine. I have to show it to them the day after tomorrow so the sooner we can complete our little chat, the better."

Cannon picked up the subtlety in her voice. She smiled but he knew she didn't really want him wasting her time. She had agreed to see him but reluctantly.

"I understand," he said.

"What is it that I can do for you?" she asked. "Our last conversation was supposed to be that, our last. As I told you on the phone the other day, I don't really have anything to say about my father. You said it was about something else?"

"Yes."

"Well?"

"You know that the name of the contact you gave me, to allow me to get hold of your father, a Mr. Perkel, was murdered the other day?"

"Yes, the police told me. It was a terrible shock," she said.

"And what did you think?"

"What do you mean?" she replied, her face showing confusion at his question.

"Well, you gave *me* his phone number, and shortly thereafter, he was dead."

"Yes? What of it?"

"Do you think I had something to do with it?" he asked.

"Did you?"

Cannon smiled inwardly at her answering every question he had with one of her own. It seemed everyone he talked to nowadays had an agenda. Where was the honesty? Was she really so different from her father? Did the apple

After the Fire

really fall far from the tree?
"No, I didn't, but I got the impression when I was told about it by the police that they didn't totally believe me."
"Why not?"
Cannon pondered the question. He realized that he had let her take control of the conversation he had initiated. It was he who should be finding out what he needed to. He decided not to answer.
"Your father?" he said, trying to wrest back control of the conversation, noticing her bristle straight away when he was mentioned, her body reacting.
She stood up from where she had been sitting, taking a few steps away from him, turning her back.
"If this is about my father, I told you last time that I don't want to speak about him," she said angrily. Turning around to face him, she reiterated her position, pointed a finger at him. "You assured me that you wanted to see me because of something else entirely, something that couldn't be discussed over the phone. If that is not the case, then I would like you to leave now!"
"It's about a horse," he said quietly, trying to diffuse her anger.
"A horse?" she answered, bemusement in her voice. "I know nothing about horses."
"Well, this one is owned by your father. It is one of the horses that I train, and its next race is in the Grand National."
She seemed genuinely surprised. Impressed almost. Her demeanour softened.
"And, you are telling me this, why?"
"Because I need your help," he said.
"My help?"
"Yes."
"And how can *I*, help *you*?" she asked.
He had thought about what he was going to say. How he needed to be careful in not giving away too much, but making sure he was able to extract what he needed from her.
"I need some information. Something personal," he went on, "about your father."
"I've just *told* you," she interrupted, "that I.."
Cannon raised his hands in defense of himself. He knew that it was a gamble but one he needed to take. He had no choice.
"I know, I know," he continued calmly, trying to get her to listen to him, "but this is really important. I wouldn't ask you if I didn't need to," he explained. "It has nothing to do with your relationship, it's about what you know about your father's *personal* circumstances."
He waited as she mentally processed his request. Was there a switch to her? A button to press in order to get her to calm down? He wasn't sure, but

maybe he had made some connection. She took a deep breath, sat down again, holding her hands in her lap. She sat on the edge of her chair. He was conscious that she was unhappy with him, but the anger in her eyes and the creases that had been on her face only seconds before had disappeared. He wasn't sure for how long, but he would take what he could get.

"I'm sorry if I upset you," he continued, "and I am not here under false pretenses, I *really* do need your help."

Lucy Flint looked down at her hands. Did she trust him? Would she cooperate with him, given how he had managed to manipulate the conversation?

"Go on," she said without expression.

Cannon knew it was a risk to share what he was about to, but it was a gamble he decided to take. He hoped he had made the right call.

"From what I've been advised by the BHA, the British Horseracing Authority, your father amongst others, and his horses plus anyone associated with them, have been the subject of an ongoing internal BHA investigation in relation to race-fixing. By inference, that includes me," he said, his annoyance clear to her.

"That means three things," he continued forcefully. "One. That I could lose my license and my livelihood, if it was ever considered or deemed, even in the slightest, that I was a party to any such race-fixing activity. Two, that a possible once in a lifetime horse that your father owns, and I train, could be banned and/or suspended from running in the upcoming Grand National. And thirdly, probably most importantly, that I could face a trial and even jail for something that I am not a party too. That makes me very angry," he concluded. "So, do you see now why I need your help?"

Lucy Flint kept her head down. Cannon waited for a response as she considered his appeal to her. He could sense her weighing up her options. He had a feeling that there was something inside her that she needed to release. That she had buried deep within her.

"What do you need from me?" she eventually replied.

"I need you to tell me all you can about your father. His business interests, anything you know about his personal life, whether you think he was capable of being a party to such a thing as race-fixing. Anything."

She looked up from her chair, meeting his eyes. Her face showed resignation, defeat, then as soon as it had surfaced, it was gone again. Whatever it was would remain buried.

"Mr. Cannon, I'm sorry but I don't think I'm going to be of much help. As I told you before, my father and I don't speak, don't communicate."

"But you must have something to do with him surely?"

"No, we don't. I have no interest in him and likewise him in me."

"Nothing at all?"

"No, nothing. And that's the way I prefer it," she answered.

After the Fire

Cannon could still see something in her eyes. It was hidden deeply. What was it? He tried again, another approach.

"Your father is highly successful, yes?'

"To some," she answered.

"Could I ask what happened to your mother?"

"She died, a car accident while holidaying in the Far East. I was only eight at the time. She and my father had divorced a year or so earlier. He had been given custody of me as my mother was an alcoholic apparently. At least that is what he told me."

"Your father?"

"Yes,"

"So how was he able to build up a successful stockbroking business and yet still have time to be a father. To look after you?"

"Who said he was?"

"What?"

"A father?"

"I just assumed," said Cannon, thinking about how he struggled with bringing up Cassie alone.

"Well," she said, "he wasn't. I most mostly brought up by nannies. Many different ones at that."

"Because?" he asked.

"Because they were dismissed or let go by him. If they got too close to me, he would just ask them to leave. Or even make them," she added.

"Do you know why?"

She didn't immediately answer, remained silent before saying, "At the time he told me that they had stolen from us, or had decided to move on. That I had outgrown them. All sorts of reasons."

"And you believed him?"

"Of course, he was my father."

Cannon was intrigued. "At what stage did you no longer need a nanny then?"

"When he sent me to boarding school without notice. Around the age of eleven," she said. The recalling of the event and its impact on her, clearly evident. He thought about some of the girls at Michelle's school. Their ages. He realized that she was teaching girls of that age. Some of whom were boarders. It hadn't really been something he had thought about before. Young girls being shipped off for others to look after, teach and help become young women.

"Mr. Cannon," she said, invading his thoughts. "These questions are almost investigative and seem to be more about me than anything else. May I ask why?"

"I'm sorry," he answered. "I was just trying to find out what motivates your father. What makes him tick I suppose."

After the Fire

Cannon was starting to form a stronger opinion of Charles Flint, his arrogance, his motivations. Lucy was providing more than she realized.

"I'm not sure I am of much help, to be honest," she said, "however, if you can take anything from this conversation, it is that money does not motivate him. He has enough, he is already wealthy. My father is more motivated by power, influence," she emphasized. "He likes to dominate, own things, then cast them aside when he has finished with them."

Cannon considered this last comment and the spite which was inherent in the way she spat out the words. It rounded out the conversation. Concluded it. Cannon knew instantly that he wouldn't get anything else from her now. She had said too much already. His experience with witnesses and criminals, the general public and even police personnel themselves, showed that they naturally found their balance as to how much they would say and to whom. Then they just stopped. He knew that Lucy Flint had reached that point.

"May I ask if he did that to you?" he asked as gently as he could.

She looked at him, holding his stare for a number of seconds. Then smiled, a sad line across her face. Her lips held tightly together. He waited.

"I think I had better get on with my work," she said finally, standing up as she did so. She walked towards her canvases, stopping at the one she had been working on when he arrived.

Cannon sighed inwardly. He looked at the cold tea still on the small table next to him, then placing his hands on the arms of his chair he pushed himself up and walked in silence to where she was standing. She had wrapped her arms around herself as if to keep warm. He knew it was an instinctive sign of self-preservation.

She watched him intently as he stood next to her looking at the unfinished work.

Having no idea about art, be it traditional, abstract, modern, impressionistic, he just knew what he liked and what he didn't.

What he was looking at was an abstract design. It meant nothing to him.

"It's a logo," she said.

"Oh," he replied, staring at the picture. A square, the bottom two thirds in red and the top third in black. Through the middle from bottom left to top right, a white thunderbolt.

"For an international motor company and their potential new electric car offshoot. It's a competition."

He wasn't sure what to say. He had no view on it either way.

"Hope you win," he said smiling. There was no response, she just kept looking at the picture.

Cannon took the hint. She remained silent as he thanked her for her time and left her studio home. It had proven fruitful in some ways. It had affirmed the view he had formed the day before when he had met with

Flint. What was inconclusive however was whether Charles Flint had anything to do with race-fixing.

CHAPTER 39

"Have you seen the Racing Post this morning?"
It was Rich on the phone to Cannon. The call had woken him. It was just after eight am. Cannon had spent the night in London after his meeting with Lucy. It was only ten days before the *National* itself and just on a week before the meeting began.
He had planned to meet with Walsh, but unfortunately, it was now postponed until the following day. He had called him after his conversation with Lucy but Walsh was unavailable. Apparently, he had flown to Amsterdam and would only be back the next day. It meant that Cannon had needed to stay for two nights. He wasn't happy about it but it was the best that he could do.
Cannon still didn't know whether Flint was involved in any race-fixing at all, but he needed to find out what Walsh was thinking. Something was bothering him. He had slept badly, tossing and turning, eventually falling asleep in the early hours, hence why he had missed his normal wake up time.
"No, I haven't Rich," he said as he lay in the bed, yawning, and struggling to insert his phone earpiece into his ear, the cord still twisted. "What's happened?"
"*Viking Spirit* has been scratched," Rich conveyed down the line, his voice expressing his excitement at the news.
Cannon processed this in his mind. The *favourite*, out of the biggest race of the year. It meant that *RockGod* would be much better fancied in the betting now.
"The *'God* is now up to second-favourite," Rich continued, "so no pressure

then Mike."

Cannon asked the question he needed to and got the answer he expected.

"So, what happened to Bramley's horse then?"

Sam Bramley, being the trainer of *Viking Spirit*.

"Found lame this morning, after gallops yesterday. Apparently spread a shoe during exercise and injured the near side hind foot."

"Umm, that's a shame," answered Cannon, thinking back to the list of horses he had compiled that suspiciously ended up lame during races.

"Yes," answered Rich, "but it does mean that *RockGod* is in with a much better chance now, Mike."

"Rich, you know as well as I do that anything can happen during the race. No one can ever take anything for granted at Aintree."

"I know Mike, believe me, I know. I've been around this game long enough to expect the unexpected. But still, it can only help our chances."

Cannon rolled over in his bed, grabbed his watch and checked the time.

"Oh, by the way," he asked, "who are the owners of *Viking Spirit* anyway? They must be devastated."

Rich didn't respond immediately. Cannon could hear him typing on a keyboard calling up the details of the horse and its ownership.

After thirty seconds, Rich came back on the line.

"It says here that it's owned by a syndicate, there are ten names listed," he noted. Rich then started to rattle them off individually down the line to Cannon. Initials, and surnames. It was when Rich mentioned '*C. Flint*' that Cannon took serious notice. Was it *the* Charles Flint who owned *RockGod* or was it someone else? Cannon had no idea how widespread Flint's investment in racehorses was. However, it seemed too coincidental for Cannon's liking.

He sat up in bed, told Rich of his concerns and asked him to keep *RockGod* in his sight at all times, even sleep in his stall with him if necessary. He also asked him to make sure that there were no unexpected visitors to the stables and to check to see if there was anyone hanging about on the gallops when the strings were exercising. He wanted his entire string of horses in lockdown.

Cannon planned to be back at his stables the next day after his meeting with Walsh that was scheduled for the morning.

Cannon called Michelle at school. After a long wait, she came onto the line, admonishing him for interrupting her first class of the day. He noted her comments then advised her to be careful and stay vigilant once she got home. He asked her not to let anyone into the house. He also told her that he had spoken with Rich about his concerns.

"What's going on, Mike?" she asked.

"I'm not sure yet, but I've got a feeling that someone may try to get at *RockGod* in the next couple of days and also possibly some of the other horses. Please just take care tonight," he said, "I'll call you around seven just to check if everything is okay."

"Mike, you're scaring me," she answered, "what if anything *does* happen. If I'm on my own what should I do?"

"Look, love," he answered. "I'm not trying to upset you, and honestly I'd rather be there with you than be here, but I've got no choice. I don't think anything *will* happen but I'm just being a little careful. I'll be back tomorrow anyway. Besides, Rich will be around."

They continued to talk for a little while longer, eventually, she accepted that he was not being paranoid, just sensible. The arrangements he had made with Rich and the additional lockdown precautions being taken for the one night that he was not at home seemed to placate her.

"Have you looked into what happened with *Viking Spirit?*" he asked.

"We've got an investigator at the stables right now," answered Timms.

Cannon was sitting at a table in a Starbucks. The coffee was terrible but the servings large, which made him feel that it was okay to sit where he was, for as long as he needed to. He was concerned about Michelle in particular. His mind had been was racing since his discussion with Rich and the additional information about Flint's apparent association with *Viking Spirit*.

"Do you have any suspicions?" he asked Timms.

"It's too early to speculate Mike, it could just be a simple accident. The vet that Sam Bramley uses at his stables is straight up and down. He'll be able to tell if there was anything unusual about the injury."

"Any idea when you will have any feedback?"

"I suspect it will be within the hour. Before the news broke this morning, I got a call from Sam's assistant, Fred Beck around eleven last night. We have been working on this matter for quite some time now as you know. Our main problem has been evidence. Most of what we have found to date has been inconclusive, speculation in some ways."

"Especially when it isn't drug-related, I suspect."

"Exactly. Banned substances even if masked, may show up in some way through blood and urine sampling, but injuries in training or in a race that have somehow been caused deliberately, are very difficult, if not impossible to prove."

Cannon realized that Timms was being extremely open with him about what was happening with Sam Bramley's horse. He felt as is there had been a shift in the relationship between them. He wasn't totally sure how or why, particularly as Cannon himself had not achieved much in the way of solving anything, but he got the impression that a bond of trust had been created between the two of them.

"Did you know Charles Flint had a stake in *Viking Spirit*?"

"Yes, I did," replied Timms, "we have checked with the ROA, and we have a list of the horses that Mr. Flint has in training or has some form of ownership in. As I mentioned a while ago, he has been a person of interest for quite some time, along with several other people, not all of which are actual owners."

"Are there others in that syndicate that are on your list?"

Timms did not reply. He stayed quiet. Cannon eventually broke the silence.

"Apart from me, are you prepared to share if Sam Bramley is on your watch list?"

"Mike, you know as well as I that I can't answer that. While we appreciate your help in this matter, divulging information about others is impossible. Apart from the privacy matters, should there ever be a legal case, criminal or otherwise, the last thing we want is someone to get away with things on the basis of a technicality. One of those being the breaching of confidentiality. Even in the Flint matter, until we prove anything it is just a question mark over the man. We could be subject to all sorts of legal claims if we get this wrong."

"Okay, okay," replied Cannon, "but surely Flint can't be the only person involved?"

"That's true," said Timms, "we think this is much wider, much better organized."

"Why didn't you tell me this before?" asked Cannon.

"Tell you what Mike?"

"That this whole thing is more than just about Flint."

"Well when we first met, it wasn't just Flint. It was you *and* Flint we were looking into."

Cannon remembered the first meeting in his office. Was it only just a month or so ago?

"And now?" he asked.

"Look, Mike, as we discussed at the Disciplinary Board meeting, we *did* say that we felt the matter was much wider than just Charles Flint himself and that's why we sought your help."

"Yes but…"

"But we didn't say it was organized as we now fear it is," interrupted Timms.

"Exactly."

"I don't think we knew how broad or widespread it was then. It's just become more evident in recent times."

"Like what happened at Worcester and Sandown?"

"Worcester yes, as we discussed already," Timms concurred. "Sandown we are not sure about yet. We are still looking into it."

Cannon picked up his paper cup and drained the last of his coffee. He was glad he wasn't living close to the chain. He didn't enjoy what they had to offer. His preference was for tea or for the coffee in pods that he and Michelle used in their own machine at home.

After putting the empty cup down he told Timms of his concern for Michelle and of his meeting the next day with Walsh. He didn't consider it necessary to mention the conversation he had had with Lucy the previous afternoon. Her view of her father wasn't directly relevant to Timms. To Cannon, however, it was a different story.

CHAPTER 40

"Can I have the photographs?"

"Just a minute, Mr. Flint," answered Jack Williams, "don't be so impatient. I'm expecting a little bit *more* from you. We still need to cut a deal."

They were meeting at *Gaucho's* restaurant near Tower Bridge. For his own added security Williams had gotten one of his staff to make the arrangements in their name, not his. With the restaurant being close to the Shard, Williams realized too late that his meeting with Madzia would have been better suited here. Being a steak restaurant, and not Chinese, perhaps his guest would have preferred it? Maybe next time?

They were sitting in a small private room inside the premises. It was enclosed glass with a single door through which waiters entered and left when instructed to do so by Sam Teal. It was well away from the large windows where diners could look out at the Thames, the Tower of London and Tower Bridge itself. The main part of the restaurant was busy, noisy, people enjoying themselves. The weekend had arrived. Seated inside their own bubble, the only noise they could hear was a gentle murmur coming from the other diners. It was just past eight in the evening.

The weather had been reasonable during the day. The drying wind which had blown across the city had now dropped leaving the sky relatively clear, the night crisp and cool. Flint, however, felt uncomfortably warm.

He had received a call shortly after he had arrived back at his office post his

After the Fire

meeting with Cannon. It was clear that someone had been watching him. The disembodied voice that Jean had put through had mentioned that they knew of his meeting with the police and also his just-concluded meeting with Cannon. He had been instructed to meet at the restaurant. It was clear that there was to be no debate.

"What do you want? What type of *deal*?" asked Flint. He was trying to keep calm. His natural confidence, however, was blunted. He had never been in such a situation and was trying really hard to maintain an image of a man in control. A man who didn't care what others thought of him. He believed the police were still unaware of the photographs. If they had been, he would have had a knock on his door already. That was at least something still in his favour. What he didn't know however was whether he could trust the man seated in front of him. Why should he? How could he?

Williams had introduced himself as Simon *Dootson*, but Flint wasn't convinced it was the man's real name. It didn't seem to fit.

"Money pre-dominantly," was Williams' response.

"I would hardly have expected anything less," replied Flint cockily.

Williams sat back in his chair. He took a sip of the beer that he had been brought to him by Sam Teal, and which sat on the table between them. The choice of drink contrasted with the gin and tonic of Flint. The difference between the two men could not have been starker, yet in some ways, they were both the same. Ruthless, devious, self-centered, arrogant. Similarly, they both had a problem, not that Williams would let Flint know about his.

"Mr. Flint, *Charles*," said Williams, leaning forward across the table, "I think you need to understand something. You are in a very precarious position here, if I may say so. I don't think being smug is a particularly clever thing to be doing if I was you," he went on, "they do awful things to paedophiles in prison, as I'm sure you are aware."

Flint didn't answer, he looked into Williams's face. They locked eyes. Flint was crumbling inside but, he refused to show it to the man across the table. Flint was in self-preservation mode. He was trying to read his nemesis. He knew that it was all about money, but he couldn't understand why *Dootson* if that was his real name, would want to meet with him face to face. Flint was wealthy, but he wasn't a fountain of cash. Everyone had limits. There must be something more to it than a simple money-for-photograph transaction, he thought. Although he would have preferred it if it was that way, he doubted it. He needed to find out what was going on. Eventually, he lowered his eyes, asking, "so what does this *deal* you are referring to constitute, *apart* from money?

"Glad to hear that you are being sensible Mr. Flint. I'm sure our little business transaction will be mutually beneficial, don't you?" Williams added with a grin. "In fact, I'm sure of it, though it's a pity that Mr. Perkel didn't see it that way," he added menacingly.

The acknowledgment that Perkel had been a victim of the man opposite made Flint shudder. He didn't know what to say. The threat had been less than subtle. Before he had time to respond, Williams picked up the menu on the table and said, "I'm hungry, let's eat."

It was as if the two men were best friends just out for dinner, however, Williams' behaviour left Flint both bemused and frightened. He scanned the menu as quickly as he could. He wanted to get away, get some fresh air, but he was trapped in a glass box, inside a glass-fronted restaurant with no way out until he was allowed too.

Williams told Teal what he wanted and then, without consultation, ordered for Flint. Teal left the room briefly to let the waiting staff know what food to serve. Eventually, Flint plucked up the courage to ask the obvious question.

"So, what do you want from me, if *this*," he waved his arm towards the empty space in the room, "is not solely about money?"

"I want your cooperation," came the reply.

"To do what?"

"All in good time," answered Williams, just as Teal returned, nodding to his boss, "all in good time," he repeated, letting the echoed comment drift.

Flint began to feel even more nervous than when he had first walked into the restaurant. Being a very popular establishment, well patronized, he thought that he would feel safe in public. However, now that he was in the private room, the isolation he felt, being so close yet so far from the other diners was becoming more of a concern. He was starting to feel nauseous. He sipped from his drink. The silence between the men was deafening. The babble of noise from the *outside* diners seeped through the door jamb, creeping its way into the room.

Williams smiled cynically at Flint. His teeth seemed like fangs to Flint, whose imagination was starting to play tricks on him.

Suddenly the door to the room opened. Two men, two waiters, brought in food on trays. Ribs, steak, French fries, steamed vegetables. They placed the dishes from the trays onto a side table that one of the waiters pulled across from the other side of the room. After they had left, Teal stood by the door, his back to the entrance. No one was expected but Teal would not be letting anyone in, unless he was advised by Williams, to do so.

Without any invitation, Williams launched into the various dishes. Flint watched on. He wasn't hungry anymore, but he knew he needed to eat. He knew he needed to show that he did not feel intimidated.

After Williams had filled his plate, Flint carefully chose what he wanted and began to eat. Fifteen minutes later both men had finished their meals. Williams dabbed his mouth with a napkin, then drank the last of his beer.

He placed the glass down heavily upon the table demanding Flints' attention.

"A quarter of a million pounds upfront, that's the first payment," he said.

Flint nearly choked on his drink, coughing in response to Williams' demand.

"Are you fucking mad?" Flint asked once he had regained the ability to speak.

"Are you?" was Williams' riposte.

"I don't have that kind of money!" Flint argued.

Williams knew otherwise, had done the homework, obtained the detail. He knew Flint was a wealthy man. He knew he had a significant share portfolio, and he knew of the cash investments and the property Flint owned. While it may not have been immediately liquid, it was possible to get the amount Williams needed, in the time that Williams had available to him.

Madzia had agreed with Williams that he had until the end of April.

"Come, come, Mr. Flint," he said, "don't lie to me. I find that most ungracious, and somewhat disappointing that you would try to dupe me like that."

"I'm not," answered Flint.

"Three hundred thousand plus extra's," Williams replied.

"What?"

"You heard me, Mr. Flint. For trying to be clever, the debt has risen fifty thousand pounds!"

"You *are* out of your mind!" Flint replied.

"Umm," responded the large man, rubbing his chin, then scratching his forehead. He was ridiculing and intimidating Flint, noting that fear was beginning to show on Flint's face. "I wonder....?" he continued, a scowl slowly beginning to form on his face.

Flint became even more uneasy, he felt that he couldn't sit still for too much longer. He had to get out somehow.

"What do I get in return?" he asked. "What assurances?"

"Assurances?"

"Yes,"

"You'll have my word," said a smiling Williams.

"And what if I told you that it wasn't enough?"

Williams looked exaggeratedly around the room. Apart from Teal, there was just the two of them. He opened his palms outwards in a gesture suggesting that he couldn't care less what Flint thought.

"Well then, Mr. Flint. If you can't trust me then who can you trust? If you feel so strongly about it then I'm afraid I will have to do my civic duty and pass on the photographs to the relevant authorities."

"No!" shouted Flint, placing his hand on Williams' arm.

After the Fire

Williams looked at Flint, who slowly withdrew the hand.

"Wise decision, *Charles,*" he said.

Williams outlined his requirements. Flint listened to the ask. In return for payment, he would get the hard copy photographs, the negatives, but not any digital copies. They would be held in safekeeping by Williams. If Flint continued paying an additional hundred thousand pounds a year for the next ten years then he could rely on Williams' verbal guarantee that he would not be harassed again. No further pictures would be taken of him, *in fragrante delicto*. It wasn't much but Flint had nothing else to offer, he didn't know that the ongoing income stream was part of Williams' retirement plan.

The assurance Flint really wanted was that all digital copies be deleted or destroyed and that no additional physical copies of the photographs would be made, but he reluctantly decided not to push the issue. He could be dead in ten years and, as time passes things move on and so do the parties, including the girl!

The money, wanted immediately by Williams was now well over a quarter of a million pounds. In fact, fifty thousand pounds over. It could be gotten hold of. However, it was the *extras*, the addition to the upfront and ongoing payments, that he wasn't prepared for. It came out of the blue. Williams dropped the bombshell on him after he had already agreed to pay the three hundred thousand.

"There is one more thing," Williams added, "I forgot to mention it earlier. As part of the deal!"

"What is that?" Flint asked cautiously.

"Your horse, *RockGod*."

"What about him?"

"You need to make sure that he doesn't win the Grand National."

Flint laughed out loud. He considered the very notion absurd. He knew that no one could guarantee the winner of the race. There were way too many things that could affect *any* horse from winning. The weather, the race-day track condition, injury, other runners falling, the horse itself not being up to the rigours of the event, bad decision making by a jockey. A multitude of reasons. It was, however, the easier of the conditions set by Williams, to accept. He wasn't sure why it was so important, but it clearly was. He grasped the nettle with both hands.

Was there another horse required to win the race? And if so, why?

Money laundering perhaps? Flint wasn't sure. He was just speculating. He wasn't totally devastated by the request. What was he really giving away? It would be disappointing, yes, and winning the race itself was extremely satisfying, almost life-changing. However, he wasn't willing to let his predilection for young female flesh be negated by winning a horse race. No matter what the potential benefit of the race was.

He knew he had made a mistake. He hadn't realized at the time that his actions, his fantasies, his needs, would put him in so much danger.

Next time he would be much more careful. Do the things he wanted, in private.

"Once we get everything that we have discussed today resolved," Williams said, "including the three hundred k, paid as discussed, in small amounts into the accounts I gave you a list of, then you'll get all the photographs I have hand-delivered, by courier, the Friday after the *National.*"

Flint did not respond. He remained silent, taking in what was being said. Williams carried on.

"To ensure that you keep the other part of *our* agreement next Saturday at Aintree, my colleague and I and several others will be there at that meeting. We *expect* to see you there Mr. Flint," he said, the threat clear in his tone. "We will be watching you throughout the day to ensure that our investment, *RockGod,* is protected, and remains so," he carried on. "Any error in your judgment either on the Saturday, prior or even post the race, *will* result in copies of the photographs, being hand-delivered to the police, the national press and other interested parties. Am I making myself clear?" Williams emphatically asked.

Flint nodded his understanding, reluctantly acquiescing to the demands.

"You have my word," he said weakly.

Williams watched Flint squirm. He could see in his eyes a beaten man. The colour had drained from the face. All the confidence and cockiness had been sucked from him as the conversation had progressed. He stood up from the table and nodded to Teal who brought him his coat.

The two men turned away from the table, both remaining silent. They left the private room walking straight out of the front door of the restaurant and into the night.

Flint remained seated, stunned.

A waiter came into the room and asked if he needed anything else as he collected up the plates, the utensils, and the empty glasses. Flint shook his head. The bill eventually arrived. Williams had left him to pay for the meal. Flint saw this as the ultimate insult. He eventually left for home feeling numb. Being so deep in thought, he didn't notice the man and woman walking behind him. They had left their table at the same time as he did and had held the door open for him as he tried to find a taxi.

They kept enough distance away from him as their training had taught them.

CHAPTER 41

"We've had a breakthrough," Walsh said.
The team was gathered in the incident room. Expectations were high.
"However, let's not get too far ahead of ourselves," he continued cautiously, "there is still a lot of work to do. But at least it's something."
He had flown back from Schipol late the previous evening. He and Sedgefield having spent the whole day with various Dutch police authorities, the *Dienst Nationale Recherche* (National Crime Squad) and the *Dienst IPOL* (National Police Intelligence Service) amongst others. In addition, whilst in Amsterdam, they had been invited to share in an audio conference with a lead investigator from Interpol who was at the Lyon headquarters. The conversation was in relation to an investigation they were running, one that Interpol believed was relevant to the Perkel murder.
Walsh was keen to share the information so that the team could get to work.
"Let's start with the bad news," began Sedgefield, wanting to emphasize

After the Fire

that what they were about to share didn't mean that the next phase of their investigation was going to be a walk in the park. That the team should slack off. "The two men we were looking for have disappeared," he continued, to a collective groan from the team. "At this stage, we, nor the Dutch police, have any idea where they are. They've gone to ground somewhere. It's even possible that they have left the Netherlands and could be in anywhere in Europe right now."

"Sorry Sarge," called out Fitch, "excuse my asking, but wasn't that the very reason for the visit? To try and find out first-hand what information the Dutch had about these guys, who they are? Their possible whereabouts, their connections, etcetera?"

Having allowed Sedgefield to start the meeting, Walsh took over.

"That's precisely what we did, Constable," he responded in answer to the question, "and it brought up some surprising results. Unfortunately, as you've just been advised, the men we are looking for have somehow slipped the net, but," he added with some satisfaction, "we now know who they are."

The feeling in the room, already heightened, was becoming more positive.

"The men are known to police across the Balkans. Croatia, Serbia, Albania and Slovenia, and possibly further afield. We have some more details about them which we will share shortly."

Walsh looked around the room at expectant faces. "What we didn't know until yesterday was who these men were associated with," he continued. "This is where it gets interesting. Unfortunately for us what we thought was a murder case on our turf, now turns out to be a wider investigation going beyond our jurisdiction."

Sedgefield handed around a set of photographs to each member of the team, then turned on the electronic screen attached to a laptop that was sitting on a desk at the side of the room. He inserted a USB stick. Sitting down next to the computer, the Sergeant managed the keyboard on behalf of Walsh.

The screen showed the same faces as the photographs that had just handed out.

"The men you see on the screen were identified as one *Jeton Shehu* and the other *Sokol Lami*, both Albanian. What they were doing in the UK we do not know, but what we do know now, thanks to our friends at Interpol is that they have an association with one, Zymon Madzia."

Sedgefield pressed another key on the laptop and a picture of two men seated at a table in what looked like an expensive restaurant popped onto the screen. Walsh pointed to Madzia.

"This picture was taken just a few days ago," Walsh continued. "The man sitting with Madzia is *one* Jack Williams."

Williams was not really known to the team. His name had been mentioned, over the years, but only in passing.

Did he really have a wider reach, an association with the big players in Europe? Up until now, he was thought to be a local thug. A player yes, but was always on the periphery of anything large scale. A bit player.

"Where was this taken Sir?" asked Wendy Carmichael, the PSO, "as I'm a little confused about the link between Madzia, Williams and our murder victim," she said.

"In answer to your question," Walsh replied, "the picture was taken at the Shard. It was taken by an undercover officer of the NCA who has been following a trail of incoming drug shipments. Recently they intercepted a shipment that it has now been discovered was destined to be delivered to Williams. A much bigger haul than anyone would have imagined. That shipment was believed to be sent by Madzia."

"And the link to Mr. Perkel?" she questioned.

"At this stage, we are not one hundred percent sure, but from the information we have received overnight, we think Perkel became a victim due to another matter. Nothing to do with the drugs."

Fitch, his face in a frown reflected his lack of understanding of what was being said. He was confused and said so. "Sir, like Wendy here, I don't see any link between what we are investigating and this fellow Madzia. What is the relevance?"

Walsh answered the best way he could.

"As I indicated earlier," he said, "there is a larger investigation underway outside of our area of responsibility, our jurisdiction. However, what we have been able to piece together is that the body of our victim, Perkel, was dumped by two men associated with Madzia who just happened to be in town meeting with Williams at the time. So, the question is, did Williams arrange the killing and use Madzia's men to carry it out so as to stay as far away as possible from it? Or did an associate of Williams commit the murder and just use Madzia's men to dump the body and then disappear? The answer is, we don't know, but," he paused and looked around the room. The atmosphere and the anticipation of the team as to any further revelations he was going to make was electric. "But," he repeated, "what we now know, thanks to SOCA who were trailing Williams, is that Williams had dinner with Charles Flint less than forty-eight hours ago. They met privately at a restaurant near Tower Bridge," he went on. "Charles Flint and Henry Perkel were long-time friends. We now think that Flint and Perkel were being blackmailed by Williams. We don't know why yet, but we can only conclude that to be the case as there was no obvious reason for Flint and Williams to be associated with each other."

"Could it not be just a case of a stockbroker meeting with his client?" asked Fitch.

"It could be, I suppose, but Williams is a known criminal, albeit we originally thought him to be *small* fry." replied Walsh, "Add that to the recent erratic behavior of Flint, just disappearing as he did, and it seems to suggest otherwise. Remember this was around the time that Perkel was murdered," he went on. "No, we think there is a definite link. What we don't know yet is how?"

"Not forgetting," added Sedgefield, "that there is still the strange association between Mike Cannon, Flint's daughter, and her Polish boyfriend, Kaminski. We still don't understand that yet either."

"Indeed," agreed Walsh rubbing a hand across his chin. "We need to get Flint and Williams in. Put some pressure on both of them. Let's see if we can get one of them to crack."

"And Cannon?"

"We're meeting with him later today anyway," Walsh indicated, "so let's leave that as planned. Arrange for Williams to be picked up for a chat tomorrow. And do the same for Flint," he added.

Walsh addressed the team. "Let's find out as much as we can about Williams. Plus, I want to know more about Flint. Adrian," he said, turning to the IT expert who had stayed quiet throughout the briefing, "Interpol has provided more information about the tattoos on the two bodies we still need to identify. We now know that one of them is not who Lucy Flint thought he was. Could you look into it further for me and let me know what you can find out asap?"

"Yes, of course," answered Windsor.

"Thanks," replied Walsh. "Now Sergeant," he said turning to Sedgefield, "Mike Cannon and his association with Charles Flint, what do we know?"

She still had no answer from Pete. It had been weeks now. Had he gone back home? Why? Lucy Flint was confused, angry. She needed to tell him what had happened. He needed to know the truth about his friend.

CHAPTER 42

It was all too familiar to Cannon. Meeting with the police was becoming a habit, something he was not enjoying. He was a racehorse trainer now. It was as if the past wouldn't leave him alone. It kept dragging him back to places he didn't want to be. Yet somehow, he was part of the problem. He knew that when the line went tight, once he had grabbed the bait, he couldn't let go. Had Timms' planned to get him involved in order to help solve the mystery or had the mystery developed the more he got involved? Was he being reeled in or had become the fisherman, the hunter? He wasn't sure which, but he knew that things didn't add up and he was determined to find out the reasons why.

It had been a positive morning so far for Walsh and team. The DNA results were in from the lab after the post mortem on the two bodies found in the Thames. *Body A*, and *Body B* as they had become known within the team. They were brothers! In addition, it was confirmed using the DNA database profile that they were definitely from Eastern Europe.

Walsh knew that when leads turn to answers, progress was often swift, fast-moving. What they needed now were names. The bodies still didn't have any, at least not real ones. After confirming that *Body B* was not Stefan Kaminski it meant they needed to follow other angles. One step at a time. They would need to speak with Lucy Flint again to see if she knew her boyfriend had a brother in the UK.

"You wanted to see us," said Walsh.

"Yes."

"About what exactly?"

"A number of things to be honest," answered Cannon, "and hopefully some assistance from you as well."

They were in a meeting room. Surprisingly available. It included a table with six chairs, an easel with a few permanent markers in a clear plastic packet resting on its lip and a whiteboard positioned at one end of the room. Along one wall was a three-door sideboard on top of which sat a speakerphone. The room was so much larger than Walsh's office. They had space to stand and walk around if needed. With just the three of them, the room seemed almost empty, too big. There was no recording device that Cannon could see. Sedgefield had a notebook on the table, pen in hand. Walsh sat in his chair, hands together, fingers pointing upwards like a steeple. Attentive.

"Go on," he requested.

"I need to share some information with you that I haven't been able to disclose so far. Plus…"
"And why would that be?" interjected Walsh.
"What?"
"Why you couldn't share this *information* with us earlier?"
Cannon considered the question for a second. This was going to be harder than he imagined. He knew the police didn't like things being withheld from them, especially where a murder was involved. When he had first met with Timms they were essentially talking about fraud. Cannon realized now that things had gone much further than either of them had ever imagined it would. Perhaps he shouldn't be so surprised? Human nature didn't change just because he was out of the Force.
"It wasn't the right time," he said. The argument sounded silly, almost naïve, to him now.
"And now is the time?"
"Yes."
The policemen looked at each other. Walsh then opened his palms like a priest, encouraging Cannon with a nod to continue.
"Over to you then Mike," he said.
"I think Perkel's murder was over money."
"Money?"
"More specifically it's to do with money to be made via a horse under my care. A horse owned by Charles Flint."
"A gambling debt resulting in murder? What makes you draw that conclusion?" asked Walsh, noting that Sedgefield had begun writing in his notebook.
"It's me putting two and two together and hopefully coming up with four," he answered.
"I'm not sure I'm following Mike. It's all a bit vague to me. Is this based on fact or is it just speculation?" he asked. "And before you answer, you know the drill. If you are wasting my time, getting involved when you shouldn't be or are holding back information pertinent to our investigation about Perkel's death then understand this, I won't be happy!"
Cannon held up his hands in mock surrender.
"Okay," he retorted, "I'll tell you what I know and why then it's over to you to do with as you please. I'll just walk away after that."
He knew he couldn't, wouldn't, but he needed Walsh and his team to be an ally, not a hindrance. He had thought about how best to tell Walsh how he had connected the dots. How to put his thoughts across in a way that didn't seem fanciful. He knew he needed evidence, solid evidence. At the moment it was a feeling. An ominous one at that, and one that disturbed him. He decided he would go for it and let Walsh decide the next steps.
"A number of weeks ago now I was approached by the BHA in relation to

a race-fixing investigation they were running which ultimately, they think, has uncovered a betting scam. They believed that it included horses that I trained plus those from other yards," he said. "The horses concerned were all owned by Charles Flint."

"And the BHA believed you were part of it?" enquired Sedgefield.

"Yes, or least had some doubts."

"Why?"

"I think primarily because I'd had a poor season. In fact, over the past eighteen months or so I'd had limited success. They would have been able to see that my income was down as a consequence, so they looked into the results of the races and decided to investigate further."

"And were you?"

"Involved?"

"Yes."

"Of course not," Cannon responded, "but it did spark my interest."

"Which resulted in..?" Walsh asked.

"To cut a long story short, it resulted in me working with the BHA after one of my other horses was the subject of an attack at Worcester racecourse. And before you ask, yes, the local police were informed and were involved in the investigation," he said.

"And what was the outcome?"

"It's still being looked at but they have established that there was a definite intent to do something to my horse."

"Look, Mike, this is all very interesting but I still don't see the link with Perkel's murder," Walsh remarked.

Walsh didn't know how much Cannon was aware of Flints' association with Jack Williams or even if he knew at all and he doubted Cannon would know of the connection between Williams and Madzia. Thinking about it though, Walsh was starting to see how a possible tie in with racing, money owed and blackmail could apply to what Cannon had said.

"I met with Lucy Flint yesterday," Cannon continued, "there was something she said, implied, that made me think was relevant to all this, but I can't yet work out what it was. So, I wanted to ask you if there was anything you had uncovered that perhaps you could share?"

"Such as?"

"I don't know," he replied, "but I do think she knows more than she has let on and I thought if we put everything on the table, perhaps we can help each other?"

Walsh sat silently. He lowered his hands onto the table and wiped away an imaginary speck of dust. Sedgefield watched intently, looking at the faces of both men in turn, as he waited for Walsh to respond. He couldn't read what either was thinking. A clock on the wall ticked off the seconds. Finally, Walsh answered Cannons' question.

After the Fire

"Mike, you understand that I may get into serious trouble if I share too much of what we know about this case, so whatever I tell you is *completely off the record*," he emphasized.

"Of course, Inspector," Cannon replied, "I know what you mean, and to be honest, I've been there myself," he continued, trying to lighten Walsh's load. "None of us," he pointed to his own chest, then to Walsh and Sedgefield in sequence, "could ever consider doing the job alone. It's an occupational hazard. and at times we need to trust others. It's how the system works. One person can't know everything, and sometimes the need to share information is with individuals outside of the *machine*. Outside of the process, outside of the rules," he said. "I know, believe me, I learnt the hard way."

Cannon felt he had overstepped the mark, telling Walsh how to do his job, but he couldn't help himself. He needed to take the chance. He needed to have Walsh on his side. Having had his say, Cannon knew he needed to stay silent, let the words sink in. Despite his openness, he wasn't completely willing to expand on some of his career failings. He had said what he hoped was enough.

There was a pause as Walsh considered Cannons' position.

"Give me your perspective on Lucy Flint," asked Walsh.

"In what way?"

"Well, you said she seems to know more than she is letting on. What do you mean by that?"

"I'm not sure," he answered, "but there was a sadness about her that seemed to be deeper than I would have imagined when I talked to her about the relationship with her father."

"Did she say anything about her boyfriend?" asked Walsh.

"Her boyfriend? No, she didn't. What about him?"

Walsh nodded imperceptibly across the table.

"He's dead," relayed Sedgefield, "found a few weeks ago in the Thames. Drowned."

"She never mentioned it," responded Cannon, "but it's not surprising then that she seemed so...so distant, almost melancholy. I guess between my asking about her father, plus the loss of her boyfriend, anyone would feel their world was crumbling around them."

"It will get worse for her shortly. We need to talk with her again now that we know more about her boyfriend," Sedgefield continued.

"It's part of the puzzle we are trying to piece together," interjected Walsh before Cannon could ask a question that would inevitably come. "I'll explain," he said, seeing the query on Cannon's face.

Walsh relayed the details of Lucy Flint's boyfriend's death, the query with the tattoo. He highlighted the anomaly about his name, his apparent place of work and his overall identity. Sharing the information with Cannon didn't seem like breaking protocol. It seemed right. Cannon was part of the solution.

"You said the tattoo was similar to another body also found in the Thames?" Cannon asked.
"Yes, that's one of the links we have, but as of this morning, we now know that they were related. Brothers. We believe both men are Polish, but we are struggling to find out their real identities."
Cannon sat silently for a moment. He was trying to tie up what he had just heard, with the very reason he had asked to see Walsh.
"Is that not the connection?"
"What connection?" asked Walsh, "and connection to what?"
"The murder of Perkel with the deaths of these two Polish men. The two brothers?"
"How do you come to that conclusion?"
"It's not a conclusion. Just a theory at this point," he answered. "The link between my investigation on behalf of the BHA and these murders, Perkel and the brothers. There seems to be a link with Lucy Flint or at least her Father."
"Not sure I'm with you, Mike," said Walsh.
"Well, let me put it this way," suggested Cannon. "If Charles Flint needed money, what better way than to influence the outcomes of races and profit from them? Particularly via betting?"
Walsh and Sedgefield weren't convinced.
"Isn't that all a bit extreme?" asked Walsh, "Flint is a wealthy man. If he needed money surely there was an easier way to get it than impacting horse racing results?"
"I guess so," conceded Cannon, reconsidering his theory, "but Flint is very ego-driven. Perhaps it appealed to his nature, to be able to pull off something so extreme?"
"I think you are grasping at straws, Mike. How *exactly* does that tie in with the deaths of two men anyway?" asked Walsh.
Despite liking Cannon and their shared backgrounds, he was getting irritated with the conversation.
"Sorry Mike, but I'm beginning to think we've been wasting our time with this discussion," he went on. "A theory is great, but I need facts." Standing up from the desk, he added, "We can sit around all day filling it with conjecture, but that won't help us resolve anything. I'm getting pressure from upstairs to solve these cases and sitting around gas-bagging, hypothecating, is not going to help me close them. I understand how you might *think* the cases are linked, but frankly, it's a long bow to draw."
Cannon realized his chance may have gone, blown. He didn't want to mention Flint's link with *Viking Spirit* and the implication on *RockGod,* the

horses' standing in the betting and his increased chances of winning. That was the information he needed to digest first. He tried one last question.

"So, if this boyfriend of Lucy Flint isn't the person she thought he was but he had all the personal information about the real and very much alive Stefan Kaminski, have you been able to establish how he was able to do that?"

"No Mike we haven't," responded Walsh edging towards the door, "he's dead. Unfortunately, he hasn't been able to tell us," he continued sarcastically.

"Perhaps they knew each other?"

"We've checked that," came the response, "they didn't." An emphatic put down.

Walsh's hand was on the door handle. Sedgefield had also stood up from the table.

Suddenly there was a knock on the door. Walsh stepped back to allow the person to enter. It was Windsor, from IT.

"Sir," he said, looking at Cannon still sitting. "Sorry to interrupt."

"That's okay," answered Walsh, "we were just concluding our discussion," he said looking back at Cannon. "What's the rush, can't it wait?"

"I guess it could Sir, but I knew you were meeting with Mr. Cannon here," nodding towards the trainer, "so I thought that you might find what I've uncovered may be of use? To both of you," he continued.

"Okay, let's hear it," Walsh responded, "take a seat," he said, closing the door.

The four men sat at the table, the three others waiting expectantly for Windsor to say his piece.

"As you asked me too, Sir, I've been following up and doing some research on those tattoo's that we have been trying to understand. Those on the two victims we know as *Body A* and *Body B*."

"Yes, yes," said Walsh impatiently, "get to the point Windsor, we don't have all day, and I'm sure Mr. Cannon needs to get back to his horses asap."

Cannon smiled inwardly. He understood why Walsh wanted him gone, having been there himself in the past. Watching the dynamics of the three others, he remembered what he had left behind. He didn't miss it.

"Well Sir, that's exactly the point," Windsor relayed.

"What is?"

"The tattoos."

"What?" said Walsh, "*what* is the point?"

"The tattoos," he stated, "they are about horses."

"Uh?"

"Well one horse in particular," Windsor emphasized confidently.

Cannon was intrigued. He sat up straight in his chair. Was his gut feeling right?

"Remember we thought that the words of the tattoo were in Polish, but then the Chef, the real Kaminski, told you it may be something *else?*" continued Windsor.

"Yes."

"Well, it was. It's Czech!"

"And?"

"Well, I did some investigation. I tried *googling* a few things to get some ideas then eventually after liaising with my colleagues at Interpol in Lyon and in Warsaw I found out what the tattoo is about. It's the name of a horse. It took longer than I expected because we thought the first letter of the tattoo was an S. Once I worked out it was actually a Z, things fell into place."

Windsor was in his element. An IT specialist who loved to surf the internet and search databases providing supporting information for detectives. What he had uncovered was like gold to him. He loved the theatre of the reveal.

"What horse?" asked Cannon.

"It's a horse called *Zeleznik,*" he said trying to get his tongue around the correct pronunciation. After trying a couple of times and failing, he eventually spelled it out. "It was a steeplechaser, from the old Czechoslovakia."

Cannon was encouraged. The link he had surmised and that Walsh was unconvinced of, could possibly lie in what Windsor was saying.

"Anything else?" asked Walsh.

"Yes, Sir. The horse was famous because it won the *Grand Paradubice Steeplechase*, which is similar to our Grand National, a record four times in what is now the Czech Republic. That was in 1987, 88, 89 and 91. Overall it won thirty times out of fifty-eight races that it competed in."

Walsh and Cannon looked at each other. From experience, they both knew instinctively that what Windsor had revealed was pertinent to the bigger picture that Cannon had alluded to.

"Anything else?" asked Walsh.

"Yes, Sir. Apparently, in 1987 the horse came to England to run in *our* National but due to some blood *irregularity* was not able to do so. This was the same year the horse won the first of its four Czech Nationals. The jockey on all four occasions and on four other times was a man called Josef Vana Snr. He was born in 1952. As of today, we believe he may still be alive."

"I doubt the horse is still alive?" enquired the Inspector.

"No Sir, it died in 2004. It was 26 years old."

Walsh thanked Windsor for his effort. Another piece of the puzzle revealed.

"Good work," he said as Windsor left the room. Turning to Cannon he asked, "what do you think?"

"It's all about the *National*," he replied, "no doubt about it. What we just heard has made me more convinced than ever. And we've only got nine days to go before we find out if I'm right."

"Umm," replied Walsh, "I see a connection but it's still only tenuous and could just be coincidental."

"Plus, we haven't yet established any possible motive," interjected Sedgefield, "for the killings of *Body A* or Perkel. Plus, we're still not sure if *Body B* was in fact murdered or his death was just an accident."

"Believe me," Cannon replied, "it's all about money, nothing else. I'm sure of it."

"Well if it is, let's hope we can find out why and who is behind it before we have any more killings," stated Walsh.

"Agreed," replied Cannon, "it's only a week before the meeting starts and if we are not careful, something big will go down, I'm sure of it."

CHAPTER 43

She wasn't sure what to do.
Should she go to the police and register him as a missing person or should she wait and see if he tries to contact her?
Lucy was getting desperate to know what had happened to him.
She was feeling more alone each day.
She needed to tell him all about it.
The visits from the police had unsettled her.
The meetings with Mike Cannon and his questions about her father had made her even more uneasy.
She decided to wait.

"No comment," answered Jack Williams.
The formal process of cautioning Williams had concluded and the recording started. Walsh and Sedgefield had begun their questioning of Jack Williams.
He and Sam Teal had presented themselves at the station voluntarily. Williams was supported by his lawyer Kenneth Bookman who sat beside his client. Teal had been told to wait outside in the public waiting area. He decided to stand in the sun outside the building.
"Okay, let me ask you another question, Mr. Williams," Walsh said, "how well do you know Mr. Charles Flint?"
He had placed a photo on the table of the two of them sitting inside *Gauchos*. Williams looked at it in disdain. *How the hell?* he thought.
"You don't have to answer that or any other questions Jack," jumped in Bookman.
Williams ignored the lawyer.
"Barely," he said.
"Barely? Meaning what exactly?" asked Walsh.
"Look, Inspector, I'm not sure what this is all about, but I've come here on my own volition as per your request on the phone last night. You started by asking me questions about some bullshit story I know nothing about and now you are prying into my personal life. What the hell is going on here?!"
Walsh could tell that he had hit a nerve, but decided to keep his powder dry.
"You said you barely know Charles Flint."
"Yes."

After the Fire

Bookman looked at Williams. He knew Walsh was drawing more out of his client than Bookman felt comfortable with. Given Williams was under caution, he needed to get his client to limit is responses.

"Jack, I suggest you let me do the talking," he said, "remember you are under caution, which means the Inspector must have a reason for doing so. However, from what I can see here," he nodded at the photograph, "is that there has been a breach of privacy and the Inspector knows it. The police can't just go around taking pictures of honest citizens conducting their daily business without any justification," he added.

Williams looked into Walsh's eyes. Both men stared at each other across the table. Sedgefield and Bookman could sense the animosity, the atmosphere between the men stiffen.

"I've got nothing to hide," Williams eventually responded. He had a lot to lose if his plans didn't work out. He needed to get Walsh off his back. He would play the game.

"Glad to hear that, Mr. Williams. So, going back to my question. What does *barely* mean?"

"We had dinner a couple of nights ago. I was introduced to him by a mutual friend. That's it."

"What did you discuss, at your dinner?" Walsh asked.

"No need to answer that Jack," interrupted Bookman, "a private conversation is exactly that."

Walsh glared at the lawyer. It was always the same, he thought. Lawyers were supposed to be a profession holding up the law not preventing it from being applied. It never failed to amaze him how often he found himself in this position. The right to have representation was one thing, but sometimes it could go way too far.

"We talked about many things Inspector," Williams said confidently, with a swagger. He knew how the game was played. In fact, he enjoyed playing it. It wasn't the first time he had been interviewed, and he had never been charged before. He decided to humour Walsh.

"Mostly we spoke about an investment I wanted to make. Mr. Flint is a stockbroker you know," he said smiling.

"Yes, we know. Anything else?"

"No!" Emphatic.

Walsh knew he needed to ask the question. Now was the time.

"Do you know a man called Henry Perkel?"

Williams frowned in an exaggerated fashion. Pretended to be thinking. Part of the game.

"No," he replied eventually, "why do you ask?"

"He was murdered. He was a friend of Charles Flint."

Walsh watched Williams for any tell-tale signs to his comment. Any changes in body language, any reaction at all to the statement. Williams sat like a statue.

"Did it never get raised in your conversation?" Walsh asked.

"No, should it have?"

"It surprises me that it wouldn't have been mentioned. It's not something one forgets that easily. I would have thought Mr. Flint would have at least shown some reaction, shared how he felt?"

Williams sat quietly for a second. Ruminating. His face blank, no sign of the smugness he felt inside.

"No, nothing. We talked business predominantly," he eventually responded while shrugging his shoulders. "Anyway Inspector, you still haven't told me what this is all about."

"It's about a murder, Mr. Williams. Mr. Perkel's murder in fact."

Walsh looked towards Sedgefield who was studying Williams like the proverbial hawk. Staring at the man.

Williams remained unmoved. Still.

"Sorry Inspector, can't help you," he said. "I didn't know the man. Never met him."

Walsh and Sedgefield had discussed their interview tactics before the meeting. It was agreed that Sedgefield's role was not to ask questions, but to try to make Williams feel uneasy. To try and put thoughts into Williams' head about what the police knew or didn't know regarding the relationship between him and Flint.

It wasn't yet the time to mention what they knew about Williams and Madzia and it still wasn't clear yet who had killed Perkel and where. Walsh was sure however that somehow Williams was involved.

The linkage with Madzia was unfortunately outside of their jurisdiction, it was a drug squad matter and that investigation was out of his Walsh's hands.

Knowing that the questioning had not been particularly successful, in fact, had achieved very little so far. Walsh decided to try one last tack.

"Okay Mr. Williams, I think that's about all. You've been very helpful, thank you," he said, then began to close a folder after inserting a few loose A4 pages that had been placed on the table between them as a prop. A prop designed to make Williams and his lawyer think.

The two policemen stood up, Williams and Brookman doing likewise, scraping their chair legs on the tiled floor.

"Oh," Walsh said, acting as if he had just remembered something, "one last thing. Something I nearly forgot. Did Mr. Flint mention anything about his good fortune with his racehorse *RockGod,* the one running in the Grand National next week?"

Walsh noticed the brief quiver in Williams's cheek.

"No, should he have?"

"No not really," Walsh said, a slight pout on his lips. A no-care lilt in his body language, "I'm just surprised given he has so much going on in his life that he didn't mention it. Must have been a boring evening."

"Well, he didn't talk about it, Inspector. But for your information, it was a very enjoyable dinner." Williams smiled at the two policemen but inside he was trying to understand Walsh's comments about *RockGod*.

"Good to know," replied Walsh, "but if I was Mr. Flint and I had heard that the favourite and last years' winner is now out of the race, giving his horse a much better chance of winning, I'd be really happy about that and I'd probably be talking about it. Wouldn't you?" he asked, a smirk on his face.

CHAPTER 44

"Only four days to go," she said, "are you getting excited?"
"More nervous than anything else," he replied.
Cannon and Michelle were sitting in the lounge at home. Dinner was over. The TV was off. They were enjoying each other's company. It wasn't often that they had the chance to do so. Especially recently. It had been a busy day. Arrangements had been made for *RockGod* to be transported up to Liverpool on Friday morning, the third day of the race meeting. Cannon and Michelle would travel by car the same day. Rich would ride with the horse to make sure he arrived fit and well at the Aintree racecourse.
The gallops that morning, were as normal as Cannon would have expected them to be, though it was clear that the excitement was beginning to build with the stable staff. There was a genuine belief that *RockGod* could win the *National*. His training for the race was now tapering off. Today he had been sent out to just have a long hard blow, galloping rather than jumping. He knew how to jump. He was a brave horse and that bravery would serve him well. The fences at Aintree were special. Replicating them in training was hard to do and unnecessary in Cannon's mind. *RockGod* knew his capabilities. He would adapt. Cannon just hoped the jockey would. The weather forecast for race day was good. Crisp and cold in the morning but dry all day, a slight breeze expected from the west and it would be partly cloudy. A maximum temperature of about 9 degrees centigrade. Perfect conditions.
RockGod was still the second favourite in the ante-post betting, at 10 to 1. Cannon knew that the staff was taking up the offer. He wasn't allowed too under the rules of racing and he never did anyway, despite what Timms had originally thought. Was it only just a few short weeks ago that Timms had first walked into Cannon's office?
"What are you thinking?" Michelle asked.
"Not much," he replied, "well not about the race anyway. What will be will be."
"I guess the TV media will want a few quotes from you on the day?" she asked, smiling.
"I guess they will. I never really liked all that stuff, but it's part of the theatre. I just hope I don't come across stupidly."
"Well, whatever happens, I'm so proud of you," she reached over and touched his hand. He took her hand in his own. The warmth of her skin on his felt so pleasing, comforting. It eased his mind.
He changed the subject slightly.

"I'm looking forward to seeing Cassie again."
"Yes, that will be nice," she replied.
Letting go of her hand he asked, "what do know about Blake?"
"Nothing really," she said, "though she looks a very pretty girl."
"How do you know that?"
"From Facebook," she answered, "God Mike, you need to get with it," she teased.
Michelle picked up her smartphone that was sitting on a small table next to the couch. Cannon grasped a mug of tea that he had placed on the same table.
After a few seconds, she moved closer to him until they were side by side. He could feel her body heat. It made him feel good.
"See," she said, "look."
Holding her phone in her hand, she showed him a selfie that Cassie had obviously taken of Blake and herself at some pub they were in.
"You see. Cassie *tagged* Blake in this photo."
Cannon looked at the image. Blake was indeed pretty. Long, light brown wavy hair surrounding a thin face. She was smiling, showing white teeth. Her grin seemed to brighten the picture. Her eyes were brown, sparkling in the flash of the camera. Her zest for life and fun obvious. He could see she had a green jacket on over a white tee-shirt. Yes, she was *very* pretty. He looked at Cassie too. She looked confident, happy. She reminded him of her mother. He still missed Sally.
"I still don't get all this Facebooking," he said eventually, "but I do like to see where my money is going," he stated jokingly.
Michelle tapped him playfully on his arm. He put his arm around her shoulder, kissing her on the head as he pulled her towards him. It was a gesture he did regularly, without thinking.
"Saturday could be a game-changer for us," he said, suddenly more aware of the race implications. He had tried to block it out of his mind and not get too far ahead of himself. He had been concentrating on the Flint issue, the impact it was having on him. The queries and the questions. Somehow, he knew there was more to Saturday than just the race. What had happened at Tony Campbell's stables, at Worcester and the sense he had felt after his second conversation with Lucy Flint, were all swirling around in his head. What it all meant, he didn't know. What he did know though was that Charles Flint was the key to it all.
The brief conversation about *RockGod's* entry into the *National* he had held with Flint after Perkel's murder came to light, then, the subsequent conversation with Walsh and the issue of the tattoo's all led to something big. Something that Timms had initially failed to warn Cannon of. Would he have gotten involved if he knew then what he knew now? *Probably*, he thought, though he still wasn't sure why. Wasn't sure where it was all going

to lead.

Michelle nuzzled closer to him, wrapping her arms around his body.

They sat in silence, enjoying the moment. The stillness, the quiet.

Suddenly Cannon's mobile phone rang.

Looking at the screen, he saw that it was Lucy Flint's number, which he had saved as a contact when he had first called her. Looking at the time on his watch it was just before 9 pm.

"Hello?" he answered. "Lucy?"

He nodded to Michelle as she headed towards the kitchen taking away Cannons' empty mug.

"I'm sorry to call so late Mike, but I just realized that you have a big day on Saturday. It's come around so quickly since we last spoke and I wanted to wish you well."

Cannon was pleasantly surprised and told her so.

"No problem," she said, "and I hope your investigations with the BHA are fruitful," she went on.

"Thanks again," he replied.

There was a silence between them for a few seconds as if one of them needed to initiate the goodbyes.

Eventually, Cannon said, "I'm sorry to have heard about your boyfriend's brother."

"Excuse me?" she replied.

"Your boyfriend," he restated. "Inspector Walsh explained to me a couple of days ago when I was in a meeting with him, that your boyfriend had a brother and that they had only identified his body…" Cannon realized he had spoken out of turn. He wasn't in the force anymore. It wasn't his job to inform loved ones, next of kin or anyone else associated with a victim of violence or murder, about that individuals' demise, that was the authorities' job.

"His brother?" she asked.

Cannon was unsure what to say. He had already crossed the line. If she hadn't already been advised, then once he found out, Walsh would be really pissed off with him.

"Sorry, I shouldn't have said anything. I apologize if you didn't already know."

"He told me he didn't have a brother," she answered blandly, robotically.

Cannon decided to remain silent. He could hear her breathing on the phone. Thinking.

After a few seconds, she put down the receiver on him, saying nothing.

Cannon listened to the silence of the dead phone for a few seconds then pressed the red dot on the screen and closed the phone app.

CHAPTER 45

Pete, dead?
A brother?
Were he and Stefan related?
They had some physical similarities, even had the same tattoo though Pete did have one from his days in the Polish armed forces. Stefan didn't.
They never said they were brothers. She only knew that they were both from Poland. No wonder she had been unable to reach him.
He had left her apartment some weeks ago. He said he was going to work.
She doubted now if either of them had ever told her the truth.
What was it with men?

"Thank you for being sensible," said the voice down the phone line.
It was *Dootson*, or whatever his real name was?
Flint was locked in his own office. Three hundred thousand pounds had been paid in small amounts through an offshore account he had set up.
Flint had raided a trust account he had access too. He had used it in the past for emergencies, moving money back into the account once the emergency was over. The trustees never knew. Didn't ask. It was an account of an *old-money* family. He had spent most of the day fielding calls from some of his partners in *Viking Spirit*, including the trainer. Sam Bramley had called each part owner, in turn, to apologize about *Viking Spirit* being scratched and advise them about the horse's welfare. Bramley told Flint that he had asked his farrier how the shoe that came off had come loose, but the farrier had no idea. It was just an accident. It happens in racing. Bramley felt that he needed to let everyone know the circumstances about the horse, because a favourite for the *National* dropping out so late, just a few days before the race, was very unusual.
Flint's partners in *Viking Spirit* were lawyers, doctors, farmers. Ten owners each with a ten percent share. Despite their own disappointment, they wished him well with *RockGod*. The advantage of being the sole-owner of

RockGod was that he had the freedom to make decisions about the horse. He just never did. As with all his other horses, he let the trainers make all the decisions.

Frankly, the horses were normally the furthest from his mind. He used them predominantly to impress. Especially young women who liked the glamour, the chance to mingle with rich people and drink champagne despite being on the arm of a much older man. For him, the younger the girl the better.

Yes, when you had money and needed a way to get what you wanted plus have a chance to get a financial return as well, it was a *worthy* investment.

He was unnerved by the call from *Dootson*. It was unexpected. Jean had already gone home.

"What do you want?" Flint asked, trying to sound more confident than he was feeling.

"I just wanted to let you know that I had a little chat with Inspector Walsh yesterday and he showed me something I didn't like," said Williams.

Flint had no idea to what *Dootson* was referring too and said so.

"He showed me a photo of you and me together. Taken at our little dinner, the one we had the other night," he replied. "I'm not very happy about that!" he concluded angrily.

Flint didn't know what to say other than to deny he had anything to do with it. "I didn't arrange for any photo's to be taken," he said in defense of himself.

"Well somehow, someone knew we were going to be there."

"What did Walsh say?" asked Flint, trying to change the subject.

"He said things I didn't like. He knows more than he let on and he asked about your horse as well," he said.

"What did he say?"

"Nothing in particular, other than whether we had spoken about it."

"We didn't."

"I know that," responded Williams, "but I think he knows more than he is saying. And that *annoys* me!"

Flint felt extremely uncomfortable. He knew Perkel had paid the ultimate price. He went into self-preservation mode.

"Do you want me to speak to the Inspector?"

"Now why would I want you to do that?"

"I don't know. Try and get him to focus on other things? Persuade him that it was purely a business meeting?"

"I told him that already, and by the way, if he does ask you why you met with Jack Williams, yes that's me," he said, his voice quivering with anger, "then keep it simple. It *was* a business meeting and I was looking to invest in the stock market. That's it. Nothing else!"

Flint agreed.

After the Fire

He didn't know who Jack Williams was but at least now that he had a name, he could find out a bit more. Perhaps learn something that could be of use in the future? Clearly, the man was more than just a common thug. He had standing. Flint decided he would ask a couple of his lawyer friends over the next day or so if they knew anything about the man. He was looking for ammunition that he could use to defend himself. His main focus, however, was to get the photographs back.

"And another thing," said Williams.

"Yes?"

"Just remember that on Saturday I will be there at Aintree. I'll be following your every move. Wherever you are, I'll be watching. I'll have my men all throughout the course. It's a big day and there are sixty thousand people plus expected. Despite this, you won't be out of my sight at all throughout the day. Wherever you are."

Flint didn't see the need.

"Why would you do that?" he asked.

"Because I don't trust anyone."

"Well, I've got no reason to do anything stupid. Why would I?"

"You know about Perkel now. It was my mistake in telling you what happened to him. So, just remember this, if you don't want to end up the same way he did. You just need to make sure you keep to the rest of the deal. If not, the *photos* are pretty clear, you dirty bastard!"

Flint flinched at the aggression coming down the line. It was clear that Williams was under pressure. Whatever was being promised by Williams was riding on *RockGod's* back. Ironic, Flint thought.

"Just remember, *RockGod* must not win the race," Williams said.

Flint was about to respond but the line went dead. The message was received, loud and clear.

Walsh sat alone contemplating what he knew. It was late, the situation room was empty. The team, including Sedgefield, had all gone home. Walsh had been invited to join a couple of them for a drink down the road but had declined. Others had gone directly home to family. Some like himself had no family to go home to. They would spend an evening in front of the TV or maybe alone with a drink. Each to his own.

He looked at the file in front of him, various pages and reports. The computer on his desk was on but had gone into sleep mode, the screen blank.

Walsh rubbed the back of his neck as he sat back in his chair.

What did they know?

Henry Perkel, murdered and body dumped. Suspects disappeared somewhere in Europe. Known to authorities there, and known associates of Madzia.

Madzia in the UK at the time of the murder, meeting with Jack Williams.

Then there was the Williams and Flint relationship and the reaction of the former to the comment about Flint's horse at the end of the interview.

Was Cannon, right?

If he was, how did that tie-up with the two bodies, now confirmed as brothers? The DNA analysis report received that morning verified it to be the case with a 99.999% accuracy.

One-shot in the head, the other drowned. Unclear as to where the latter died.

Though their nationality was not yet factually established they were likely Polish, based on the evidence to date. However until the verification sought from the Polish authorities came through, they could not be totally certain.

They had also asked the authorities via Interpol in the Czech Republic to check if Josef Vana Snr had any relatives, either immediate or indirect. Hopefully, the DNA evidence would confirm things one way or the other.

Perhaps Walsh hoped, it wasn't even necessary.

Perhaps through birth, death and marriage records, enough detail would establish a reason as to why the two men had tattoos of a racehorse on them. It clearly meant something.

The problem he was still struggling with was who had killed the men and why?

The only link with the men was Lucy Flint, and she had only ever talked about one of them.

Instinctively Walsh picked up the phone and called her number. He wasn't sure if she would answer.

On the third ring, she did.

"Good evening Lucy, it's Jeremy Walsh here, Balham CID. Sorry to have called you so late."

He could sense her smile as she responded, "It's not too late Inspector. Just after nine isn't late at all. How can I help you?"

"I just wanted to ask you something. Something perhaps I should have asked or at least had my team follow up on yesterday," he said, "unfortunately, due to circumstances, it seems to have fallen through the cracks," he continued apologetically. "We have been following up some information received in relation to another matter and finally established a link between that issue and the case of your boyfriend. For some unknown reason, it looks like we forgot to make you aware."

"Yes, what is it?"

He wasn't sure how she would react, especially given the confusion around her boyfriend's identity.

"Did you know your boyfriend had a brother?" he asked.

After the Fire

He could sense the hesitation in her.
He had expected an immediate reaction.
"Well," she finally responded, "I didn't know until I spoke with Mike Cannon last night. He let it slip, obviously accidentally. It came as a big shock."
Cannon, he thought? What the hell?
He tried to remain calm despite his anger.
"I do apologize for this Lucy, it's really unfortunate that you found out this way. It's not how it should be and I will certainly take this up with Mr. Cannon directly."
Lucy Flint had no issue with what Cannon had done and told Walsh that it wasn't a problem. He didn't see it the same way but decided not to say so.
"Mr. Cannon indicated that something had happened to this *brother*," she said, "Is that why you needed to speak to me about Stefan?"
Walsh decided that it was best to lay the cards on the table and fill her in on what they knew. He wasn't sure what Cannon had told her. Perhaps she was already aware?
"I may as well let you know," he said. "Stefan's brother's death is, unfortunately, now the subject of a murder inquiry."
Silence.
Walsh waited for a few seconds before saying.
"Are you there Lucy?"
"Yes, yes," came the reply. "I was just thinking about things. Sorry Inspector but it's a lot to take in. Do you know what happened?"
"At this stage, we are still investigating. We are following up some leads but now that we know that there was a link between the two inquiries we have been conducting, we believe we are getting closer to an answer."
"Is there anything else you need from me then?"
"No, not just yet. We may need to speak with you again, once we have more information but at this stage, I don't think I need to bother you in the short term. I just wanted to keep you informed as necessary."
Lucy Flint thanked him for the call and he hung up the phone.

Seconds later he picked up the receiver again. He was going to blast Cannon for his interference.

After an earful from Walsh, Cannon called Timms.
Timms acknowledged and understood the position that Cannon was in and accepted that his focus was on *RockGod's* final preparations for the *National* now only three days away.
Cannon relayed his suspicions about Flint.

In return, Timms shared the information that he and his team had been gathering and collating in relation to the races that they believe had been fixed over the past few weeks. This included *RockGod's* recent win at Sandown.
"You still don't think I had anything to do with what happened at Sandown, do you?" asked Cannon.
"No Mike, I don't. We think we know what happened, but I'll share it with you once confirmed."
"Thank God for small mercies," Cannon replied and put down the phone.
He was beginning to form an idea as to how the races were being manipulated but he needed to sleep on it.

He slept fitfully. It was becoming a habit. Michelle decided to sleep on the couch in the lounge as his tossing and turning kept waking her.
Was it the excitement or fear, the questions still unanswered or something else that swirled in his mind? Whatever it was, it was still unclear when he woke up. He noticed the empty space beside him. He walked into the lounge in the darkness and apologized.

CHAPTER 46

Cannon watched through his binoculars.

His mind was not on the second lot as they went through their paces and he was struggling to concentrate. He should have been at Aintree by now but his horse *Visitation* had been scratched the day he spoke with Lucy and let slip the finding of the two brothers. The horse had come down with a temperature and it was not possible to race. To some extent given what had happened since then, it was probably a good thing. The Airbnb would stay empty until they arrived tomorrow. The meeting had started. With brighter weather expected during the festival, despite it being cold, clear and with no rain, that would ensure a good crowd would attend every day.

Rich, who stood beside him as the horses thundered by in pairs, had continued to run the day to day operation of the stables while Cannon was down in London. As always, Rich had done a great job.

Despite the big race on Saturday, there were still other races beyond the coming weekend. Much more racing. The industry didn't stop after the Aintree festival. *Harvester*, *TheMan* plus other horses in the stable had races that they had been accepted for. Some of Cannon's less experienced horses had been nominated for easier, lower grade races at the more remote courses.

Today, despite the season's *official* end, compared to twenty years ago when jumps racing ceased for several months, the sport continues in some capacity throughout the year, even if on some days there are only point-to-point meetings held. There is now a much more expanded program throughout the year and thank God it is. Better tracks, improved hurdles and fences, making racing less dangerous, have given the industry new life. Without it, many a stable without *flat* horses in their mix would have gone to the wall.

Cannon looked up at the sky. The earlier mist had already begun to dissipate, it was going to be a fine day here too.

"How are you feeling Mike?" asked Telside.

"A bit nervous to be honest Rich. After what I've seen down in London and what happened at Worcester, I have a bad feeling about Saturday."

Telside stayed quiet for a second before saying, "It's the *National* Mike, they'll be so many people around, security will be tight. I can't see how anyone will be able to get at the horse. Plus, I'll be there with him every second until he's on the track."

"I know Rich, and I appreciate that. It's just that we don't know what we are dealing with. Who we are dealing with! I have a view, a theory, which I

gave an outline to Timms last night, but I could be totally wrong."
"Well I wouldn't worry Mike, only time will tell," answered Telside.
"I guess it will," Cannon answered.

The second lot were back in their individual stables after their cooldown, wash and rub. The stables were beginning to quieten down. The staff had predominantly dispersed. Some had gone home to rest before they came back to muck out, before preparing food for the evening stables. Others took time out to catch up with their emails and other social media activities, call friends, play cards. Those with residual energy had gone to ride work elsewhere.
Cannon was back in his office.
Michelle had gone off to school. She would be back a little earlier than normal as she wanted to pack and get ready for the morning. Friday was going to be a long day. They would be leaving for Liverpool at six the next morning while *RockGod* and Rich would be taken by horse transport up to Aintree leaving an hour earlier. The horse would stable there overnight.
Michelle had told Cannon how excited she was about the dinner they would be attending the following evening. The annual Grand National gala dinner for the owners and friends, trainers, and jockeys of the horses entered into the race.
She had bought herself a new dress for the gala evening that she wanted to show off. This was in addition to the suit that she had put away some time ago for a special occasion. She would wear the suit the next day.
The biggest race of the year, with the biggest crowd of the year, was just such an occasion.

Cannon still couldn't concentrate, there were things in his mind that just didn't add up.
Since the call from Walsh, he had struggled with the various thoughts in his head. Flint, Perkel, Lucy, *RockGod*, Worcester, Sandown, Timms, the two unknown brothers with tattoos, *Zeleznik*. Something was missing, he thought.
He picked up the phone on his desk and called Walsh on his mobile.
"The brothers?" he asked without even waiting for a hello from Walsh. "How exactly were they killed?"
Walsh took Umbridge to the question.
"I beg your pardon Mike, I told you to stay out of it," Walsh responded angrily. "The investigation regarding the two brothers as well as that of Perkel is a police matter. It has nothing to do with you!"
Cannon would not be stopped. He asked again, insisted.
Walsh sighed. "One was shot, and as you know already the other drowned. Look, Mike, I'm not sure what you think you're doing but its…"

"Trust me with this Inspector. Something doesn't add up here," he said, "and before you ask me why I want to know, it's quite simple. I have obligations to my family, my team, my owners, the BHA and to myself. I will *not* put any of my family at risk nor have anyone else do the same," he stated animatedly. "I take those responsibilities very seriously. So, I ask again apart from what you have told me to date is there anything unusual about the deaths of the two brothers?"

Walsh looked at the toxicology reports now on his desk. They were as Dr. Davidson had mentioned at the various autopsies. He read out the pertinent parts to Cannon finishing with the conclusions.

"Thank you," Cannon responded, "you've given me what I needed."

"Mike," said Walsh, knowing that Cannon was about to put the phone down, "Mike!" he repeated.

"Yes?"

"I'm not sure what you are up to and I hope you realize that I can arrest you if you get in my way regarding these cases."

"Yes, I know," said Cannon, "but I'm convinced you won't. After all, we are on the same side."

"That may well be, but if you have anything that you think is pertinent to these cases, you need to share it," he said, "I'll remind you I did the same for you, at potential risk to my own career."

"Yes, I know and I appreciate it," Cannon replied. "As I told you myself, I think this is all about money and it has been all along. The only thing I've not been able to work out so far is who has been benefitting. I think I know that now," he said.

"Are you going to tell me?"

"I think it was the two brothers," he said.

Walsh wasn't prepared for the answer. Nor did he agree.

"How did you work that out?" he asked.

"It just fits," Cannon continued, "the use of fictitious names, the tattoos, the lies they obviously told Lucy Flint. Why would they do that if they didn't have anything to hide?"

"But hang on Mike. You haven't said *how* they were benefitting, in fact not even given me anything to believe you even know *what* they were doing."

"I'm still working on it."

"And what about *who* killed them"

"I believe I know that now."

"And?"

"After the *National*," he said by way of closing the conversation.

"Mike!" shouted Walsh down the phone "Mike, you can't! I'll have you arrested....,"

Cannon had swiftly ended the conversation and was already picking up the phone again to call Timms by the time Walsh looked at his mobile and realized the connection had been severed.

CHAPTER 47

They had originally all met up at the Airbnb in Chester that morning. Michelle, Cassie and Blake spending the afternoon enjoying each other's company and getting ready for the race eve dinner, while Cannon had been at the course waiting, then arranging, for *RockGod* to be properly stabled once he arrived.
According to Rich who travelled with the horse, the trip had been uneventful though it had taken them nearly 5 hours to get to the track due to the increased traffic heading towards Liverpool.
"Tomorrow could be a nightmare for you," said Telside once they had settled the horse in his stable for the rest of the day.
"Don't worry Rich," Cannon had responded, "I'll be there just after seven in the morning, no matter how late the dinner goes tonight."

Now they were seated at a table of six in the restaurant of the Hilton City Centre Hotel, just off Strand Street on Thomas Steers Way. It had been chosen by the Jockey Club for the annual Grand National eve gala dinner. Normally attended by owners and friends, trainers, and their families. In the past, most jockeys would make an appearance and then get away early but in recent times some jockeys preferred to stay away completely. Cannon wasn't sure if he would see Timms at the event, he had not seen him so far.
Blake was indeed a very pretty girl. Eighteen in years but much more adult than Cassie. In fact, Cannon thought, she seemed too sophisticated for his daughter. Despite that, he also noticed how Cassie had grown, changed from the girl who left for university only seven months ago. She seemed to have suddenly matured, no longer his baby. He hadn't really been able to spend too much time with them during the day, but now he had a few hours where he could relax and catch up with his daughter, but first, he had to entertain Flint.
RockGod's owner had arrived at the function just as the pre-dinner drinks were concluding and people were being encouraged to move to their tables. He joined them after excusing himself for being late, saying that his train had been delayed leaving London mid-afternoon. He took the empty seat between Blake on his left and Simon McCorkindale, *RockGods'* jockey, to his right. Cannon was sitting directly opposite him between Cassie and Michelle. During the evening Cannon spent an inordinate amount of time watching Flint. The man showed no signs of pressure or nervousness, despite recent events. There was no evidence to suggest that Flint was even excited about the race the following day. When Cannon asked him about

Viking Spirit and his injury, Flint just shrugged it off, preferring not to discuss it, but rather spending more time talking with Blake. Initially, it just seemed like friendly banter, but as the evening went on, Cannon could see Blake was beginning to become more uncomfortable. Growing up too fast was not always a good idea. Most of the conversation in the room was about the festival results over the past couple of days and how the track was holding up to the big field of horses in each race. There had been a few fallers as expected and a number of well-fancied runners not having run up to expectations. The noise in the room grew as the evening progressed. People came and went to various tables, wishing the best of luck to the connections of their opposition. It was like a family gathering. Many of the larger stables had multiple entries in the race, and having had runners for successive years, the evening had become a regular event to them. To Michelle and Cassie, the night was magical just being part of it. The drying weather expected the next day was also talked about. Cannon discussed tactics with his jockey but knew that it would be more about luck in running than anything else. Forty runners jumping over the famous fences meant anything could happen. The only advice Cannon could give was to stay wide and stay out of trouble. The rest he would leave to his experienced rider. Flint showed only cursory interest in the discussion about the race. His mind was elsewhere.

Simon McCorkindale left the table early to go back to his hotel around 9:30 pm, with the formal part of the evening coming to an end just after 10 pm.

A wish from the stage where the festivities for the evening were managed from, that all in the race came back safe, was welcomed with a cheer and a final toast.

He had always believed that no one would be able to trace him. He swapped phones often enough, only giving the number applicable for a specific period to those he trusted most. Yet there it was. A message, from Madzia's people reminding him of the debt that was due. Williams only had a few weeks left before he needed to settle. They *knew* he needed the right result tomorrow. It was a warning.

Darkness surrounded them. Cannon lay in bed, with Michelle's head on his chest, his arm around her shoulders. It was just before midnight. His day starting in less than five hours.

"Did you enjoy the evening?" he asked.

"Of course, I did Mike," she answered enthusiastically. "I think we all did. Even Cassie said so when we went to use the bathroom. It was amazing to see all those personalities, sense all the excitement. Yes, it was a wonderful

evening. Didn't you have a good time?"
Cannon didn't respond immediately.
"What about Blake?" he asked, "do you think she enjoyed it too?"
Michelle turned towards him, resting slightly on her hip, head up off the pillow trying to see his face. Her eyes adjusting to the slight sliver of light coming through the curtains from a streetlamp outside.
"That's a strange question Mike, why do you ask?"
"Just asking," he responded nonchalantly.
"She seemed to enjoy it, yes."
"Good."
The answer wasn't the right one. She knew him too well.
"Mike!" she said, raising her voice from their initial whispered conversation, "what is it? What's bothering you?"
Cannon sighed. He was never sure what to say when it came to his gut feeling about women, especially younger ones.
"I think she's too old for Cassie," he said eventually.
Michelle smiled, giving him a brief kiss on the lips before falling back to put her head on the pillow.
"You're getting old Mike," she said jokingly. He could sense a smile on her face.
Thinking about it for a few seconds he then said, "I guess you're right. I must be."
"I wouldn't worry about Cassie if I were you," she encouraged him, "she's a smart girl."
"What do you mean?" he asked, "I'm just worried about her...."
"Growing up?" she interrupted.
"Yes, I suppose so," he answered.
They both lay silently for a minute. Cannon wasn't sure if she had fallen asleep. His eyes were heavy as well. The few drinks he had had over the evening beginning to take their toll. It had been a really long day.
"She's aware of what she is doing Mike," Michelle eventually said softly. "Believe me, she's already worked it out. Blake may be a friend, a bit more grown-up than Cassie, bit more *experienced* shall we say, but believe me Cassie knows what's right and what's' wrong. She knows a lot more than you will probably give her credit for. Blake won't be around forever, Cassie will move on, she's got her head screwed on properly."
"She looked gorgeous tonight, didn't she?"
"Yes, she did."
"You both did," he added.
"Thank you, Mike, you didn't look too bad yourself."
He laughed, pulling her closer to him.
"You should be proud," she continued, snuggling into his arms, "you've done a great job with Cassie. A great job."

CHAPTER 48

He was walking the course, the full *National* track. All 16 fences. The horses had to go around twice, fortunately only jumping the *Chair* and the *Water* jumps once, but they had to navigate over *Beechers Brook, Foinavon* and the *Canal Turn* twice.

Cannon had left the house while Michelle and the girls were still sleeping. They would make their own way to the course. He expected them around midday. The first race was off just before two pm.

He had already been to see *RockGod*. Rich had spent the whole night sleeping next to him along with his groom Ted Seedle who would parade him to the masses when the big race came. They did not want to take any chances.

Fortunately, they were not disturbed. Just the soft sneeze of the horse and a snort every now and again had broken the quiet, the stillness.

RockGod was primed. He appeared to know what was coming and all the noise rippling across to the stables from inside and outside the course was reaching the horses' ears. Media trucks, police sirens, the hum and bustle of human activity still in its earliest stages of the day were intruding on the relative quiet of the night which was now losing traction to the morning. It was up to Rich and Ted to keep him calm. The race itself was still 9 hours plus away.

They were two of many. Hundreds of people, spread over two-and-a-half miles who were braving the early morning chill just as Cannon and McCorkindale were. Cannon wrapped his unbuttoned coat around himself, a habit of a lifetime. He hardly ever buttoned them up, preferring to tie together the attached belt, if there was one. If not, he would hold it closed with his hands.

They were walking up the straight heading towards the *Chair,* the most feared fence of all. A stretch across an 11 foot or 3.5m spread. This was due to a 6 foot, 1.83m ditch, directly in front of the 5 foot 3 inch, or 1.6m high fence.

The sun was trying to burn off the mist, working together with the slight breeze that blew in over the North Sea. The temperature was hovering around 5 degrees centigrade but was still expected to reach around 12 by the time of the race.

The grass on the course was damp. The going, the state of the track, was expected to be classed as *Good*. There had been no rain over the past three days and the track had dried out quite well. Cannon thought back to only a short while ago when the incessant rain resulted in race meetings across the

After the Fire

country being cancelled or abandoned. At one point he had his doubts as to whether the race would even take place, or indeed if he would ever get *RockGod* race fit in time.

"What do you think?" he asked McCorkindale.

"Should be okay Guv'nor," he answered, "he doesn't mind it when there is a bit of spring in the ground. If it dries out a bit more though it will be perfect for him."

"And for a couple of the others, I suspect?"

"Yes, it works both ways I suppose," answered the jockey, who already had had a winner and a second over the past few days of the festival. He'd also had a fall.

"How's your shoulder?" asked Cannon.

"It's fine this morning," he answered. "It was a bit stiff last night, but I slept okay and the massage immediately after the fall helped ease it, so I'm good to go. Don't worry," he smiled.

"Glad to hear."

They continued walking up the track towards the finishing line. Grey outlines of buildings poked out of the mist in the distance. The flags flew half-heartedly, fluttering slightly now and again on their poles that sat on top of the famous grandstands to the right.

Various groups were standing at irregular intervals alongside the course straight, looking at the ground, talking quietly amongst themselves. Trainers, owners, and jockeys all discussing race tactics now that the big day had dawned. The weather always plays a big part in the outcome of the race and it created all manner of different scenarios depending upon whether a runner enjoyed muddy or soft tracks or dryer and more firm ones. It seemed that today the race would be run on a track that was drying out. Cannon was pleased, he didn't need it to rain, that would ruin their chances.

"Time for breakfast?" he asked.

"For some," answered McCorkindale a wry smile on his face, "I've got a few pounds to shed, unfortunately, due to an early ride in race one. I don't want to carry overweight," he said, "it's a three-and-a-half-mile hurdle and I've got a chance in it."

"Well good luck," said Cannon and they shook hands, "I'll see you later."

He watched his jockey walk away towards the stands, slowly disappearing in the mist still lingering in places at ground level. McCorkindale seemed to disappear like a ghost. One minute he was there, the next he was gone.

For a second Cannon felt alone, isolated, a cold shiver ran up his back. A premonition? Of what? He hoped it wasn't a sign. He didn't believe in that type of thing. He had slept peacefully and woken in a positive mood.

As he had driven to the track he had gone over the events of the previous evening, then he had switched his thoughts to today. The biggest day of his training career. Was it possible for them to win the most famous

After the Fire

steeplechase in the world? It was his first attempt. Time would tell.

It was the phone call he had expected but dreaded. An unknown number on his mobile, but he knew who it was. Flints' normal confidence was being shattered. Did he really trust Williams? And what options did he have anyway? At this stage he had none. He hoped the deal they had struck was enough, but he doubted it. He needed to find a way out of it but was that even possible?
That was a question was for another day.
The prevailing question needing an answer to, was how to prevent *RockGod* from winning the race?
It was out of his hands. It always had been. He could try and have the horse scratched, but on what basis?
He didn't think it was an option anyway. Whatever Williams was planning, he needed the horse to run. So many questions and so few answers. Flint felt trapped. Was he being hung by his own petard?
"Good morning, *Charles,*" said Williams.
The voice sounded so remote, so removed, so robotic. He realized he was no longer Mr. Flint, he was now *owned,* a commodity. At least that's what it felt like. He didn't like it.
"Fuck off!"
"Tut-tut," Williams replied, "such language! That's not like you, *Charles,*" he continued, re-emphasizing Flint's name, sarcasm dripping down the line.
Flint had even surprised himself at his vitriolic response.
He felt slightly emboldened, his self-belief returning.
"What do you want?" he asked.
"Did you enjoy the evening last night?"
"What is it to you?" Flint reacted angrily.
"Young girls hey? So delicate, so easily used. So easily…consumed," Williams said lasciviously.
Flint knew what he meant. God, had they been watching him?
He couldn't help himself, could he? She had been so attentive initially. She had flirted with him. He had touched her leg with his hand. He had enjoyed the feel of her skin, just above the knee. But she had reacted. Negatively. Moving away. Closer to the other girl, Cannons daughter. Had Cannon noticed?
"You see Charles, I have eyes everywhere. I'm watching everything you do. It could a waiter, a taxi driver, just someone standing next to you," Williams said through gritted teeth. "So, don't fuck with me, or you'll be hearing a knock on your door anytime soon, and it won't be your local pizza delivery man. Do you hear me?!"
Flint sudden felt small, alone. The bravado he has built up was gone in an

instant. Burst like a balloon popping.

He stayed silent. Noise from the corridor of his hotel room as people passed by the only sound. He sat on his bed waiting. It was nearly ten o'clock. He had eaten breakfast in his room, was almost dressed and was ready to leave for the racecourse. His transport, a private car, booked for 10:15.

Williams continued, his words precise, more measured. "It's quite a simple proposition, one which we've discussed before. I want you to back your horse. I want you to put on as much money on it as possible. To win!" he said, "but just make sure it doesn't."

"You know I can't do that," Flint wailed, "winning the race is out of my hands."

"I know," replied Williams, laughing as he disconnected the call.

He hadn't seen Timms the previous evening, so he called him once McCorkindale had left.

"I'm on track already Mike," came the reply when asked where he was. "My team and I have a lot of work to do today as you can imagine. We'll be watching the betting throughout the day on all the races."

"What about the exchanges?" Cannon asked.

"Those as well. Any plunges, or unusual patterns we'll hopefully be able to spot."

"So, across all platforms?"

"Yes, on course, and on the web."

"What about betting shops?"

"That will be a little bit harder, but what happens there should flow through to the exchanges."

Cannon didn't know how things would play out, but he believed he was getting close.

While he had told Walsh some of his theory, he had expanded upon it with Timms. He hoped he was right.

"Okay, I don't think I will have time to see you until after the race. I've got a couple of TV, radio and press interviews to go to now, and then lunch with Flint and the family. After that, until the race itself I'll be with the horse," he said. "Unfortunately, it means leaving the girls in the company of Flint."

"How are *you* feeling Mike?" asked Timms.

"Nervous," he replied, "very very nervous. And not just about the race."

Their early lunch was nearly over. They were in the 1839 restaurant, situated in the Dodson and Horrell Owners and Trainers suite, directly opposite the

After the Fire

parade ring. The noise both inside and outside the facility was unbelievable. 75000 people were expected at the meeting. Traffic around the course was being managed as it always was. Effective and efficiently, but with a few broken down cars causing hold-ups in certain roads leading towards approved parking areas, the authorities had their hands full.

It seemed like everyone wanted to arrive at the same time. Passes needed to be checked. Many of those streaming to the course went to the wrong gates. Those with the wrong tickets or passes were sent in the appropriate direction. It was just after 1 O'clock but some of the women, despite being dressed in their finery already looked the worse for wear. This was before they had the chance to get into the course. Many were carrying their high heeled shoes in their hands as they walked bare feet, despite the cold, to try and find their correct gate. Men likewise, ties skewed, coats and waistcoats open, struggled to find where they needed to be. Nothing new. Those too intoxicated were turned away. Shouts and arguments ensued. Voices raised added to the cacophony.

Thank God they had arrived early. Cannon had told Michelle to make sure she and the girls were settled inside the dining area before 11:30 am and had scoped out the best vantage points to watch the races. They had decided to stand on the steps of the Queen Mother Stand. They preferred standing despite Cannon advising Michelle of the likely impact on their feet if they didn't find a seat.

Flint had seemed subdued at lunch. He had tried to hide it.
Blake had stayed away from him when they sat down to eat, preferring to sit between Michelle and Cassie.
"How have you enjoyed things so far?" Cannon asked her.
"It's been lovely," Blake answered, "my mum and dad were so happy for me when Cassie asked me to come."
"Well we are happy to have you here," Cannon said, noticing that behind Blake's eyes he could see the girl. She had been intimidated, frightened by Flint the previous evening and though she had tried to hide it, from Cassie, and even herself, Cannon could see it, sense it. Michelle could see it too. Cannon and Michelle looked at each other. With an imperceptible nod of agreement, they excused themselves from the table. Michelle and the girls went off towards the stands and Cannon walked off towards the stables. He felt even angrier towards Flint. He would meet him again in the parade ring in just over two hours.

Talking to the media about *RockGod's* chances took longer than he had expected but eventually, Cannon was able to make his way through the

After the Fire

crowds, past the various security checks and reach the stable block where he caught up with Rich and Ted Seedle.

Inside the stable block, a number of horses were being walked the length of the building by their grooms, then turned and walked to the opposite end. It looked like organized chaos but in fact was just a gentle warm-up, a simple walk. Some of the other *National* runners remained in their allocated stable, resting.

All the horses would spend at least 15 minutes walking around the parade ring before they then got onto the track and were able to stretch their legs a little more. Nearly all would be ridden up to the first fence to have a look at the obstacle. Most jockeys liked to look beyond it, into the distance towards *Beechers Brook* where the challenge really lay. The neat piles of birch spreading across the whole width of the track looked like rows of fallen trees. The majority of each fence was about to be smashed and strewn across the track as the field of 40 runners stormed towards and through them.

Cannon hoped that nothing would go wrong and that his horse and rider would come home safely. He had a feeling of trepidation, however.

"How is it going?" he asked.

"Old boy is taking everything in his stride," replied Rich smiling, "he's the consummate professional, aren't you boy?" he continued, slapping the horse on the neck and rubbing the side of his face. A bright, deep brown eye twitched as if to answer back.

"Anything odd happened? Any sign of anyone hanging around?"

"With all the security around the place Mike, I don't think anyone would try."

"How about the farrier?"

"Been and gone Mr. Cannon," said Ted. "The *'God* has got his racing plates on. Both Mr. Telside here and I watched him do it. Finished about 20 minutes ago," Ted explained.

Cannon heaved a sigh of relief, but he still wasn't convinced that they were in the clear. Something was going to happen. He just had that feeling. He didn't know what to expect, but he was being extremely cautious. Winning the *National* could be a huge fillip for the stable but if *RockGod* fell and hurt himself, who knew how that would affect the future.

"Can I see his feet?"

Rich picked up the horses' back legs in succession. Cannon was satisfied that the farrier had done a good job. In turn, Rich did the same with the front legs. Cannon standing behind Rich as his assistant bent the legs and was able to show Cannon the feet. Ted held *RockGod's* head.

"I guess it's up to McCorkindale now," Cannon said.

"Yep," replied Rich, "it's in the lap-of-the-God's now."

After the Fire

The sun had been slow to make an appearance. The earlier races had been run in a grey gloom. The silks of the jockeys had seemed dull and most came back after each race with black mud and dirt on them. The course was cutting up a little making the race seem a little longer. Heavy ground meant a race was often about stamina, as much as it was about bravery and jumping ability.

During the running of the fourth race, a Grade 1 Stayers Hurdle, the sun eventually broke through. Melting away the cloud. The shadows they had been creating over the track disappearing like ghosts retreating from the coming dawn. The crowd roared as much for the suns arrival as it did for the horses contesting the event.

Along with the breeze, the sun would help the track dry out to ensure a *Good* track condition in time for the main race.

Flint wandered around, pushing his way through the crowds. Was he beginning to become a little paranoid? Had Cannon looked at him strangely at lunch? Had the girl said anything about last night? He remembered the tingle of pleasure that ran through him when he felt the girl's thigh. He wanted to feel that pleasure again.

He looked around at the women sitting in the seats of the Princess Royal Stand and managed to find an empty spot to sit down. A patron had suddenly stood up as he walked by so he quickly took the seat.

The women intrigued him. He noticed how flimsy some of the dresses were and how the younger ones, in particular, were not wearing coats or jackets despite the cold. It excited him. For a moment he forgot Cannon and Williams. His eyes focused on a girl seated two rows ahead of him and to his right. She was no older than 15 he thought. She sat with a party of four others. Two sisters he estimated at between 18 and 21, and what he guessed were the parents. They seemed to be discussing what was happening on the track, pointing at their racecards and the runners contesting the event.

Flint couldn't hear the commentary, the roar of the crowd, he could only see the young girl. He began fantasizing in his mind about her, then suddenly his mobile rang, breaking his concentration. Williams again.

Despite putting his phone to his right ear and pressing a finger to his left, he couldn't hear what was being said. He shouted down the phone telling Williams that he couldn't hear. As he waited for the crescendo of noise to die down as the race concluded, he realized the line was already dead. A message was already on his screen. He looked at it in terror. *'I'm watching you,'* the screen displayed. *'If this goes wrong, You're DEAD.'*

Flint looked around, scanning faces. His mind was beginning to play tricks on him. Everywhere he looked people were staring at him. Were they? Or did he imagine it? Then he saw a face. Williams, ten rows below him, looking back at him. Then suddenly he was gone. How could such a big man just disappear like that? Flint was beginning to crumble inside. Crack. He didn't know what to do. He needed to think.

CHAPTER 49

Up to 600 million viewers in over 140 countries worldwide would be watching them race for over half a million pounds first prize. Forty runners with the hopes of millions riding on their backs. *RockGod* was still the second favourite but had firmed in the betting to 9 to 1. The favourite *Silver Surfer* was at 8 to 1.
Cannon stood in the parade ring along with Michelle, the girls, and Flint. McCorkindale was already aboard the horse who was prancing around, up on his toes, letting the public and the other runners know that he was ready for the race.
"Cocky, isn't he?" he said to Flint.
The owner appeared miles away. It was beginning to warm up a little, especially when standing in full sun but Cannon noticed how pale Flint was looking. How he kept scanning the crowd as *RockGod* walked around parading with the other runners.
"Oh, sorry," replied Flint. "I was just enjoying the moment. Got carried away." he lied. "Yes, he's looking really well. You've done an excellent job, Mike."
"Are you having a bet, Mr. Flint?" asked Cassie, "on *RockGod?*"
"Just a small one," he answered, without enthusiasm, "I don't want to jinx him."
The runners were called to leave the ring and parade on the track itself so that the majority of the crowd, as well as the TV audience, could get a better view of the powerful equine athletes.
Tradition dictated a walk from the ring to the winning post of each runner which then allowed them to turn 180 degrees and head towards the starting line.
The crowd roared as each of the runners were turned around by their grooms then bucked or kicked as they cantered away. The colours of the jockey's silks initially in a shadow from the main grandstand blazed in the sunlight. A mixture of reds, yellows, blues, pinks, purples, and blacks contrasted with the whites of the jockey's breeches.

Around the starting line, people gathered on either side of the track. It was five minutes before the *off* time.

People were crossing the track, some going to the inside, others to the outer. Each had a preference as to where they were going to watch the spectacle. For many, they had no choice. Their tickets or passes allowed them limited access to the various parts of the course. Others such as owners and trainers had extensive access to wherever they wanted to go.

"Are you watching the race with us Charles?" asked Cannon. He was beginning to wonder whether his suspicions were true or had he been wrong. He was convinced of part of the answer, but time would tell if he was right with the rest. He had shared some of them with Timms and Walsh during the course of their recent conversations.

"No, I'm going to watch in the owners and trainers bar," he said. "as you know I normally stay away from the track itself. Too many people, too much noise. I prefer to watch it in relative peace."

Cannon was suspicious. He doubted whether the bar in question would be as quiet as Flint expected it to be and said so. He was trying to keep him close but had no way of doing so without it becoming obvious.

"Okay," he replied. "I hope to see you later then. Maybe in the winner's box?" he said smiling.

He noticed Flint's reaction. A short look of dread on his face before a false smile replaced it.

"Yes, I do hope so," Flint responded, "I will see you later. Good luck."

They shook hands and Flint said his goodbyes to Cannon and Michelle. The girls had already gone off to find their viewing spot.

Michelle looked at Cannon, surprised that Flint had decided to wander off into the crowd and not watch the race with them.

"What's all that about?" she asked. "The man seems lost, almost as if he doesn't care."

"Umm," responded Mike. "I'm sure he cares," he said, looking towards the place where he had last seen Flint disappearing into the crowd. "The question is. About what?"

Thirty fences, four-and-a-quarter miles and between nine to ten minutes of racing lay ahead of the horses as they waited in line for the starter to raise the tapes standing between them and the first fence.

The crowd was now at its maximum. Seventy-five thousand excited racegoers. A heaving massing of humanity crammed into pens, shouting out the names of the horses or jockeys that their hopes were literally riding on.

As the starter climbed the famous platform to start the race, the noise rose as the excitement built. TV audiences and commentators around the world

held their collective breath for what seemed like an eternity but was less than a second before the field was sent on its way.
In an instant, the roar of the crowd magnified and whips cracked against flanks as jockeys changed positions from sitting on their mounts' backs to standing in their stirrups. The biggest most popular steeplechase in the world was underway.
Cannon tracked *RockGod* through his binoculars as the field raced in cavalry charge formation towards the first fence. As the horses left the ground at the first obstacle, Cannon lost sight of his horse in the blur of colour. At first, he thought the horse had fallen but Michelle quickly pointed out where the horse was and Cannon relaxed a little. McCorkindale had done exactly as he was asked to do. He had taken the horse to the outside of the course, keeping away from trouble and the tight bunching of the leaders sticking to the inside. He was staying in the back half of the runners for now. There was a long way to go.

Flint was relatively calm. His horse was racing fifteen lengths off the leaders and in about 18th position as the wall of horses headed towards *Beechers Brook*.
He had noticed Williams' minder, Teal, been following him. The man had an earpiece in and despite the noise around him was talking to someone. Flint guessed it was Williams.
Flint pushed his way through the crowd, bumping and shoving.
Teal followed.

After *Beechers* for the first time, there was still a large contingent of horses vying for the lead. At least four of them ran abreast as the pace continued unrelentingly towards the Canal Turn, the ninety-degree angle which the runners had to cross before heading back towards the stands, the *Chair*, and the *Water* jump.
As they crashed over the fence two runners came down in a tangle of legs and bodies. Jockeys being separated from their mounts, rolling across the turf like armadillo's, arms and heads tucked in to prevent being kicked or stood on by the remaining contestants.

Cannon noticed that the field of horses was starting to string out already. At least three had already pulled up and there were six fallers so far. The race was more brutal it seemed this year than last. At the head of the field, *Silver Surfer*, the favourite sat quietly in third position. *RockGod* was in ninth position about 6 lengths off the pace, but still going strongly. The jockey sitting quietly on his back.

Flint looked up at the big screen that stood on the inside of the track. He watched his own colours successfully clear fence twelve. He was now standing in a virtual sea of people, lower down from the stands, towards the track itself. He looked around him. He couldn't see Teal. As he turned back to face the screen again, he knocked a man's arm and spilt some of the beer the man was holding over himself. Expletives were shouted at him as he continued to push through the crowd. Out of the corner of his eye, he saw Williams. He continued pushing through the mass of people. He needed to get away. He didn't have a plan, but the stalking was unsettling him, he was beginning to panic. He had no control about what was happening on the track, but the outcome of the race could determine his fate. He had been in control most of his life. Now it appeared to be spinning out of control. What would happen to him if *RockGod* did win? His judgment was starting to leave him. He didn't know what he was doing. This wasn't a place he was comfortable with. There were too many people he had no power over. Somehow, he needed to get away. He continued pushing his way through the masses.

What was Flint up too, Williams thought? Where was he going? He knew that if *RockGod* won the race, Flint was dead. He would kill him himself. Before he himself needed to run. To get away from Madzia. He would disappear and find a place in the sun somewhere.

The leaders headed towards the *Chair*. There were still twenty-eight horses still racing, spread out over a distance of about two hundred metres. At the fence, two more came down, though *Silver Surfer* sailed over it in second place. *RockGod* in fifth. The crowd roared even louder as the runners passed the stands heading out on the second circuit. The favourite now leading.

Cannon admired *RockGod's* incessant rhythm, his action. Michelle, Cassie, and Blake screamed their support as they stood alongside him. Everyone in the stands now on their feet. Flint's racing colours stood out as the horses wheeled away back towards fence number one, now fence number seventeen. As he watched, it suddenly hit him.
He now knew what was going on. It had been there right in front of his eyes.
Michelle grabbed his arm, shouting above the noise as she did so.
"Mike! Mike! The horse is jumping so well. He going to win, I know it!"
"Still a long way to go," he shouted back.

Flint watched the screen as *Silver Surfer* fell at *Fioinavon,* brought down by a loose horse that was a few lengths ahead and that suddenly swerved in front of him refusing to jump at the last minute. The favourite's jockey had no chance, landing heavily as he crashed through the birch, sending pieces of it flying in all directions. A huge groan erupted from the stands. A large sigh of relief drifted silently from the bookmakers stands on course and in the betting shops around the country.

There were now only three horses in the leading group. *RockGod* had moved up into second place and was still running strongly. Behind the front trio, a further five horses raced on. The remaining runners had no real chance of winning. The jockeys persisted. Finishing the race was the best that they could hope for.

Cannon was getting excited, but not too far ahead of himself. His confidence was growing. Three fences to go then the run home.

Flint was wide-eyed. No! He had reached the railing separating the track from the public. He looked to his left and could see the horses running towards him, towards the last two fences. Around him, arms were waving. People screaming. Everyone looking towards the big screen to get a better perspective of how the final moments of the race were unfolding. *RockGod* and two other horses were disputing the lead. Jockeys furiously urging their mounts on towards victory, immortality.
Looking around, Teal and Williams were less than five yards away. Both looking towards him. Eyes darting between their target and the big screen. Images that could potentially seal their fates.

Cannon began to shout. He punched the air as *RockGod* cleared the penultimate fence, taking the lead from the forty-to-one shot, *Arthurs Sword*. Only one to go.

Flint was stunned. What was happening, he thought? The recent threats he had been trying to escape were now so real. All because of a horse that *he* owned! His worst nightmare coming true. He had visions of being exposed for his excesses, his perversions. Fear filled his head. Trials. Humiliation. Prison. Loss of liberty. His freedom, gone! Life was not worth living! He climbed under the railing onto the track. He ran towards the last fence.

Williams realized what was happening before anyone else did. It couldn't happen. He wouldn't let it. Not when he was so close.
Flint was trying to stop the race. Doing so would void the outcome. A no result, as in 1993. His investment would be lost. No one would win. He would be dead.
He scrambled under the railing. He needed to catch Flint quickly.

Cannon, like millions around TV screens, and those on course, watched in horror as two men, one behind the other ran, arms flailing, towards the final fence.

The jockeys, head down, arms pumping, shouting, screaming, urged their mounts on towards the last barrier and on to glory. *RockGod* still a half-length ahead of *Arthurs Sword*.

The two men didn't stand a chance. A half a ton of muscle travelling at over thirty miles an hour hit them on the landing side of the fence. Williams had tried to wrestle Flint away from the obstacle just as the runners reached it. Security men in orange jackets had been too late to reach them or indeed notify the jockeys of what was happening. Flint was killed on impact, his neck snapping as he was crumpled under *RockGod*, a hoof smashing into his face as the horse thrashed out as it tried to stand up, post-impact. Williams had tried to dive out of the way as he saw the shadow of the horses from out of the corner of his eye as they leapt the fence. He broke his back when *Arthurs Sword* trampled him. He died later on the way to the hospital, never regaining consciousness.

Silence abounded. The course attendees seeing the carnage unfold on the big screen, but not really believing it.

Cannon shook his head. He had his arms around Michelle and the girls. They were sobbing. No one on the stand that they were watching the race from had moved. *RockGod* had been caught after losing his jockey. From a distance, it looked to Cannon that the horse was okay. He had checked through his binoculars a short while earlier that McCorkindale was up and walking around okay. *Arthurs Sword* it appeared was still down on the ground, a blue curtain had quickly been pulled around the scene now being played out at the final fence. Ambulances, Paramedics busying themselves.

An announcement about the result of the race being postponed was relayed over the public address system.

It didn't matter anymore.

Cannon's mobile began to ring. He asked the girls if he could take it. It was Walsh.

"You were right," he said.

Cannon closed the call without responding. There would be time for conversation later. As he went to put the phone back into his jacket pocket, he saw the text from Timms. *I'm so sorry,* it said.

CHAPTER 50

They were standing on the pavement outside her building.
It was going to be a difficult conversation. Sad in a way thought Cannon. He, Walsh and Sedgefield. It seemed unnecessary for all of them to be there.
She opened the door, letting them in.
"I didn't expect all three of you," she said.
"I guess not," replied Walsh, "but Mr. Cannon, *Mike* has something to say."
She invited them to sit down where they could. Lucy sat in the same chair she had done when Cannon last visited. She again sat with her hands in her lap. Looking down.
Cannon and Walsh took a seat on the couch. Sedgefield remained standing. She smiled at him after he declined another chair.
"Firstly, let me say I am so sorry for your loss," Cannon said. "I know you may not have been on speaking terms with your father, but nonetheless, losing him on Saturday in the way that he died must be difficult for you?"
She didn't respond immediately, continuing to look at her hands.
They waited for her to react.
Eventually, she proffered a simple, "Thank you."
Cannon looked at Walsh, who gave him the briefest of nods to continue. It was his theory after all.
"Why did you do it?" he asked.
She looked up, looking straight into his eyes, then asked, "I'm sorry Mr. Cannon, I'm not sure what you mean? Do what?"
Cannon pointed towards Walsh and Sedgefield in turn.
"Give the police the run-around. Fob them off?"
She frowned her face blank, then a change reflecting confusion.
"I really have no clue what you are talking about, *Mike*."
He had expected it to be difficult, it always was. He knew he had to be bold. It was still a theory, but he believed it was the right one.

After the Fire

"Lucy," he said. "I'm referring to you telling Inspector Walsh here that your boyfriend was Stefan Kaminski, and that he was a part-time chef and a Masters student."

"He was," she answered, insisting, "that's what he told me. Believe me," she pleaded.

"But it wasn't true, was it?" he asked.

"It was. It was," she repeated, running her hands through her hair. The pink and green streaks that she was wearing merging together.

"So why did you kill him?" he asked pointedly.

Sitting as she was, she stared at him. Her eyes darkened, then glistened. Tears formed. She held them back as best she could.

"I didn't kill my boyfriend, Mr. Cannon," she replied, her shoulders beginning to slowly heave and up and down. Her body was beginning to tremble slightly.

"Then it was his brother," Cannon stated. "You killed his brother. Why?"

Walsh was about to speak. He wasn't sure this was the right place for this conversation. Maybe it was better down at the police station? He opened his mouth to say so but Cannon hushed him, with a wave of his hand.

Slowly she lifted her head. Tears slowly ran down her cheeks. She sniffed, wiping her nose on the back of her hand before she took a rag from her pocket. Cannon noticed the paint on it.

She took a deep breath.

"Because he raped me," she said angrily. "The bastard raped me, Mr. Cannon. He took advantage of me, like so many others have and so I killed him," she stated unemotionally, robotically.

Walsh sat on the edge of the chair and leaned forward.

"He was a big man," he said almost incredulously, disbelieving. "What stopped him killing you? And why didn't you just report the rape to the police?" he asked.

"Because I had had enough. The lies, the abuse. I couldn't take it anymore."

"Are you going to tell us what happened?" asked Cannon.

"I think you know what happened," she said, "otherwise you wouldn't be here."

Cannon nodded. She had a sad smile on her face. They waited.

"After he had finished with me, he left me like a rag doll, a piece of shit lying on the floor. I was finished, broken. It brought back memories."

Cannon was about to ask something, but he let her continue.

"I lay for about half an hour on the floor, not moving, scared in case he did it again. I could hear him drinking. Vodka. After a while, I heard the bath running. Then he got in."

"And fell asleep?" suggested Cannon.

"Yes."

"And what did you do?"

After the Fire

Lucy thought back to the incident, reliving it in her mind.

"I had some caustic soda under the sink. I poured it down his throat as he lay sleeping in the bath. He was snoring with his mouth open. Then I held him under the water until he was dead. Simple really," she said, nonchalantly.

Hard to believe she could be so callous.

Walsh remembered the swelling in the throat of *Body B*, Davidson had mentioned it in his report. A fact that Walsh had shared with Cannon.

"The next day I hired a minivan. Dumped him that night in the Thames. I used the fire escape at the back of the building to drag him out of here. It was difficult but I managed it. I often have to move large canvases out through that door at night and into a van, so no one bothered me." She seemed to be enjoying telling her story. Was it relief, or bravado?

"And yet, it was your idea all along?"

"Sorry Mr. Cannon," she queried, "to do what?"

"To target your father," he argued.

"No, that was Pete's idea."

"Your *real* boyfriend," Walsh said.

"That's right. My *real* boyfriend. My *lover*."

"Until it all got too much," Cannon said. "Until they got greedy."

Silence descended over them. The theory was being tested. Cannon had played most of his cards. Would she really tell the full story?

Slowly she shared what he had hoped.

"Pete was the real mastermind. He was an electronics wizard. I don't know what their real names were. I just knew them as Pete and Rick. They were Polish, I didn't know they were brothers. They just said they were related. I think that was the only part that was true. Everything else they told me was probably a lie. Even Pete, I don't think he ever loved me," she continued sadly. "Even where they worked, what they did for a living. I think most of it was made up. They used me."

"So, *Stefan* was made up by you?" asked Walsh.

"The name yes. All the other detail is what Rick told me about himself. It was part of the lie I suppose. When Pete disappeared and you came to see me, I didn't know what was going on at the time, so I just made out that Rick was my boyfriend."

"To protect Pete?"

"Yes, Inspector. How naïve was I?"

"Yet it was too late," Cannon stated.

"It seems they got involved with some people they shouldn't have and things started to go south soon after that. I told them to stop, but they wouldn't, they couldn't. It went on for a few months."

"I assume that was Williams," Walsh said.

"Probably," she answered, "but I didn't know anything about that initially."

"They were targeting your father's horses at first, weren't they? Until it got out of hand?" Cannon believed he knew why but wanted her to tell the story. Walsh also needed to hear it from her.

"It seems that through people they knew, they were able to get access to stables and to my father's horses," she said.

Builders! realized Cannon. The piece he had been unsure of. Polish builders. They always had people coming and going on-site all the time he now understood. His own house repairs had continued to go on longer than they really should have. Cannon surmised that somehow the brothers were able to pay-off the builder just to allow them on site. Ease of access without suspicion.

"What did they do?" he asked.

She smiled sadly. What she was about to share had intrigued her. She didn't know how it worked, she just admired it.

"Somehow Pete had developed a way of inserting a small electronic chip onto a hoof, just inside the foot. It was attached to a small charge that when triggered would somehow blow off a horse's shoe. I don't know how it worked," she went on, "but apparently it could be set off remotely by someone being on the racecourse."

The reason why the list of horses he had originally compiled some weeks back, all ended up lame, Cannon realized. It must have been why *Harvester* was targeted at Worcester.

"So, it was all about money?" Cannon insisted, "Being able to ensure at least one of the runners didn't or couldn't win?" he went on. "If you know which, then you could bet against it. Taking the bigger odds perhaps, especially if the horse targeted was low in the betting. Particularly the favourite."

"Yes," she said.

"Making much more money with less risk."

"Yes," she repeated. "It was okay when they just targeted my father's horses, but Rick opened his mouth too wide and I think it got them into trouble. A local thug came to see them one day and it escalated. I think it was a warning. Pete tried to shut it down and was going to see someone. I don't know who. I never saw him after that."

"From what we now know," Walsh said, "that was probably Williams."

"Who was likely the one who arranged for him to be killed. If he didn't do it himself," said Cannon, aware of how fragile Lucy was. "What Williams didn't know was that Rick was dead. He must have thought your father knew what was going on and was also part of it," he continued. "The fact that Williams was making money from your father's horses didn't concern him. It was ironic that your father didn't care either."

They watched her. Waiting. She said nothing. It had to be said.

"Why Lucy? Why your father? Why focus on him?" Cannon asked

eventually.

"Because..." she started to say, 'because, he..."

"Because he abused you too?" Cannon asked. "He abused you, didn't he?" he repeated. "He sexually abused you. When you were younger. Didn't he!"

She couldn't take it anymore.

The memories, the pain, the guilt.

"Stop! Stop!" she shouted. "Stop!"

Tears ran down her face like little rivulets. She curled up in the chair as if folding into herself. From the sound of her screams to the silent sobs, the atmosphere in the room changed. It felt like a vacuum had sucked out all the air from each of them. They felt flat.

The policemen looked towards Cannon. So far, they only had a verbal confession to what may have been a revenge killing for being raped. A mental aberration. A crime committed under extreme circumstances. Duress almost. A good lawyer could find some form of out, some mitigating circumstance. No longer a murder charge perhaps, but self-defense due to extreme provocation?

She needed to be taken back to the police station.

"It was the painting," Cannon said eventually.

She raised her eyes. Walsh and Sedgefield appeared confused.

"The painting," he repeated. "It was a clue. I didn't realize it at the time, but eventually, it struck me. When I was watching *RockGod* on the track, on Saturday.

Cannon stood up and walked over to the easel that was still in the same spot as previously. The picture wasn't going anywhere. There was never any intention.

Lucy Flint watched him.

He stopped in front of the painting. Smiled sadly and then turned the easel around facing the policeman. She looked away. She knew what the picture was, there was no need to see it again.

It was still the same. A square the bottom two thirds in red and the top third in black. Through the middle from bottom left to top right, a white thunderbolt.

"I don't get it," said Walsh looking confused.

"Lucy told me that this painting was her entry into a competition. A logo for a new electric car," Cannon replied, "but it's not, it's Flint racing colours," he said. "The only difference is that the white is normally a chevron on the red jacket. Black is the colour of the cap. I think the thunderbolt here is really Lucy's way of putting something like it through her father's heart. It's symbolic as much as representative of her anger."

Lucy smiled. A sad smile. One of resignation.

Cannon understood. He had seen this before. Fathers abusing their daughters. He was saddened, he had hoped never to see it again.

"I think we need to go down to the police station," Walsh said. "Lucy, I need to caution you…"

"Before you do," she interrupted, "can I use the bathroom for a second. I need to wash my face. Use the toilet."

They had no objections.

Lucy stood, crossed the room, rubbing her face with her hands. Sniffing back tears.

They watched her enter the bathroom. They knew it only had a small window and a grill to allow airflow. There was no concern of her trying to run, to escape. Where would she go anyway? The door clicked closed and the lock turned.

Cannon, Walsh, and Sedgefield spoke briefly amongst themselves about what they had heard. What they now knew. Sedgefield made a call to the station to ask for a police car. She was to be taken into custody and held on remand until charges were laid.

As they waited it suddenly dawned on them that she was taking way too long. Much longer than she should have.

Walsh walked to the bathroom door and knocked.

"Lucy?" he called, "Lucy? Are you okay?"

A murmur came from the other side of the door. He couldn't make out what she was saying, but he took it as a sign that she would be out shortly.

He went to sit down again.

As they waited, they heard a crash coming from the bathroom. Glass hitting the floor, breaking. Bottles disgorging their contents upon the tiles.

The three men rushed to the door. They hammered upon it. Eventually their combined weight and the force from kicks and shoulders hitting wood, the door jamb splintered and they were in.

It was too late.

Lucy Flint sat slumped on the toilet seat. Her face screwed up in death. Her tongue was swollen and covered in dark saliva. Her eyes were open but unseeing. Green vomit ran down her chin.

Cannon found what he was looking for. Two bottles still intact but opened amongst the rest of the detritus of perfume, handwash and face cream jars covering the floor. He picked up each of them in turn and with a handkerchief placed them on the bathroom vanity. One of the bottles was labelled Scheele's Green, the other labelled Strychnine. They must have been stored under the sink. Did she know what was coming? Had she prepared for this moment? These were questions they would never get answers too. Cannon looked again at Lucy, her sad corpse. He knew that Strychnine was deadly when ingested. Small amounts could kill in 2-3 hours. They later established through toxicology analysis that Scheele's Green was a rarely used paint colour. It contained arsenic.

Lucy knew what she had in her midst. Some of what she used in her studio was poisonous. Many artists know that the paints and chemicals they use each day in their work can have deadly consequences.

Readily available if you knew where to look. Easily bought on the internet. An artist like Lucy would often use various them along with other chemicals. Sometimes just to create an effect. She knew what they could do. Cannon kicked himself as he remembered the smells when he first visited her in her studio. Was that also a clue? After all, she had already used caustic soda on Rick when she killed him. Was she trying to get caught or just showing how clever she was?

Cannon looked again. How much had she taken for her to die so quickly? She would have died in agony.

Did it matter?

Did anything matter anymore, he thought.

ABOUT THE AUTHOR

An ex Accountant with a lifelong love of horseracing. He has lived on three continents and has been passionate about the sport wherever he resided. Having grown up in England he was educated in South Africa where he played soccer professionally. Moving to Australia, he expanded his love for racing through becoming a syndicate member in several racehorses.
In addition, he began a hobby which quickly became extremely successful, that of making award-winning red wine with a close friend.
In mid-2014 he moved with his employer to England for just over four years, during which time he became a member of the British Racing Club (BRC).
He has now moved back to Australia, where he continues to write, and also presents a regular music show on local community radio.
He shares his life with his beautiful wife Rebecca.
He has two sons, one who lives in the UK and one who lives in Australia. This is his second novel.

Printed in Great Britain
by Amazon